P9-CLB-993

HITLER'S
SECRET

HITLER'S SECRET

A NOVEL

WILLIAM OSBORNE

Chicken House

SCHOLASTIC INC. | NEW YORK

First published in the United Kingdom in 2012 as *Hitler's Angel* by Chicken House,
2 Palmer Street, Frome, Somerset BA11 1DS.
www.doublecluck.com

Library of Congress Cataloging-in-Publication Data

Osborne, William (William Hanslow), 1960–
[Hitler's angel]
Hitler's secret / William Osborne. — 1st American ed.
p. cm.
Originally published as: Hitler's angel; Frome, England : Chicken House, (c) 2012.
Summary: In June 1941, Otto and Leni, two young refugees from the Nazis living in England, are sent on a secret mission to Bavaria, to extract a young girl attending a summer camp, and who may hold the key to the war.
ISBN 978-0-545-49646-9 1. World War, 1939–1945 — Refugees — Juvenile fiction. 2. World War, 1939–1945 — Juvenile fiction. 3. Undercover operations — Juvenile fiction. [1. World War, 1939–1945 — Fiction. 2. Refugees — Fiction. 3. Undercover operations — Fiction. 4. Secrets — Fiction.] I. Title.

PZ7.O8645Hit 2013
823.914–dc23

2012040706

10 9 8 7 6 5 4 3 2 1   13 14 15 16 17

Printed in the U.S.A.   23
First American edition, October 2013

The text type was set in Constantia.
Book design by Yaffa Jaskoll

DEDICATION

For C, D, E, F

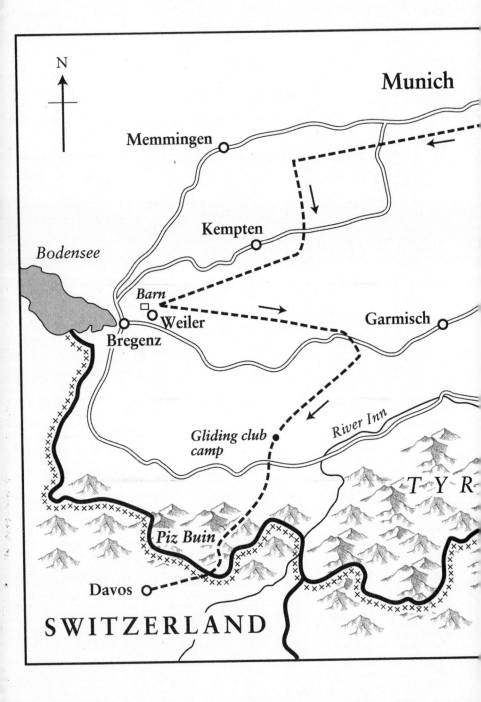

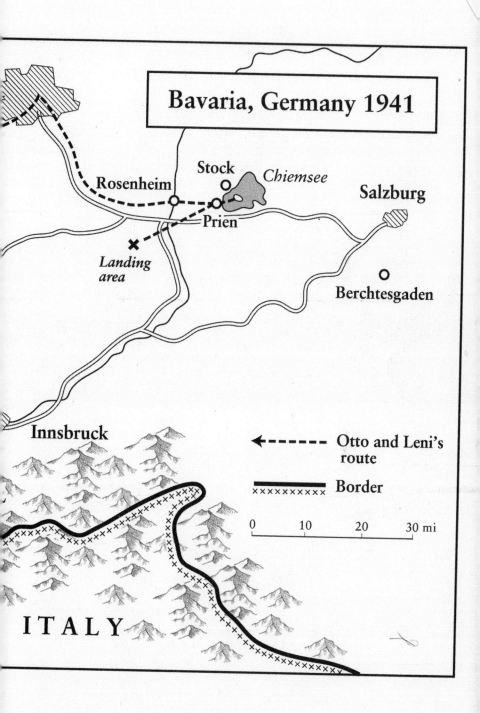

Bavaria, Germany 1941

Rosenheim
Stock
Chiemsee
Salzburg
Prien
Landing area
Berchtesgaden
Innsbruck

←------- Otto and Leni's route
××××××××× Border

0   10   20   30 mi

ITALY

1

The boy's lungs were burning, and his eyes streaming with tears.

He had to get to England. It was now or never. The smoke was all around him, acrid cordite and sulphurous petrol. He kept on running, every breath a sharp stab in his chest. He had to keep going, had to reach the water's edge, had to get beyond the upturned burning vehicles and the dead and dying men lying on the beach. He kept his eyes fixed on the hundreds of boats of every shape and size anchored in the water: barges and sailing yachts, naval destroyers and passenger liners. It seemed every boat in Britain had made the journey across the Channel to help its soldiers escape the advancing German Army.

He stumbled over discarded equipment, soldiers' canvas packs, ammunition boxes and piles of guns. Then the boy heard the sharp roar of aeroplane engines at close range. He turned. Three Messerschmitt fighters were racing straight towards him, and they were no more than fifty feet above his head.

The water was only about two hundred yards away now. He was so close. The boy tripped and stumbled as the planes flashed overhead. Suddenly he realized he'd lost his money belt. Its zipped compartment contained his whole life, everything he had managed to snatch from home the afternoon he had made his escape: photos of his parents and brother, his identity card and German passport, the last of his money.

He crawled over the sand on his knees, searching for it, machine-gun fire kicking up columns of sand around him. Something glinted a few feet away. He snaked towards it on elbows and knees. It was his father's gold wristwatch, which had been tucked inside the belt for safekeeping. At least he had found that. The Nazis had taken everything else.

There was a sudden blast of whistles along the foreshore, and the sound of orders bellowed above the explosions and gunfire. The rescue boats were leaving.

He sprinted the last few feet to the water, plunging into the surf. Another wave of German planes circled to the west, lining up for an attack. He spotted a small wooden riverboat with a green hull and white trim. It was only about fifty yards away but it was already completely overloaded with troops. Its skipper, a duffle-coated man with a pipe clenched between his teeth, was pulling up the anchor.

The boy waded out. Within a few steps he was out of his depth. He was a strong swimmer, and the cold water revived him. He lifted his head to check his position and saw a plume of black exhaust appear from the back of the riverboat as the skipper engaged the propellers.

"Bitte warten Sie!" the boy shouted at the top of his voice.

But they didn't understand. They weren't going to wait for him. The boat was beginning to move forward on the swell, the captain looking to maneuver through the burning wreckage of other sinking boats.

The boy knew if he let go of his father's watch he could gain a little more speed, but he refused to do it. It was all he had left. Instead he plunged his head into the water and kicked harder. He had to keep going. He had to make it.

And then his arm struck the side of the boat and he pulled his head up. The boat was so overloaded it was only a foot above the water. He grabbed the rope around the side with one hand, fighting for breath, and found himself being dragged along.

A plume of water erupted in front of the boat. A bomb. The skipper spun the wheel. The boy thought his arm would be torn from his shoulder as the boat rode into the swell from the bomb's impact. His head slammed against the hull.

"*Hilfe! Hilf mir!*" he yelled. He felt his grip on the sodden rope weaken, knew he couldn't hold on much longer. His head sank beneath the waves.

Suddenly, strong hands grabbed him under his armpits and he found himself being hauled up over the side of the boat. He opened his eyes. He was lying on his back on the deck, gasping for breath, retching. A group of British soldiers was staring down at him. They were all bandaged and bloodied. He smelled cigarette smoke. One of them kicked him lightly in the ribs.

"*Hilfe?* You said, '*Hilf mir.*' What are you, a Kraut?"

The boy nodded and staggered to his feet. "Please, I am also from Herr Hitler escaping." He had to convince them to take him with them. "Victory for England!" he shouted desperately. Then his eyes rolled up into his head and he pitched forward onto the deck.

LONDON, ENGLAND — 1 JUNE 1940 — 4:30 P.M.

A girl with long chestnut hair leaned right out of the passenger window of a black car as it hurtled down Haverstock Hill towards the center of London. In large white letters on the car's bodywork were the words *Blood Transfusion Service*. The girl was proud to be finally helping with the war effort. She gripped the doorframe with one hand and rang a large brass bell for all it was worth with the other.

"Hold on tight!" yelled her driver, Judy, a plucky young woman from Mill Hill, as the car shot over Regent's Canal Bridge. A double-decker bus appeared directly in front of them, and they swerved to pass it, meeting a black taxi coming the other way. The bell ringer squeezed her eyes shut as the driver floored the accelerator, and ducked back in before the two cars collided. A traffic policeman was frantically blowing his whistle and waving them through a junction. The girl grinned from ear to ear. She'd just started working on the "Blood Run" with Judy on her Wednesday half-day from school. Judy was great: She was nearly twenty and drove like the wind. The girl had started this job as a way of repaying the Brits for saving her and family, but now she realized it was very exciting, too!

Less than ten minutes later, the car skidded to a halt at the entrance of St. George's Hospital at Hyde Park Corner. It was a chaotic mass of activity, ambulances arriving with wounded and others departing, their bells jangling. Hospital staff jostled between patients and visitors. Soldiers sat smoking at their guard posts, surrounded by sandbags. Buckingham Palace was just a stone's throw from the hospital, so the whole place was bristling with anti-aircraft guns.

The girl jumped out and ran to the back of the car to open the trunk. Resting inside was a large wooden ice chest and some crates. The girl swung up the lid of the chest. Inside were thirty large glass bottles filled with dark red fluid, and they were all still intact. Relieved, the girl deftly selected eight bottles and filled two crates. She sprinted for the entrance.

"Urgent blood! Emergency, urgent blood!" she shouted like a market trader, and the crowd outside parted without complaint to let her through. Her voice, high and clear, had just a trace of an Austrian accent.

Inside, a nurse was waiting for her by the operating theater. "You took your time," she said, sounding harassed.

"Sorry," the girl said, feeling a little stung. They'd got here as quickly as they could.

"No, I'm sorry," replied the nurse, sighing. "It's just that we need the blood pronto." She took the crates from the girl and pushed the theater's swing door open with her hip. The girl caught a glimpse of the surgeon inside. There was blood on his rubber apron.

"Is it bad?" she whispered.

The nurse paused at the door. "They're bringing the wounded up from the coast on the trains," she said quietly. "This one's lost both legs. Still, this should save him. See you."

The door swung shut.

Back outside, Judy had turned the car around and was revving the engine impatiently.

"*Mein Gott*, it is big mess in there," said the girl, clambering back in, glad to be away from the carnage inside. "Where to now?" she asked.

"Whitechapel," Judy replied, stepping on the accelerator, and the car shot back out into the traffic. "Just be thankful you're not at Dunkirk, duckie, or back in Austria. Them Nazis 'ave got us on the run, but we're not beaten yet. Churchill will save us, you mark my words."

2

The prime minister, Winston Churchill, strode briskly up the path leading directly from the River Thames to the Tower of London. His visit was supposed to be incognito, but in spite of a common beige gabardine raincoat and a dark Homburg hat pulled low, he was an unmistakable figure. The guards in kilts and bearskins who were guarding the entrance of the White Tower saluted crisply as he approached.

At Churchill's side was another man. At least twenty years younger, he was tall with a pronounced nose, his receding hair a mousy brown. His eyes were gray, with dark shadows beneath them, perhaps from lack of sleep. He wore the uniform of an admiral of the Royal Navy, but was in fact a key member of the London Controlling Section, the prime minister's ultra-secret intelligence and operations group, dedicated to defeating Adolf Hitler by covert means.

The admiral showed one of the guards his identification. It seemed perhaps a little unnecessary, given whom he was accompanying, but nevertheless the guard observed strict protocol and inspected the document carefully before saluting smartly once more and unlocking the heavy oak door.

"Well, MacPherson," Churchill said as they stepped inside, "perhaps we will find a way of profiting from this strange business."

A minute later they stood in a small soundproofed anteroom staring through a two-way mirror on the wall. In the cell beyond the mirror a dark-haired man limped from one wall to another with the help of a cane. Jet-black on top, his hair was shorn at the sides, but his eyebrows were thick, almost meeting above his piercing eyes. Rudolf Hess, Deputy Führer of the Third Reich.

Admiral MacPherson couldn't help but feel a strange sense of wonder that the second most powerful man in Nazi Germany had flown solo from Germany by night, parachuted into Scotland, and was now imprisoned here in the Tower of London. It was a very strange set of circumstances indeed. His unexpected arrival had stunned not just the British but, if the press were to be believed, the Germans as well.

Hess had managed to break his ankle when landing in Scotland, and it was now in a plaster cast. This didn't seem to stop his pacing, and he shot an occasional look at the mirror, his brow furrowed. He appeared to be deep in thought.

"Is he insane?" Churchill wasn't wasting any time.

"We don't think so," replied MacPherson. He had just read a report of the latest interrogation to discover the reasons for Hess's defection.

"Well, his ideas sound pretty far-fetched. He might have defected because he didn't agree with Hitler's invasion of the Balkans. But to have organized some incredible plot to depose the Führer so he can save his life? And that somehow this girl will set the ball rolling?" Churchill shook his head.

"I agree, it does sound less than rational." MacPherson shrugged. "But it is clear he felt it was achievable — with our help."

"Well, whatever harebrained plan the man thought up is irrelevant now. He has made his bed and he will have to lie in it. In the meantime the only matter that concerns us is this child." The prime minister paused. "Admiral, do you believe she is who he says she is?"

MacPherson nodded. "I do. We have gone over the facts with him a dozen times. Besides, he has no reason to lie."

"In that case, she is invaluable." Churchill turned to the door. He had made up his mind. "Come along, MacPherson, we have work to do."

They walked back down the path towards Traitors' Gate, where the river launch had waited on the incoming tide to take the prime minister back to Westminster.

"Are we managing to keep Herr Hess's whereabouts secret from Schellenberg's agents in London?" Churchill asked.

"I'm confident of that, Prime Minister," replied MacPherson. "So far as the German security service is aware, the Deputy Führer was moved from here to Windsor five days ago. We have a serviceable double there to keep their spies occupied."

"Excellent work, Admiral."

"You really think this girl can help us?" asked MacPherson as they approached the boat.

Churchill glanced up at the barrage balloons before he answered. "In the last month, Greece has fallen, Crete has fallen, and the Afrika Korps have us on the run in the Western Desert, so perhaps Egypt and the oil fields of Arabia will fall, too. Hitler's U-boats are sinking half a million tons of shipping a week in the Atlantic, and our planes are being shot out of the sky faster than we can build them." He took out a cigar and rolled it between his fingers. "Not only that, but the Americans steadfastly refuse to declare war on Germany, so we stand alone. And we are losing, let us make no bones about it. Having this girl will give us a victory we badly need, a propaganda victory. It will stiffen our side's morale, win the hearts and minds of decent people in Germany, and deal a blow to the Führer that will strike at his very core."

"He'll never let her out of Germany alive if he so much as suspects our intentions," said MacPherson.

"Then you must ensure he does not get a whiff of our plans, Admiral. This matter is above and beyond top secret, for your eyes only. Time is short. I assume you have agents on standby for instant action?"

"Of course, Prime Minister," he replied smoothly.

"Good chap. I knew I could rely on you." Churchill patted him on the arm and stepped onto the gangplank.

MacPherson saluted the prime minister smartly, but already his mind was spinning.

He didn't have agents on standby. Not the kind he would need, anyway. German-speaking agents were thin on the ground, to say the least, and the ones they had were already known to Hitler's security services. Now he had no more than two weeks to find and train top-class operatives that could get into Germany and back out again — with the most precious cargo in the Reich. How on earth could it be done?

3

The boy was running across his school's cobbled courtyard as fast as he had across the bullet-riddled sands of Dunkirk a year ago.

He reached the entrance to the chapel tower and took the stone steps three at a time. It wasn't easy. The treads were narrow, worn in the middle, and he was wearing studded cricket boots, which made him slide. He was still wearing his cricket whites, too, the knees scuffed green from a fumbled catch earlier in the afternoon. The air was stifling and he was dripping with sweat. He reached the door to the roof, and slammed back the bolt with the side of his hand. He gasped in pain as his knuckles, skinned red and raw, slid along the rough wooden door. Behind him he could hear the clatter of other cricket boots.

He stumbled onto the roof of the chapel. The English countryside lay spread out around him, the playing fields and cricket pitch away to the left. He heard a shout behind, and turned. Four members of his team were advancing towards him. The captain, Catchpole, was wielding a cricket bat.

"I'm really going to kill you this time," he said.

"Just leave me alone, Catchpole," said the boy. His accent had improved considerably since he had been dragged from the water at Dunkirk, and he was almost a young man now, taller and thinner. On arrival in England he had given the authorities the name of his father's English friend, a chemistry professor at Cambridge, who had greeted him kindly, then sent him to this place. He must have thought he was being generous.

"Why should I, Nazi Boy?" sneered Catchpole. If there was one insult he hated above all the ones that were hurled at him, it was "Nazi Boy." And they knew it. The boy looked around for some kind of weapon, but there was nothing to hand. It was fight or run, and, as there didn't seemed to be anywhere to run to, fight it was, even though he knew he would take a beating. He raised his fists and planted his feet anyway, waiting for their charge.

Then his eye caught something behind them. New scaffolding up the side of the tower. A rope hung from it.

As the youths charged, the boy darted to his right and was past his pursuers before they could turn and give chase. He reached the end of the roof and climbed onto the crenellated parapet. The scaffolding was about six feet away; the ground beneath many more. He could make it. He threw himself forward across the gap, landing with a thud on wooden planks, then grabbed hold of the rope. He turned. Catchpole was standing on the parapet, looking at the gap. He didn't seem in any hurry to jump.

The boy tightened his grip on the rope and swung out. He sailed through the air like a pirate swooping between two ships, dropped with a satisfying thump on the roof of the dining hall, then scrambled down onto the main school roof. He turned on his heel and ran blindly on — missing the open skylight in his path . . .

With a startled yell, he fell straight through the hole, landing on a large round table, then crashing onto the floor, papers cascading around him.

Grimacing with the pain and trying to catch his breath, he glanced up at the skylight. Catchpole was staring down at him. The cricket captain slowly ran his finger across his throat, then disappeared from view.

"So glad you could drop in," said Professor Maddox.

The boy scrambled to his feet and smoothed back his hair as the dust settled in the room. He was really in trouble now.

"You know, your behavior continues to confound all standards of English decency," continued the headmaster. As he spoke, the boy noticed there was another man in the room, sitting opposite. A tall, thin man, with keen gray eyes. He was dressed in a light summer suit and puffing on a cigar.

"Sorry, sir."

"Stand up straight when you speak to me!" Maddox barked, his eyes darkening. "This is Admiral MacPherson of His Majesty's Royal Navy."

The young man stood to attention and swiveled his eyes to the other man.

MacPherson was studying him carefully. "That was quite an entrance," he said.

Maddox rose from his chair. "Incredible as it seems, the admiral has a proposition for you." He couldn't hide the disdain in his voice. "I'll tell you again, Admiral," he added in an acid tone, "this boy is trouble."

"That's the sort we need," MacPherson replied.

"Yes," said the boy. "The answer is yes."

Both men looked at him sharply.

"What?" Maddox said.

"To the admiral's proposition, sir, yes."

"You don't even know what he's going to ask you, you foolish child!" Maddox said, exasperated.

"Does it get me out of this place, sir?" the boy asked.

MacPherson nodded. "It does."

"Then my answer is yes."

"I told you he was a half-wit. I'm afraid your journey's been wasted, Admiral."

MacPherson ignored the headmaster. He stubbed his cigar out in the ashtray. "Go and clean up, get your things, young man. My car is outside."

"I'll do that, sir." The boy grinned, then looked at the headmaster, waiting to be dismissed.

Maddox was incandescent with rage, but could do nothing. "Get out," he said.

The boy needed no second invitation.

Back in his dormitory, he changed out of his cricket whites and pulled on a short-sleeved gray Aertex shirt, a dark blazer, gray trousers, and black shoes. Then he slid under the metal-framed single bed and pried up the floorboard he'd previously loosened to use as a hiding place. He reached down into the cavity and retrieved a small metal tin. Inside were a five-pound note, some coins, his father's gold watch, and a new British identity card. He glanced at the watch's face, the hands still frozen at 3:20 P.M.

The dormitory was hot and airless and mercifully silent. He put the watch into his blazer pocket, and everything else into a canvas backpack, along with a few other clothes. He left the school uniform behind.

The boy hurried back through the school, past a group of classmates who jeered and gave him the Nazi salute. He ignored them and kept walking until he reached the dining hall. He stopped outside the main door and listened. The two cricket teams were inside having tea. He could hear the familiar voices and laughter of his tormentors. He peeked inside.

". . . And then the dirty little sausage-eater started screaming for his mummy and daddy." Catchpole was enjoying embellishing the tale. *"Mutti, Vati . . ."* The others were laughing hysterically as he leaped up from the table and began to goose-step around, holding two of his fingers horizontally under his nose, mimicking Hitler's mustache. *"Vater, Vater —"* He suddenly stopped as he saw the boy at the door. Silence fell.

The boy walked across the room. "I'll say good-bye then, Catchpole."

He landed his punch full in Catchpole's face, square on the bridge of his nose. He even heard the bone crack. Then he turned and walked calmly back to the door as Catchpole's knees hit the wooden floor and his hands rose to catch the blood spurting from his shattered septum. The other cricket players were frozen to the spot.

As soon as the boy stepped out of the hall, he sprinted towards the school's entrance. A moment later and a roar of angry voices erupted from inside. If they caught him now, he was a dead man.

Admiral MacPherson was standing beside a blue Hudson parked in the driveway.

The boy slammed to a halt beside him, his shoes skidding on the gravel.

"I'm ready to leave, sir," he said, gasping for breath.

"Now, just a minute," said MacPherson, resting a hand on the boy's shoulder. "We mustn't be too hasty here."

Behind them came the shouts and yells of the enraged cricket mob.

"Really, sir, it's fine, let's go." The boy looked anxiously back. The mob had appeared at the school's entrance, about fifty yards away. They were baying like hounds for blood.

"What the British government is asking of you," said MacPherson, "is extremely dangerous. In fact, I'll be blunt, it could be life threatening."

The mob was almost upon them. Two weeks in the sick bay was the minimum he was looking at for breaking Catchpole's nose. And when he came out, his life would be hell.

"I understand, sir. Really, I do. Can we please go?" The boy was almost pleading now.

"You're sure?" MacPherson said.

The mob was ten yards away.

"Yes!"

"As you wish."

MacPherson stepped aside and the boy threw himself inside the car. The admiral followed smartly, slamming the door behind him.

"Go!" he ordered the driver.

The car's wheels spun on the gravel as the mob reached the car. The boy turned to look back through the rear window. His tormentors were standing impotently in the driveway, sprayed by the dust thrown up from the tires. He flicked them Churchill's famous two-fingered "Victory" sign and settled back into the leather seat, for a moment savoring his settling of scores and the successful escape.

"Quite a send-off," MacPherson remarked drily.

The boy reached into his jacket and felt for his father's watch. It was still there.

"You saved my life," he said, his heart thumping.

4

The girl settled herself behind the steering wheel and turned the key. The engine fired. This was always her treat at the end of the "blood run." Judy allowed her to drive the last few miles back to her home, and now, after six months, she had become pretty good at it, it had to be said. Judy watched as she eased the car into first gear and pulled away from the bus stop where they always swapped over. She swiftly changed up to second and third with a hitch. She watched the needle on the speedometer flick up to fifty miles per hour and grinned. She loved being behind the wheel; it made her feel so grown-up, and there was the thrill of doing something illegal, too! Not that anyone cared — after all, young men only a few years older than her were being killed every minute.

"That's it, duckie," Judy said approvingly. "Feeling much smoother today."

21

The sun was just beginning to drop when the girl turned the corner into the modest suburban road where she lived. She couldn't resist accelerating the last hundred yards.

"Look out!" yelled Judy, and the girl had to slam on the brakes to avoid ramming the car parked outside her house. The car screeched to a halt, and Judy lurched forward.

"It's practically the only other car in the street. You need your eyes tested, I swear," she said, but she was smiling.

"Sorry, Judy," the girl said. "See you next week." She climbed out of the car, and Judy slid back behind the wheel.

The girl watched the car pull away, and only then did she study the blue Hudson outside the house. She knew all the different cars in London now. Hudsons were big American cars favored by the army and navy. This one had a navy pennant on one of its wings.

The girl hurried up the short path to her front door. A modest two-bedroom row house, with a vegetable patch and an Anderson air-raid shelter, which housed a zinc bath and an iron mangle to dry the clothes, it was a long way from their elegant villa in Vienna. No nanny, no maids. But it was home now. Their home.

The moment she opened the front door her two sisters, Zelda and Ruth, aged sixteen and eighteen, pulled her inside and quietly eased the door shut, their fingers on their lips.

"What's going on?" she whispered.

Zelda and Ruth were wide-eyed with excitement.

"*Es ist ein* admiral from the Royal Navy *in der Küche,*" hissed her second sister, Ruth, mixing her languages as she pointed to the room beyond the stairs. They had agreed to speak English at home, but Ruth had the most trouble keeping to this rule.

"Are you sure?" the girl said. It didn't sound very likely, but there *was* the car outside.

"We're sure. And he's come to speak to you!" said Zelda. "He's been in there with Mutti for over an hour."

"Me?" said the girl. She was astonished.

"Well, go on," said Ruth, giving her a shove towards the kitchen.

"All right," said the girl. But she didn't move. She was racking her brains trying to think why an admiral was calling to speak to a young Austrian refugee in Mill Hill. Nothing so dramatic had happened to them in the three years since their arrival in London. Well, except the Blitz, of course. But that had been terrifying rather than exciting.

"You're not moving," said Zelda.

"Stop bossing me, I'm going."

She walked down the hall and knocked on the kitchen door. Mutti opened it almost immediately and stood looking at her with a grave expression. The girl glanced past her; she was taller than her mother now, having grown a good four inches in the last two years. A tall, thin man was standing in front of the small kitchen fire grate. He was wearing a dark three-piece suit, with

23

a gold watch chain hanging in two neat loops across the waist-coat. He smiled at the girl amiably, but his gray eyes were sharp.

"This is Admiral MacPherson," said Mutti, shutting the door on Ruth and Zelda. "He is here to ask you something." She sat in her usual place at the kitchen table, her hands tightly clasped and her lips pressed together. She was clearly agitated. The girl moved to the sink and remained standing.

"That is very valuable work you are doing for the Blood Transfusion Service, young lady," MacPherson said. "And a first-class report from your school. Academic, good at lan-guages, and a first-class runner, too, I see." She noticed he was holding a small gray folder.

"Thank you, sir," she replied, wondering what else was in the folder. "I enjoy the blood work. I mean . . . I am pleased to help after all Great Britain has done for us."

"Good, we need all the help we can get right now. Which is the reason I am here. We would like you to do something even more important for the war effort."

"Important but very dangerous. She's just a girl, Admiral," added her mother, sighing heavily.

"As you can imagine, your mother is understandably against your agreeing. However, she has consented to my ask-ing you. So, do you wish to help?"

"Help with what?" the girl asked.

MacPherson smiled. "I like your bluntness. But in order

to tell you anything more, I must ask your mother to leave the room."

"What?" exclaimed the girl's mother, alarmed now.

"At present this matter is known only to myself, the prime minister, and a small number of highly trusted individuals. I can only speak of it to your daughter alone, subject to the Official Secrets Act."

Mutti reddened. "I'm sorry. I have made a mistake in allowing you to speak to her. She is far too young for such things. Far too young!"

But the girl was intrigued. "It's all right, Mutti. Let me hear what Admiral MacPherson has to say."

Her mother shook her head but, even so, she got up and walked out of the room.

Now they were alone, MacPherson wasted no time.

"We want you to go to Germany, southern Germany, and bring back an item to England. Is that something you think you could do?"

"Go to Germany?" The girl stared at the admiral.

"Just for a few days. You would be helping the war effort enormously." MacPherson added, "Helping your father and brothers, too, and all of your people left behind."

The girl turned to the sink and found a glass resting on the drainer. She turned the tap on and filled the glass, then gulped it down. It gave her time to think.

It had been a little over three years since the packet ship from Copenhagen had docked at Tilbury, three years since she had last seen her brothers and her father. Saying good-bye to them at the border between Austria and Czechoslovakia on that fateful night in 1938 was the hardest thing she had ever done. They were supposed to have followed her mother, her sisters, and her to England, but nothing had been heard of them since.

She felt her heart racing. "What is the item?" she asked.

MacPherson studied her, as if trying to decide something. "A child," he said at last.

The girl tried not to look surprised by his answer. A child? A child who was very important to the war effort? Now she felt even more intrigued. "Would I be going alone?"

"No. You would go with a boy, a German boy. And rest assured, you would be trained and prepared."

The girl could hardly think. It was all so unexpected.

"There, I have laid the matter out for you," he said. "I don't mean to pressure you but I have two other candidates to see tonight." He smiled lightly back at her.

That's exactly *what he meant to do*, she thought. *Pressure me.* "Two other candidates?" she said.

MacPherson nodded. "You happen to have the required qualities for this mission: You speak German and have the right character, as well as athletic and academic aptitude. But

I would be a fool if I had placed all my eggs in one basket, if you are familiar with that English expression?"

She wondered if he was calling her bluff. She stared at him, trying to work it out.

He met her gaze unwaveringly, then looked at his watch. "Well, I shall have to go, I think," he said.

"Mutti," she called out.

There was a pause and her mother returned to the kitchen, her face etched with worry.

"I have decided to help the admiral, Mutti."

MacPherson smiled.

"I want to do something important for Father and the boys."

5

THE FISCHERS OF SALZBURG

It was just after seven in the morning, and the girl had been awake for two hours already. She'd arrived at Wanborough Manor the day before. It was a beautiful old house, perched on a part of the Surrey North Downs called the Hog's Back. MacPherson had told her that the house had been requisitioned by the Ministry of Defense at the beginning of the war and was now one of the main training establishments for Special Operations.

Special Operations: She turned the words over in her thoughts as she took in the large, empty dining room. She couldn't quite believe that she was a part of it. Not yet.

Her room was right up in the eaves, and it had taken her almost the whole of yesterday to find her way around the rambling rooms and staircases. She'd hardly set eyes on anyone, except for one or two Royal Marines, who paid her no attention.

A member of the Women's Royal Naval Service — Wrens, as they were known — had been there to meet her and settle her in, and then she, too, had disappeared after supper. Perhaps the Wren and the marines would be training her? She also hadn't seen MacPherson since he had dropped her off.

Suddenly the door opened and a boy walked in. He was tall and quite thin, with brown eyes. His hair was wet and rather disheveled, as if he'd washed it quickly. He stopped short when he saw her, and his cheeks colored a little. He ran a hand through his hair.

"Hello," he said evenly.

"Hello," she replied.

"Who are you?" he asked.

"I'm your sister." She smiled at his look of confusion and surprise.

"What on earth are you talking about?" the boy said. His English was very good, hardly a trace of a German accent.

"I'm 'Leni,' your sister. And you're 'Otto.'"

"Otto? Who told you my name was Otto?" She could see he was beginning to get rattled.

"I did." MacPherson was standing in the doorway. "From now on you are the Fischer family from Salzburg." He handed them each a buff-colored file, and plucked a piece of toast from the rack. "I realize this is throwing you both in at the deep end, but time is rather short. You'll find your Reich passports and other items of identification inside the folders."

The girl looked at the cover of the file that bore her new name. Leni Fischer. She knew she'd have to get used to it. She flipped open the folder and withdrew a gray passport. She stared at her photograph on the inside page. A good German, a Nazi now. And nearly nine months older than her real age. Fifteen at last. The Reich's eagle was stamped across the picture, its talons holding a swastika.

She felt a familiar wave of fear return to her stomach. Living in England for the last three years had somehow blunted the feeling she had whenever she saw this hateful emblem. But now her mind flashed back to Vienna, her home, and to the Nazis parading down the street at night with their torches, their chants, and, most of all, their swastika banners held high. She closed the passport, dropped it on the table.

"It looks real," she said.

"That's because it is," MacPherson said, ignoring her look of revulsion. "We've secured a source in Berlin who can supply us with anything we need in the way of identification. All the necessary stamps and inks, blank passports, the whole shooting match. Look at the rest of the stuff."

Reluctantly Leni took out a series of documents from the folder: a membership card for the *Bund Deutscher Mädel* — the League of German Girls — and certificates for athletics and dressmaking, all made out in Leni Fischer's name, with

30

her photograph where it was required. From a despised *Jude* to one of the master race. She glanced at the boy, her so-called brother. He was looking at the documents intently, but his expression was unreadable.

"Your father, Kurt Fischer, was a captain with the Afrika Korps under General Rommel in Libya. KIA, unfortunately," said MacPherson.

"KIA?" asked Leni.

"Killed in action. Your mother is at home in Salzburg, suffering from the bereavement. Greta is her name. She has sent you to visit your godmother while she deals with her grief. All the details are contained in these files, and I would ask you to study them carefully and commit them to memory."

"Do these people really exist?" the boy asked.

"Physically, no, Otto," replied MacPherson. "Officially, absolutely. Again with a little help from Berlin, you will find birth certificates, medical and army records, electoral registers, Nazi memberships, Gestapo record cards, everything that establishes the existence of the Fischer family beyond any shadow of doubt." He watched them look through the other documents. "I understand it must be strange to be these people all of a sudden."

"To be perfect Nazis, you mean," blurted Leni. She could feel her face reddening.

"You'll get used to it," said MacPherson.

"I will never get used to it, thank you." She knew her voice had risen, and felt close to tears.

"I'm sorry, that was not what I meant." MacPherson seemed taken aback.

There was an awkward silence.

"Well then, Leni and Otto Fischer, finish your breakfast. We'll meet in the drawing room at nine o'clock. The briefing will continue then." MacPherson swallowed down the last of his toast with a great gulp of tea, and left the room.

"Are you all right?"

Leni glanced up. The boy was looking at her with something like concern. She stuffed the documents back into the buff envelope.

"I'm fine," she said, but she felt angry and afraid and not remotely all right.

"The second island on the lake is known as Fraueninsel, and on it is a Benedictine convent. The child is being held there."

MacPherson was speaking in the darkened drawing room. The curtains had been drawn and a large screen erected in front of the marble fireplace. A projectionist stood at the back of the room. Leni and Otto were sitting next to each other on a leather sofa, staring at the grainy black-and-white image. The old sofa slumped in the middle, pushing them together like some inanimate matchmaker. Leni could feel Otto's leg

32

pressing lightly against hers. She concentrated on the photograph. The nunnery was an ancient-looking stone building with an onion-shaped bell tower.

"Her room is on the fourth floor of the west side of the main building." MacPherson paused. "Any questions?"

The briefing had begun after breakfast and it was now half past ten. Their mission was straightforward, in theory. They were to be parachuted into southern Bavaria in order to rescue a nine-year-old girl from the convent where she was being held. They were then to get the child as quickly as possible to a rendezvous point at Lake Constance — or the Bodensee — on the Swiss border. There the admiral would be waiting with a plane to fly them all back to England.

There was one question she wished to ask.

"I have a question, sir," Otto said, just as Leni was about to speak.

"Yes, Otto?" MacPherson was addressing them by their cover names at every opportunity. It was vital, he said, that they become second nature as soon as possible.

"Why me, I mean . . ." Otto shot a glance at Leni. ". . . why us? We're . . ." He hesitated, looking for the right word. ". . . untrained."

"You're right to ask," MacPherson said. "In the normal course of events, we would choose to send in two adult agents, ideally a man and a woman. With the child, they could pose as a family traveling together. But this, we feel, is an obvious cover. We believe that, in the event of the authorities searching for the girl, three children traveling together will attract the least attention and suspicion. In addition, although we have plenty of French, Flemish, and even Dutch agents to call upon — and we're sending them across into those countries as we speak — the truth is, we simply have very few suitable German agents. The Reich has agents in this country whose job it is to report on any natural-born German or Austrian they can find. We believe you two have slipped through their net."

Leni nodded. It made sense now to her. But her heart had skipped a beat at the mention of a hunt by the "authorities."

"But," said MacPherson, staring down at the two of them, "let me make this clear: We also happen to believe that both of you have what it takes to carry out this mission. If we didn't think that, then you wouldn't be sitting here. Simple as that."

Leni found herself smiling self-consciously, a little embarrassed by the gruff compliment. She glanced at Otto, but he was staring ahead at the screen, frowning, deep in thought.

"All right, moving on, next slide please," said MacPherson. A Bavarian lakeside town appeared on the screen. "Your cover story on the way in will be that you are joining the Hitler Youth — *Hitler-Jugend* — camp at the village of Stock, which lies on the west bank of the Bavarian Sea, or the Chiemsee, as the lake is known in Bavaria. The camp runs throughout the summer months for children of officers serving in the Balkans and North Africa. Nobody will question your presence — another reason for choosing people of your age. Most of the time is spent swimming and sailing."

"And singing," added Otto.

"Of course, you were a member," said MacPherson.

"Not of the Hitler-Jugend, sir, but of the *Jungvolk*."

Leni shifted on the sofa, moving away from him. The Jungvolk was the junior branch of the Nazi Party's youth wing, for children aged ten to thirteen.

"I didn't have a choice," he said defensively.

MacPherson broke in. "Once you have got the child off the island, you will follow a preplanned escape route taking you south towards the border. You will travel mostly by train. Your cover for this return part of the mission will be that you are visiting your godmother in Bregenz." A map of Bavaria and the Tyrol was now on the screen, and MacPherson pointed to the Austrian town on the shore of Lake Constance. "Your mission should take no more than three days at the most. We will wait at the rendezvous point for as long as it takes." The implication in MacPherson's last sentence was left hanging.

"When are we going?" asked Otto.

"In a little over two weeks, on the eighteenth of June," said MacPherson.

Otto and Leni looked at each other, and Leni spoke for them both. "We'll never be ready."

"It's my job to make sure you are," said MacPherson. "This opportunity will not come again, and we must seize it."

A silence fell on the room as each of them contemplated what lay ahead.

"It is only fair, now that you know the whole picture, to ask you one last time. Particularly you, Otto, as you didn't really know what you were getting yourself into when I took you from school." MacPherson spoke softly, but in a measured, calm voice, like a judge passing sentence. "If you wish to step down from this endeavor, please do so now."

Silence once again. Leni didn't dare look at Otto. Was he about to back out? If he did, she felt she most probably would, too. Then she spoke up, her voice firm.

"Who is this child?" she asked.

MacPherson pursed his lips and held up his hands. "I don't know, Leni. I have not been told her identity."

Leni studied the admiral. Did admirals lie? She supposed they did, that sometimes, in wartime, lies were necessary. But if he was lying, why?

"But I can tell you this," MacPherson went on. "Her name is Angelika. And if you succeed in your mission, you will have performed a very great service to this country, your adopted country, and to the war effort."

At that moment, the projectionist snapped back the curtains

and a shaft of sunlight cut through the darkness. Otto and Leni shielded their eyes from the brightness.

Maybe he did know who this girl was, maybe he didn't, thought Leni, but one thing was certain in her mind. She would find out.

6

TRAINING

Training began in earnest straight after lunch. MacPherson had certainly meant it when he said time was short.

They had been taken out for a long run with backpacks filled with rocks before being put through their paces on an assault course. Twice. They were nearly at the end of it now.

Otto just found the strength to climb the next obstacle in front of him, a fifteen-foot wall, hauling himself up the rope before sitting astride the top to catch his breath. He glanced down. Leni was struggling to follow him. She had easily kept pace on the run, but now looked to be in trouble. Her face was flushed, but her lips were strangely bloodless. The instructor, a stocky Royal Marine sergeant, yelled at them to keep moving.

"Take my hand," Otto said, reaching down. He was, as instructed by MacPherson, speaking in German to Leni.

"I can do it," Leni replied hoarsely. She finally managed to pull herself onto the top of the wall, and lay on it, gasping for breath.

"You should have let me help," said Otto.

He could see Leni was done in, but she wasn't going to give up, either.

"What are you waiting for? Tea and biscuits?" the instructor snapped up at them.

They looked at the last obstacle: a long pit filled with watery mud over which a lattice of barbed wire had been strung. Leni grabbed hold of the rope to slide down. But the strength in her arms gave, and instead she half slid, half fell to the ground, landing with a thud. Otto grabbed the rope and followed her down. He reached out to help her up, but she pushed him away and staggered to her feet.

"Leave me alone," she wheezed, and started wading through the mud.

Otto followed her. He was reminded of Dunkirk, of wading out to the boat, then the sodden rope in his hand and the water closing over his head. He lost his footing and stumbled forward, plunging headfirst into the mud. It seemed to pull on him, sucking him down, and for a moment he felt blind panic and terror. Fighting the instinct to breathe in, he struggled to his feet. The barbed wire caught the top of his head. He yelled in pain and ducked down again.

"Get a move on, you lazy idiot!" the instructor barked.

Up ahead Leni had crawled out of the pit and was waiting for him.

"You all right?"

Otto nodded. They were both covered from head to foot in stinking mud.

"Right! Time for a little swim," bellowed the instructor, pointing to the lake at the edge of the woods. "At the double!"

Otto looked at the dark water of the lake, surrounded by tall bulrushes. He was still fighting the panic and knew he couldn't do it. He was going to have to fake an injury, like he had done back at school when he was trying to get out of class in the gymnasium.

Trying to make it look real, he stumbled and fell to the ground, yelling out in pain and clutching his ankle.

Tutting, the instructor jogged towards them, then knelt down and examined Otto's ankle.

"I think it's broken," Otto groaned.

"Only sprained — if that." He stared at Otto, his eyes narrowed, trying to figure out whether he was faking or not. "All right, you pathetic little oik, let's call it a day. Get in the jeep. Both of you."

Leni sank to her knees, tears of relief rolling down her mud-stained cheeks. Otto slowly got to his feet. He would have to pretend to limp till they got back to the manor, but it was worth it.

———

After supper that night, which was dominated by MacPherson drilling them about their cover family, Otto and Leni climbed slowly and wearily up to their rooms at the top of the manor house. They were too tired even to talk until they reached their bedroom doors.

"You're not limping anymore," said Leni.

"Er . . . no," replied Otto. "It's feeling much better."

Leni shook her head. "You know, you didn't have to pretend to give up for me. I could have swum that lake."

"I wasn't pretending, I sprained my ankle," Otto lied, then added, truthfully, "Don't worry, it had nothing to do with you."

Leni shrugged. "Well, if I'm being truthful, you did help me really. I would have tried the lake, but it might have killed me."

Otto managed a tired smile. She returned it, then went to open her door. Otto saw there was a raw channel across her palm where the rope had burned her.

"Does it hurt a lot?" he said.

Leni put her hand behind her back. "It's fine."

But he knew it must be agonizing. She was obviously made of strong stuff.

"Good night, Leni," he said.

But he stood outside her door for a few moments after she had closed it, wondering who this girl really was and what had driven her to volunteer. All he knew for certain was that she was from Bavaria like him, or perhaps even farther west. He thought he detected a Viennese accent.

The next day they spent the morning at the lake. Not swimming it, to Otto's great relief, but being taught the rudiments of handling a motor launch by another instructor. Otto didn't like the sway of the boat on the water, and found landing the launch really difficult. He was delighted when, after lunch, they were taken to the shooting ranges instead of back to the water. This was much more his scene.

Otto pressed the butt of his Lee-Enfield rifle into his shoulder and tried to line up the sights on the paper target of a charging soldier one hundred yards away.

"Commence fire!" yelled their instructor.

Otto squeezed the trigger and the rifle kicked into his shoulder like a sharp punch. He couldn't believe how loud it sounded. He dropped it down from his shoulder and worked the bolt, expelling the spent cartridge and sliding a fresh bullet into the breach. Then he brought the gun back up and fired again. He and Leni both kept up a steady rate of fire until their magazines were empty.

They walked down to inspect their targets. Of their eleven shots each, Otto's paper soldier had nine neat holes drilled into the middle of his chest.

"Outstanding! I believe we have a budding marksman," proclaimed the instructor.

Otto couldn't help smiling. He was better at this than landing the boat.

When they inspected Leni's target, it was a different story. Only five hits, and most of them towards the edge.

The instructor shook his head.

"Probably just flesh wounds," he sniffed. "Maybe you'll be better with handguns."

But it was similar story: Otto's eight rounds from his Walther PPK in the bull's-eye; Leni's wide of the mark.

"Let's try grenades," sighed the instructor. "Nothing to them."

"All you need is some practice," said Otto as they jogged after the instructor to the grenade pit.

"It's not that," huffed Leni.

"I understand . . ." Otto nodded. ". . . you don't like guns."

"What?" said Leni. "Oh, that's so typical, thinking a girl wouldn't like a gun. It isn't that at all. It's just the target is so far away!"

But Otto wasn't convinced. It seemed to him that Leni's eyesight might be a problem.

The routine hardly varied: physical training in the morning, weapons training in the afternoon, interspersed with learning to parachute, to sail, and to find their way to a rendezvous point with map and compass. They even had some training with vehicles and motorbikes, and Otto was surprised how good Leni was with machines. They talked little, the long physical hours of training and the evenings spent with

MacPherson going over the mission's details draining them of all their energy. By the time their heads hit the pillow they were asleep.

But come the day of the mission they had developed, if not a friendship, then at least an understanding.

Otto found Leni sitting on the veranda outside the dining room after their last lunch. A car was coming in an hour to take them to the airfield. It was very warm, and swarms of mayflies were fizzing in the air. Leni was sitting in the shade. He could see there were freckles on the bridge of her nose that hadn't been there two weeks ago. They both stared across the lawn in silence.

"You don't have to do this, you know," Otto said.

"Why are you saying that now?" asked Leni. The two of them were speaking in German, as they always did when they were alone together.

Otto looked across at her. "You're Jewish, aren't you? From Vienna, I think?"

For a moment, Leni looked taken aback. She tucked a strand of her chestnut hair behind her ear and gazed at Otto with her blue eyes.

"Is it so obvious?" she said.

"Not at all," replied Otto, "but you said you'd come to England in 1938. Why else would someone want to leave Austria when their savior, Adolf Hitler, was just marching in?"

"Very clever," said Leni.

"If we get captured and they find out who you are . . ." Otto stopped. "Look, it's too dangerous."

"It's my decision, Otto," replied Leni. "And what about you? Do you think you'll get special treatment?"

Otto shrugged. "I don't know," he said flatly. In fact, he'd spent half the night lying in his bed wondering exactly that. His sheet had been soaked with perspiration when he'd woken that morning.

"Anyway, why did *you* leave?" asked Leni.

Otto sighed. "My father was a Communist — before I was born, I mean. My mother, too. That's how they met. When the Nazis came to power they went underground, tried to hide their past. He was a chemistry professor, so he was of some use to them. But eventually someone must have talked, and the Gestapo came and took him away. My mother and brother, too. I don't know where they are now." He stopped for a moment, felt his eyes pricking. "*Undermining the war effort*, that's what the Gestapo said when they arrested him."

"I'm sorry," said Leni. Her voice was soft. At that moment, MacPherson marched out of the double doors leading from the drawing room onto the veranda.

"Well, I'm afraid there's rather a lot of weather over southern Germany," he said cheerily.

Leni and Otto exchanged an anxious glance. It was easy for him to be in good spirits; he wasn't parachuting into enemy territory that night.

"But don't fret," he went on. "I've pulled some strings, managed to get hold of a prototype plane. It's being flown down from the factory this afternoon. It's called a Mosquito, and it can fly higher and faster than anything we've got at the moment. Even has Rolls-Royce engines. It'll get you there, safe as houses. Now, come along."

Leni stood up. "Do I have time to write a letter?" she asked.

"Of course. We won't set off for the airfield for half an hour, so take your time."

As Otto got up to follow Leni, MacPherson tapped him on the shoulder.

"Otto, a quick word, if you wouldn't mind."

Leni gave them a curious glance as she left the veranda. Otto sat back down again.

"She's a great girl, isn't she?" MacPherson said, looking after Leni.

"Yes, she is," said Otto.

"Nothing she can't do, eh?" continued MacPherson.

Otto began to feel on his guard. "I'd say so."

"But here's the thing, Otto. At the end of the day, she's still a girl and, well, girls, women, whatever you like, sometimes they can get emotional about things, I think you'll agree?"

Otto didn't want to agree. After all, he'd been the one who

46

panicked in the water. Besides, what was wrong with being emotional when something was important?

"I suppose so," he said.

"Exactly." MacPherson was now looking at Otto steadily. "So that's why I need to talk to you about one last matter, just us men together . . . without Leni. All right?"

7

INTO THE NIGHT

Adrenaline was making Leni's heart thud. Encased in a thick flying suit and leather helmet, she was lying inside the bomb bay of the Mosquito, on the actual bay doors. Otto was beside her. Their parachute release lines were fixed on to metal O-rings above them, next to a steady red light. Leni kept an eye on it while she wiggled her toes, trying to keep the pins and needles at bay. The light would start to flash as they reached the drop zone and then switch to green at the moment of release. At that point the doors would drop open and gravity and the slipstream would suck them out, snapping the release line tight and opening their chutes. The whole business would take no more than a few seconds.

Her heart continued to thump. It was dark inside the bay, and the noise from the engines was deafening. But that wasn't why she was scared. It was the fact that they'd never deployed by this method. In their jumps during the last two weeks they had gone out of the side of a conventional transport plane. *On the green light, stand by in the doorway, feel the slipstream, hands across your chest, and go!* That had been the drill, and she and Otto had just about got used to it. But the Mosquito wasn't a conventional transport plane, so they had had to be strapped in, literally like bombs, to be dropped from its belly.

She felt the Mosquito hit another trough of turbulence and her stomach came rushing up to her throat as the plane dropped like a stone for a dozen terrifying seconds before slamming into a trampoline of clouds and hurtling back up.

They'd been in this unpressurized, freezing craft for hours, at least three by her calculation. *Perhaps we're over the Alps,* she thought. The pilot increased the throttle and the engines roared loudly above Leni, making her whole body vibrate. She struggled to see Otto on her left. With a heavy pack on his front and a parachute on his back, he looked the way she felt: like some insect in a cocoon, waiting to hatch.

The plane shuddered and bucked again. She felt the sour taste of vomit at the back of her throat but refused to let it rise higher and gush into her mask. They'd both been given a drug called Dramamine before takeoff, but that only counteracted the motion sickness. Not the fear. She stared up at the metal panels above her head and started to count the rivets, willing the time to pass.

As if on cue, a small hatch opened above her head and the navigator's face appeared, his oxygen mask hanging to one side. He looked ludicrously young to be flying a plane, not much older than Leni.

Leni, Leni, Leni. Her new name throbbed through her head in time with the engines.

"Can you hear me?" yelled the navigator above the din.

Leni nodded and raised her gloved hand in a thumbs-up. Out of the corner of her eye she saw Otto respond similarly. She hoped he was all right.

"Five minutes to the drop zone. Understand?"

Thumbs up again. The plane gave a sudden violent lurch to the left.

"Sorry about the bumps!" the navigator went on jovially. "Bit of a storm. It's blown us south of the drop zone. But we'll soon have you down. Good luck!"

He gave them what Leni thought might have been a look of pity, then he slammed the inspection hatch shut.

Leni focused on the steady red light. Her stomach had turned to water.

The light started to flash. Her toes curled tight in her boots.

Then it turned green.

She took a deep breath. Before she knew it, she was completely weightless. Falling. Into the night.

―――――――

It was so black that when the ground came up to meet her, Leni only just managed to see it before her boots slammed down. She landed with her feet together just as she'd been taught, collapsing her knees and rolling onto her side. It really hurt, and knocked all the breath out of her. It was, she thought, a bit like being shot out of a circus cannon towards a brick wall, feetfirst. She lay still for a minute, trying to breathe, then scrambled to her feet and started gathering up her parachute. She prayed Otto had made it down safely. It had been too dark to see him, and she'd been concentrating on her own landing.

She tried to put the last few terrifying hours to the back of her mind. From the moment they'd strapped her into the Mosquito's bomb bay and the doors had slammed shut, she'd been convinced she was going to die. But she hadn't, and here she was. Which brought her back to the present. She was on a road. She frowned. There weren't supposed to be any roads near the landing zone.

She looked around, trying to get her bearings as her eyes gradually became accustomed to the dark. Soon she could see the outline of a forest to her left. Above her there was still the odd rumble of thunder, but the storm had passed through. She finished gathering in the parachute, unclipped her harness, and stepped out of it. The first thing she had to do was find somewhere to hide it. The ditch by the side of the road was the most obvious option.

It was still very dark and the moon was covered by the last of the storm clouds, but she managed to climb down into the ditch and crawled along it until she found a drain running under the road. She stuffed the parachute and harness inside it, out of sight. Next she took off her heavy flying suit, gloves, and helmet, and pushed them into the drain as well. Then she unpacked her Bund Deutscher Mädel uniform and quickly slipped on the long dark blue skirt, white short-sleeved blouse, and black neckerchief. When she had finished, she sat down in the ditch and rested for a few minutes. She suddenly felt cold as the sweat cooled her skin, and reached into her pack, pulling out the BDM woolen sweater she had also been issued.

Except for the sound of her rapid breathing, it was deathly quiet. No sounds at all. And no Otto, either. *How long have I been on the ground?* she wondered. *Half an hour? He has to be nearby, surely.* She checked the luminous hands on her watch. A nice German child's watch. *Glashütte.* Quite expensive. A present from her godmother, Frau Varbinner. The one they would be visiting in Bregenz in a couple of days. It was quarter to three. Two hours until dawn.

She didn't dare yell out his name. There was no way of knowing who might be out there in the darkness. Perhaps he was dead.

Please don't be dead, she thought.

8

Otto was thinking exactly the same thing.

If Leni was dead, or even badly hurt, then the mission was as good as finished. And so was he.

He had crashed down into a fir tree and was suspended fifty feet above the ground, his canopy hopelessly enmeshed in the higher branches. If Leni didn't turn up soon, he would have to cut himself free and face falling, wearing a full pack, through the branches to the ground below, risking a broken ankle or worse. He hissed her name again, afraid to yell. She could be anywhere. Where the hell was he, for that matter? He knew where he was supposed to be: on wide-open hop fields in the countryside twenty-five miles southeast of Munich. But he was getting a bad feeling that he was nowhere near the drop zone. When he parachuted down he'd felt the strong winds blowing him, and for a moment he had been terrified they might collapse the canopy. The rain had hammered at his face, and he'd gripped the lines for dear life. But he'd made it down in one piece, even if it was into this wretched forest.

It was just getting light now, shafts of dawn light filtering through the trees. He checked his father's wristwatch. MacPherson had had it repaired and Otto was glad to have it with him. A lucky talisman, he'd thought. But the mission hadn't exactly started well. It was a little after four o'clock. He'd been hanging here for over an hour. His legs felt numb and the harness cut painfully into his groin.

"Leni." He hissed her name one more time.

Nothing. Then he heard the sound of branches snapping beneath him. Someone was approaching.

Otto reached for the Walther PPK resting in the shoulder holster inside his flying suit. He pulled off the leather retaining strap and drew the pistol out, pointing it down to the gloomy forest floor.

"Don't move or I'll shoot," he ordered in German.

There was another sharp crack of branches.

"I mean it," he said. He swept the gun barrel, trying to find the target, every sinew in his body tense. His finger tightened on the trigger. Then he saw it. A fox staring up at him quizzically. He shooed loudly at it, and the animal darted away.

He reholstered the pistol, breathing hard. Shooting paper silhouettes was one thing; getting to ready to shoot for real had his head pounding. *Would I actually have pulled the trigger if it had been someone?* he wondered. *Perhaps instinct takes over and you just do it.*

"Otto!"

His heart jumped and then relief flooded over him. Leni. He twisted around in his harness to look down. There she was, standing below him, craning her neck up to see him in the gloom.

"Leni, thank God, you heard me!"

"Half of Bavaria probably heard you, Otto. Are you stuck?"

"No, no . . . I'm just enjoying the view." He grinned. He was so pleased to see her alive.

"What do you want me to do?" she asked, shaking her head at his silly remark.

Otto glanced down at her. "Give me a hand?"

Leni nodded and sized up the tree. She tucked her skirt into the waistband, then spat on her hands, rubbed them together, and grabbed hold of the lowest branch. Slowly she made her way up the side of the tree and edged out along the branch above him. He could see the training at Wanborough Manor had made the most of her natural agility. She took hold of the twisted parachute lines above her head, pulled on them, and built up a pendulum-like swing until Otto was able to grab hold of the branch she was sitting on, and wrap his arms and legs around it.

"Now cut the lines," he said, desperately hanging on.

Leni pulled out a short double-edged knife from a sheath

strapped to her thigh. She started to saw away at the lines. Otto watched her working, concentrating on the job, her legs clamped around the branch.

"Are you all right?" she said, severing the first of the nylon cords.

"I'm fine," he lied, though he was dripping with sweat and his skin was on fire.

At last Leni had cut all the lines. She resheathed her knife, planted her hands on the branch, and deftly swung her legs around like a gymnast on the uneven bars.

Otto couldn't hold on any longer. His hands slipped from the branch and then he was falling through the thick foliage. He landed on the soft mossy ground and lay there groaning.

"Don't move!" Leni whispered from the tree. "I'm coming."

Otto smiled weakly. "Hey, it's all right. I just decided to take the quickest way down."

Ten minutes later, after Otto had changed into his Hitler-Jugend uniform, and they'd buried his harness and flying suit as best they could, they reached the edge of the woods.

"Follow me!" said Leni, running forward from the tree line towards a farm track.

"Wait!" hissed Otto, grabbing her arm and pulling her down. "You need to be more careful."

He took a pair of binoculars out of his pack and scanned the area around them. In the dawn light he could see they had landed in rolling agricultural countryside: meadows and fields of grain, surrounded by thickly wooded hills. About a mile away he could make out a village.

"There's no one around, Otto," Leni said quietly. "It's not even five o'clock."

Otto ignored her and swept the area a second time before he stowed the binoculars. "Okay," he said, "where do you think we are?"

"Bavaria?" she said.

Otto laughed before he could stop himself. Then he found a map in his top pocket and pored over it. It was made of silk and beautifully detailed. But it wasn't much help in such poor light and with no landmarks to speak of. They'd have to take the farm track, and look out for features on the way.

Leni unwrapped a chocolate bar. "You want some?" she said, handing him a square.

He popped it in his mouth. It was the first thing he'd eaten in six hours and it tasted delicious. Too delicious, in fact. He glanced at the wrapper. Hershey's.

"Are you insane?" He turned on Leni. "You brought *American* chocolate with you? How are you going to explain that if someone stops us, searches us?"

Leni blushed. "It was just this bar, all right!" She pulled the wrapper off and screwed it up into a little ball. Then she threw it into the woods. "Satisfied?" she said.

"Let's hope no one finds it," Otto said grudgingly. He fished out his pocket compass and waited for the needle to settle.

"I think we should go east," he said.

"Fine," she said, clearly still irritated about the chocolate.

Otto knew they were only getting angry at each other because they were scared and they had no idea where they were, but they just had to make the best of it. There was no going back now.

"Sorry, all right? Can I have another piece?"

Leni handed him the rest of the chocolate and he wolfed it down. Then he stood up and adjusted his uniform, pulling up his long khaki socks and tightening the brown belt holding up his black lederhosen. The Hitler-Jugend uniform was immaculate in every detail, right down to the enamel badges on his shirt pocket for proficiency in swimming and sailing.

He remembered how upset his parents had been when his father had finally decided he and his brother would have to join. Not to have done so would have risked imprisonment for his parents and an orphanage for them. Not that it had mattered much in the long run, but right now he wished he could explain that to Leni.

"How do I look?" he asked her as he slid his service dagger with the swastika hilt into the scabbard on his belt.

"Horrible," she said.

Otto nodded. "So do you."

Together they picked up their packs and set off down the farm track.

9

THE ROAD TO PRIEN

They reached the village Otto had spotted from the woods well before six in the morning. They gave it a wide berth to avoid meeting any locals. Farmers were often up at first light. Once past it, they checked Otto's map again and were surprised to discover that the village had to be Reit im Winkl. It meant that they had at least landed west of the River Inn, which was something. Together they plotted a simple course that would take them east and then north to the town of Prien. From there they could catch a local train to the port of Stock on the Chiemsee.

It promised to be a hot day, and they were already sweating under the weight of their packs. Otto retrieved his water bottle and took a long swig before passing it to Leni. She gazed around as she drank, taking in the lush green farmland. They were almost in the foothills of the Alps, with the mountains rising up to the south. A few of the highest peaks were still covered with snow even now. She had taken summer holidays in the Alps.

Leni passed the water bottle back to Otto. "Why are you smiling like that?"

"Like what?" He stowed the bottle in his pack.

"I don't know . . ." Leni said. "Like you're at home or something . . ." She paused, staring at him. "Of course. You're from around here, aren't you?" He spoke with a Bavarian accent but he'd refused up till now to tell her exactly where his hometown was. *That must be another reason why MacPherson wanted Otto for this job*, she thought.

Otto looked as if he was wondering what to say. They weren't meant to tell each other too much about their previous lives. Now that they were in Germany again, it was vital they stuck to their aliases. They had to think of themselves as Otto and Leni Fischer of Salzburg.

"Sorry, I know we're not supposed to tell," Leni said, and walked on.

"You're right," came Otto's voice behind her. "I used to live not far from here, to the north." He sounded so sad.

Leni decided to ask no more questions, and they walked on in silence for another half an hour until they reached an enormous road. They both stopped and stared in amazement. In front of them was one of the new and famous Autobahns of which the Reich was so proud: six-lane roads that the Führer had built all across Germany. This had to be the new route between Munich and Innsbruck. They would have to cross it to keep their line east across the farmland. It was empty now, but from the south came the low rumble of vehicles.

Leni grabbed Otto's arm. "Should we hide?"

Otto shook his head, and Leni supposed he was right. It was too late, anyway.

A convoy of army vehicles was coming towards them. With a shudder, Leni recalled how such similar cold parades had rolled through the streets of Vienna three years before. First to rumble past were a dozen *Kübelwagen*, the standard German Army field car. After them came perhaps thirty Opel trucks, built to carry troops, and even more tank transporters. Otto tugged at Leni's sleeve. She glanced at him and saw he had his right arm raised in a Nazi salute. Quickly she followed suit.

But the sight was intimidating, and a shiver ran down Leni's body as she held a salute she had never imagined making in her life. She hated herself for doing it. Walking through the countryside on a bright sunny morning, she had almost forgotten the war. But seeing these tanks, with the black-and-white crosses on their turrets, she was reminded sharply of the terrible fighting going on all over the world.

When the last vehicle had passed and the rumble of engines had begun to fade, Otto and Leni decided to cross the Autobahn. As they were about to do so, a battered old Daimler car puttered towards them.

"Let's hitch," said Leni.

"It's too risky," said Otto. He looked on edge. "Remember what MacPherson told us? Avoid all unnecessary contact with strangers. He drilled it into us."

"But he also told us to use our initiative — and my feet are killing me already."

"No."

"Come on, Otto, we've got to talk to someone eventually and the driver's an old man. He looks all right."

Before he could protest any further, Leni jumped onto the road and waved enthusiastically. The car slowed to a stop.

"Just don't say anything you don't have to say, all right?" said Otto, but he still seemed reluctant.

"Good morning, sir. Are you going east by any chance?" Leni smiled politely at the grizzled old man.

"North, towards Rosenheim, but only for a few miles. Is that any good?" the man said.

"That would be perfect," replied Leni in her sweetest voice.

"Jump in, then. So long you don't mind sharing with Gunter." The man jerked his thumb towards the backseat. A large spotted pig was lying there, bold as brass.

"Oh, we don't mind," Leni said, quickly opening the front passenger door and bagging the seat next to the farmer.

Otto scowled and climbed in the back. The pig appeared to appreciate the company and farted a loud welcome.

"He's happy, going to visit his girlfriend in Rosenheim. Make some little piglets for me." The farmer chuckled and slammed the car into gear. The Daimler accelerated down the road.

"That was a big convoy," said Otto.

The driver grunted. "Been like that for the last month or more. All coming back from Italy and whatnot, heading east. Something big's about to happen, if you ask me. Where are you two headed?"

"East," said Otto shortly.

"Well, that doesn't sound like a good idea, does it?" The farmer laughed.

Leni was inclined to agree.

Half an hour later, the car pulled up on the side of the road. To the left a track led towards a Bavarian timber farmhouse. A sturdy-looking woman in a black skirt and red blouse was herding some cattle out of a pasture towards the milking shed.

"Well, young people, this is Gunter's stop."

Leni turned to the back. Otto was sound asleep, his head resting on the pig's buttocks. She giggled. The farmer whistled loudly, and both Otto and the pig woke with a start.

Otto and Leni scrambled out, and watched the car bounce down the track to the farm where Gunter's girlfriend was waiting. Then they set off down a country lane towards Prien. They walked in silence for a good ten minutes, alone with their thoughts, the only chatter coming from the birds in the hedgerows and the grasshoppers in the weeds.

"What was MacPherson talking to you about?" Leni suddenly asked.

"What do you mean?"

"Yesterday, before we left. When I went up to my room, he kept you behind. What did he say?"

"Nothing," said Otto.

"Well, he must have said something."

Otto shrugged, but Leni could see he was blushing. "He was just running through some details about our family."

"That's all?" said Leni. She was unconvinced. Otto might be good at shooting, but he was rubbish at lying.

"That's all."

They walked on. "We have to trust each other, Otto," Leni said eventually.

"I know and it wasn't important, I promise." But he was looking straight ahead and not at her. Leni decided not to push it any further for now. She'd get it out of him in the end, whatever it was.

"Fine, let's talk about something else," she said.

Otto smiled. He seemed relieved. "All right, let's practice. What do we like to do on a Sunday afternoon after lunch?"

Leni thought for a moment. "Ah, the Fischers are creatures of habit. We don't often leave Salzburg. In the summer we go to the park for the concerts in the Mirabell gardens."

"And in the winter?"

"Skating. We go skating at Hellbrunn."

"I love skating," said Otto. He sounded wistful, as if he really did. "Your turn."

"All right, what's the name of the girl you like on our street?"

"What? There isn't a girl I like," said Otto, frowning.

Leni smiled. "Good," she said.

10

FLY BOYS

Otto and Leni reached Prien by midday, keeping mostly to the lanes and walking across farmland in places. They had seen plenty of people along the route, working the land and going about their daily business in little villages, but no one had stopped or questioned them except to wish them *"Guten Tag."* Now they were waiting in Prien's pleasant main square for the train to the lakeside port of Stock. A brass band was playing military tunes.

MacPherson had briefed them about the area, and the lake in particular, but Otto already knew that the Chiemsee was the largest lake in Bavaria, nearly twenty-five miles long and three wide. It was deep, too, teeming with fish, and had three islands. The largest was the Herreninsel, and the smallest the uninhabited Krautinsel. But, as MacPherson had told them, it was on the middle island, the Fraueninsel, that the child was being held. Otto and Leni were to take a pleasure boat to visit King Ludwig's nineteenth-century summer palace on the Herreninsel in the afternoon and from there make their way across to the second island by nightfall.

After a year away from Germany, Otto found sitting in this town square strangely alien. He didn't feel connected to the country anymore. Perhaps, he thought, it was because he was there under an assumed identity. Every other person seemed to be wearing some kind of uniform, and most buildings were draped with Nazi flags. Had it been like this before he'd escaped? Maybe he was just more sensitive to it now. He listened to the brass band and tried to take his mind off the situation.

"Maybe we should walk to Stock. It's only a few miles," he said.

Leni was sitting with her bare feet in the stone fountain in the center of the square. She took her left one out and examined the blister on the side of her big toe. "My feet are on fire. I'm not walking anywhere except to the station."

"I don't like hanging around here," Otto muttered.

Leni took out a small printed timetable and consulted it. "The train'll be here in twenty minutes, and no one's taking a blind bit of notice of us." She plunged her foot back into the water. "Can't you buy us some lemonade at least?"

"All right. Wait here. I'll be back in a minute."

Otto walked across the square towards a small store. It was a traditional, family-run business with long salamis covered in peppercorns hanging above the counter. At the back was a tin tub full of ice and water and floating bottles of beer and lemonade. He plunged in his hand, took out two bottles, and went back to the front of the shop. There was a queue, and the woman in front of him in the line took an age buying her weekly groceries: a little bit of this and a little bit of that, all interspersed with a good long chat about local events. Otto shifted from one foot to the next, anxious not to be separated from Leni for too long. Five minutes later, he stepped outside and knew immediately there was something wrong.

A truck towing a glider on a trailer had arrived in the square, but for a moment Otto couldn't see Leni. Then he spotted her near the truck, surrounded by teenage boys. She was looking around nervously, trying to locate him. He hurried over, trying to stem the rising panic in his chest. There was a logo on the truck around the initials *NSFK*. A winged man, Icarus, with a swastika at his feet. Otto recognized it as the emblem of the national gliding club. The boys around Leni were tall and broad-shouldered, mostly blond or sandy-haired. They looked fit and handsome and strong. They looked like trouble.

As Otto reached Leni, he saw she'd put her shoes back on.

"Come on, let's get to the station," he said to her.

She picked up her bag. "Well, it was nice meeting you," she said to the three boys closest to her. Then she started to walk away with Otto.

He could tell she was ready to run. "Don't hurry," he whispered to her. "They'll get suspicious."

"What took you so long?" she hissed back.

"Hey, you!" one of the boys shouted.

"Just keep walking!" said Otto sharply. This was not looking good. He heard the sound of footsteps behind them. Then a hand grasped his shoulder, pulling him to a halt. He turned around. A strapping boy, who looked about sixteen, was standing in front of him, his hands on his hips. Two others stood beside him. They all had the silver Icarus badges on their shirts.

"That wasn't very polite, was it?"

Otto tried to stay calm and keep his voice even. "I'm sorry, we are in a hurry."

"Actually, we have a train to catch!" Leni said.

The boy glanced over to the station. So did Otto and Leni. The train was approaching. "So get the next one," he said casually.

"What do you want with us?" Otto asked.

The boy smiled, showing white, straight teeth. "Well, your girlfriend is very pretty . . ."

"She's not my girlfriend," said Otto.

"Really? Then you won't mind if I buy her an ice cream."

"Actually, he's my brother, and he would mind," said Leni.

The three boys stared at Otto.

"Your brother?" They didn't look convinced.

"Yes, and she's right, I do mind. So please leave us alone."

"Tell you what," the first boy said pleasantly, "I'm going to ignore your advice, *little man*, and take your sister for an ice cream anyway."

Just as the train's whistle blew, he drove his fist into Otto's solar plexus. Otto pitched down onto the ground, gasping, all the air driven from his lungs.

"No!" cried Leni, reaching down to help him.

The boy grabbed her arm and yanked her up. "There's really no need to be rude." He pulled Leni towards him, all the while smiling at Otto. "Particularly when you're so pretty. My name's Rudi. What's yours?"

"Let go of her." Otto was back on his feet, but Rudi was bigger and stronger than him, and there was no way he could beat the three boys in a straight fight.

"And what if I don't want to? What are you going to do about it?" Rudi said, laughing. His companions joined in.

For a moment Otto thought of the pistol inside his pack, then put the thought right out of his mind.

"I'll fight you," he said instead, and stepped towards him.

"As you wish." Rudi laughed. He turned to Leni. "This won't take long, beautiful, then there'll be an ice cream for you and a kiss for me, I think." He let her go. As he did so, she twisted to one side and it was then that Otto saw the glint of her knife in her hand.

The train's whistle sounded again, louder this time.

"Perhaps an apology would be better." Leni's voice was icy.

"What is this?" The young man stared down at the knife.

"It's an apology to my brother from you," she said, stepping in close and pressing the blade against his ribs.

Rudi looked into her eyes. "You wouldn't dare."

"Try me." She returned his stare and pressed the point of the blade harder into his side. He winced.

"Say it."

"Never." He spat the words back at her, a fleck of spittle hitting her on the cheek.

"As you wish," Leni repeated, then her hand moved and the boy looked down at the red stain that suddenly bloomed on his shirt. Leni had sliced through cotton and opened the skin just below his ribs. Not deep enough to do any serious damage, but sufficient to wound his pride. And hurt like hell.

"Run," she said to Otto.

He didn't need telling twice. Together they sprinted towards the station and pulled themselves up into the last carriage just as the train began to move. As they unslung their packs, Rudi appeared outside their window, hammering on the carriage's glass as he ran along the platform.

"You're dead!" he screamed at them. "You hear me? Dead!"

Then the train was clear of the platform and he was gone.

Otto sat down. He was suddenly conscious of other passengers in the carriage staring at them. "My God, Leni," he whispered, "did you have to do that?"

Leni smoothed her blouse, tucking a stray hair back behind her ear. "He won't tell anyone. Think about it, if word gets round that a younger girl got the better of him, he'll be a laughingstock." She glanced at Otto. "Are you all right?"

"Fine, I'm fine. I could have beaten him. He took me by surprise, that's all."

Leni nodded. "Of course," she said, but Otto could see she was hiding a smile.

"Well, maybe a thank-you is in order." Otto closed his eyes and sighed. "But please don't do it again."

After a while he opened his eyes and gazed out at the view. The train was traveling along the edge of the Chiemsee, and scores of little boats were bobbing on the sparkling water. His heart began to beat more calmly.

But he wasn't sure what had alarmed him most: the confrontation with the young thug, or the fact that Leni had shown herself to be tough as well as fearless. Now he couldn't help wondering: Would she get them out of danger . . . or into it?

11

BICYCLE THIEVES

Leni caught Otto staring at her during the train ride and felt herself blushing under his intent gaze. The more she thought about it, the more she couldn't quite believe what she'd done. It had just sort of happened, as if it were out of her control. When the youth had postured and bullied and then hit out at Otto, something inside her had just flipped, like a switch, and she'd found the knife in her hand. But she was pleased with herself, even if it might cause trouble down the line. It was like the time she'd come upon her youngest brother being taunted by some older boys, his shorts pulled down around his ankles. Without thinking she'd waded into them, her fists flying, feet kicking, until they turned and fled, noses bleeding and shins bruised. Her father had received several complaints, she knew, but he had kissed her on the top of the head and told her how proud he was.

The train started to slow, and she focused once more on the present. They stood up together to reach for their packs just as the train braked sharply. She lurched forward into Otto, who caught her in his arms. They stayed like that for a moment or two, frozen, then Otto stepped back, letting go of her as if he'd been scalded.

"I'll get your bag," he said, not meeting her eye.

"Thank you," Leni replied formally as he lifted it down.

They exited the station at Stock and walked the length of the promenade, carefully examining the shops and businesses before they reached the landings where the tourist ferries were moored. Just beyond them, at the end of the town, they could make out a dozen or more large tents erected in a field, with a small armada of sailing dinghies and canoes tethered at the water's edge nearby. A large group of teenagers seemed to be getting ready for an afternoon's sailing on the lake. The Hitler-Jugend sailing camp. Otto and Leni had been issued with papers to use if need be, showing their late enrollment in the camp. Leni hoped they wouldn't need them. If anyone started questioning them, the mission might be compromised before it had even begun.

"Just keep away from any more boys offering to buy you an ice cream," said Otto as they stood together, leaning on the promenade rail. Leni wondered for a moment if there wasn't a smidgeon of jealousy in his voice.

"I can take care of myself," she replied tartly.

"That's what I'm worried about," said Otto.

Leni managed a small smile. "We'd better synchronize our watches. I have ten past two . . . now."

Otto looked down at his father's gold watch and adjusted it. "Check," he said and pushed the crown in, setting the time. "See you in one hour. Good hunting."

"You, too," said Leni, and hurried back down the promenade.

Each of them had the task of stealing a bicycle to use for their getaway from the town in the early hours of the following morning. That was, of course, if everything went according to plan. The rendezvous point was at the back of a deserted boatyard they had identified while walking through the town.

Fortunately it was a little after two o'clock and people were enjoying a late luncheon in the numerous cafés along the promenade. It was only a matter of minutes before Leni found a suitable bike and satisfied herself that it was safe to steal. Minutes later she had ridden it along to the boatyard, which was still deserted. She hid the bike at the back under a large piece of canvas, then slipped out unseen, anxious to complete the other task she had been assigned.

She walked along the parade of shops and eventually found the chandlers. She went inside and the owner nodded a greeting to her as he finished serving another customer. It gave Leni time to select the sort of rope they would need later that night. Ropes of different widths and materials were on rollers by the window. She made her choice and went over to the shopkeeper once the other customer had left the shop.

"I'll like twenty yards of this one please," she said, indicating the rope she wanted.

"Twenty yards, young lady?" The shopkeeper wasn't exactly suspicious, but he was curious. He looked at Leni's BDM uniform. "Are you with the sailing club?"

"Yes, that's right."

The man nodded. "I haven't seen you before."

"No, it's my first year." Leni tried to keep her voice light.

The man nodded again and pulled the rope she had chosen off its roller, measuring the yardage with his stick.

"Are you enjoying yourself, young lady?" he asked.

"Oh, absolutely, it's great fun. I'm learning a lot."

"That's good. Here you are." The man expertly looped the rope around his arm and wound it tightly in the middle. He walked back to the counter and wrote out a receipt.

"How much?" Leni reached for her wallet.

The man frowned. "The club has an account."

"Ah, yes, that's right. I forgot. They told me that. I wasn't thinking. First time . . ."

Stop talking now! yelled a voice in Leni's head.

The man looked at her again, then slowly handed her the rope.

"Make sure you tell Frau Farbiner that I have given you a twenty percent discount."

"I will, of course, I will."

Who the hell is Frau Farbiner? thought Leni as she walked out of the shop and headed towards the sailing club tents, glancing back now and again to see if the shopkeeper was watching her. He was. She continued walking, then pretended to stop in front of a shop window. The man was still there, but then another customer stepped into the shop and he disappeared. Leni breathed a sigh of relief and doubled back as fast as she could to the boatyard. She hunkered down at the back and waited.

Otto appeared soon after, wheeling not one but two bicycles, the second one designed for a younger child.

"Can you believe it?" He laughed. "It's perfect."

Leni lifted up the canvas and helped him put the bicycles next to hers.

"They belong to a mother and her little girl. I saw them go to a café for some ice cream. When they come out their day will be ruined." He chuckled.

"Don't be so horrid," said Leni.

Otto shrugged. "I'm sorry, I didn't mean anything by it."

"Typical unfeeling boy," said Leni.

Otto ignored this. "What about the rope?" he asked.

Leni held it up.

"Why didn't you get him to wrap it up? It'll stick out on the ferry."

"He was asking a lot of questions. I needed to get out quick. All right?" said Leni defensively. "What about the church?"

"It's fine for what we need," confirmed Otto.

It was time to catch the ferry to Herreninsel. They made their way on board and the boat weighed anchor, the funnels belching black smoke as the engines started up belowdecks.

The boat was soon out in the middle of the lake, and Leni hung on the deck rail, enjoying the cool breeze off the water. Otto chose to sit on one of the slatted benches bolted to the middle section of the deck. He kept their packs wedged beneath him and the rope tucked away out of sight beside them. Apart from a few soldiers in uniform on a day out with their girl-friends, there was no sense of a world war. It seemed as though no place on earth could be more peaceful and pleasant than this sunny June afternoon in Bavaria.

When they reached the island, they joined a group of tourists walking two by two from the jetty through thick pine woods to King Ludwig's Palace. But as the party trooped towards the entrance, Otto and Leni darted away unseen to the side of the building.

They squatted down in the trees, and Otto unfolded a more detailed silk map of the two main islands, showing the footpaths through the woods as well the buildings and other structures. They studied it carefully, then made their way to the west of the island. At the water's edge there, they found the small fishing jetty marked on the map. There were a number of unattended boats moored up, as they had hoped. They agreed that one of them, a small dinghy with a bright red sail, was just what they needed.

Fraueninsel was over a mile away, but the brass onion-shaped dome of the convent's chapel rose clearly above the tree line. Even Leni with her poor eyesight could see it.

"Let's go!" she said, and started to climb down to the boat.

"No! We're to wait until sundown, remember? Less chance of anyone bothering us."

Leni looked back up at him. "You think that's a good idea? What if there's a problem with the boat in the dark? Or the weather breaks? Or the wind drops? Besides, there's only a few fishing boats around. The fishermen will think we're from the sailing club. They won't take any notice of us." She was anxious to keep moving.

Otto rubbed his chin with his thumb. "I suppose it'll give us time to survey the island before dark." But he didn't look as though he liked her taking charge.

"Whatever you say," Leni said, trying not to smile.

12

THE *AMERIKA*

At the same time as Otto and Leni were looking out to Fraueninsel, Hitler's express train, the *Führersonderzug*, also known as the *Amerika*, thundered through southern Austria, heading, if not directly at them, then in their direction. The armored carriages rattled over the points as the train blasted through a country station, its whistle shrieking a warning.

Martin Bormann, a thickset man with broad, heavy features and slicked-back dark hair, strode through the carriages. He was dressed in a gray suit with a small gold swastika badge in the buttonhole of the jacket — a recent personal gift from the Führer. Since Rudolf Hess's flight to Scotland, Bormann had seized the opportunity presented to him and replaced his former boss as Hitler's personal secretary and head of the Nazi Party's political framework. At a stroke he had taken over Hitler's paperwork, appointments, and massive but secret personal wealth. From now on, all other Party members would have to answer to him if they wished to have access to the Führer.

An SS sentry guard snapped to attention and opened the door to the Führer's carriage with a white-gloved hand. Hitler was sitting alone in his wood-paneled carriage, situated exactly in the middle of the train. It was simply furnished, like his apartment in Munich, with dark wooden tables, leather-backed seats, and a portrait of himself over the mantelpiece. As Bormann came in, he slid a series of photographs that he had been reviewing off his knees and folded his hands. One appeared to have a slight tremor.

"What is the news from London?"

"Not good, mein Führer. Our agents cannot tell us where the British are holding the Deputy Leader."

"He is no longer the Deputy Leader! Never call him that again! Never!" Hitler was suddenly spitting the words, his face contorted with rage.

"Of course." Bormann lowered his head in contrition.

Hitler sat in silence for a few moments, apparently calm. He stared out of the window. People at a crossing were standing to attention outside their vehicles, their arms raised in salute as the train roared past. He casually threw back a salute.

"Perhaps you would like to run through your appointments for the next twenty-four hours?" Bormann ventured. "I have brought the diary."

Hitler waved the suggestion away. Bormann cleared his throat and tried a different tack.

"Führer, Hess is insane. In fact, the Reichsminister for Information is at this very moment preparing a further broadcast —"

"You know nothing, nothing of what you speak!" Hitler was suddenly furious once more. "For these last weeks I have struggled with his treachery. Wondering at the purpose of it. What sword can he raise to strike against me? Only now do I see what that weapon is. And I must act quickly to deflect it."

"Forgive me, Führer." Bormann once again cast his eyes to the floor.

"Bring Heydrich to the Berghof immediately. Without delay, do you hear me? I have a mission that only he can carry out. Do you understand?"

"Yes, mein Führer, *zu Befehl*. At once."

Bormann strode from the carriage, the order ringing in his ears.

13

THE BELL TOWER

It seemed to Angelika that she could see for hundreds of miles from the top of the convent's bell tower, which had slit windows at the four points of the compass. Staring through them, she could make out the towns, villages, and mountains to the south, and the roads around the shore of the huge lake. It was wonderful to gaze at them but at the same time she felt very sad to know that she would never be allowed to paddle in the lake, let alone visit the mainland.

She crept over the wooden planks to the next window, skirting the massive bronze bell hanging in the middle of the tower. It took three nuns pulling together to make it ring, and she had been told it could be heard across the whole of the lake. The air was stifling and, even in just the white shorts and cotton undershirt she wore beneath her woolen novice's robe, she was boiling hot and thirsty. But she didn't mind. Being up here by herself, even just for an hour or two, was her favorite thing to do.

Her second favorite thing was to climb the pine trees just outside the walls of the convent. It was more fun than going up the bell tower, but if Sister Margareta caught her there she'd be furious and, anyway, you couldn't see nearly as far. Sister Margareta had been on the warpath just lately, always keeping a beady eye on her, and so Angelika had decided against sneaking out today. In fact, she felt as if she was being watched by the rest of the nuns, even the novices, most of the time. She knew they talked about her because they often fell silent when she approached. On the other hand, she was not encouraged to talk to them, and so over the years she'd become happy to spend most of her free time in her own company.

Her third favorite thing was visiting the convent's library. Most Sundays, after morning service and her walk around the gardens with the mother superior, she was allowed an hour or two before lunch to explore the rows of books in their tall oak shelves. She would pore over the atlases and encyclopedias and learn about the wonders that lay outside her little white-washed room on this tiny island. She especially loved reading about the mountains of the Alps, which she could just see from the tower.

At least she'd been lucky this afternoon and the coast had been clear in the church below, so she could slip unnoticed into the tower. She had finished weeding in the kitchen garden by three o'clock, which meant she had an hour before she had to wash and get ready for tea — just bread and goats' milk — and then evensong. She looked once more at the mountains in the distance. She longed to visit them — even if it was just for a day. That would be the best birthday present anyone could give her, she thought.

Angelika's birthday was this Sunday and she was looking forward to it. Of course, nothing was made of it by the nuns or the mother superior, but every year since she had been at the convent a visitor had come to see her. He was a very nice man who always brought a camera, a pretty dress, and a huge box of chocolates, and he would take a photograph of her in the dress. He never told her his name but she knew the chocolates were from Munich. It said so on the box.

This birthday would be her fifth at the convent. Five years stuck on this little island. At least it was summer now. In the winter, the cold and rain and fog made her feel even more of a captive, almost like a criminal in a prison. Since the war had started, the mood in the convent had changed. The nuns had become preoccupied and she'd been even more unhappy. Perhaps the mother superior sensed this and that was why she'd walk with her every week, talking to her quietly about God's purpose for her, about how special and important she was, and how she must be patient and trust in God. She felt better after these talks. The chocolates the mother superior doled out helped, too, but even so, on a day like today, when she was staring out like a bird in a cage at the world beyond, she longed to spread her wings and fly.

She moved to the last of the windows, the one that faced west towards Herreninsel. The lake was still studded with boats at the end of the day. The steam ferry on its way back to Stock, its decks crowded with tourists dressed in bright summer clothes, tiny pinpoints of color. Closer to her were fishing boats and a sailing boat that was halfway between the two islands. It had a bright red sail and was heading straight towards her. She could just make out two figures: one hunched down at the front, and another holding the tiller and the rope for the main sail. *It must be wonderful to be out there on the water like that*, she thought. Then she got up and checked on the position of the sun. She had no watch but had learned to tell the time as accurately as a sundial. It was nearly four. Time to go, or risk discovery.

Angelika quickly pulled her robe over her head, slipped on her leather sandals, and hurried back down the stone steps. *One day*, she thought. *One day I will be free.*

14

ON THE WATER

Otto and Leni's little sailing dinghy scudded nimbly over the gentle swell. To the south was a cluster of fishing boats, men hauling in their nets, but otherwise there was nothing on the water near them. They were making excellent time and the shore of Fraueninsel was now only a few hundred feet away.

Otto sat in the stern, holding the tiller, with Leni squeezed farther up on the port side. She had the packs with her and the rope stowed beside them. A light breeze filled the sail, and the dinghy's hull was heeling gently, up on its side.

In front of them was a small cove, the beach covered in large flat stones. *Nearly there*, thought Otto. He felt relief at the prospect of dry land.

Above them came the sound of an aircraft. The drone of a single-engine plane. It grew louder. Otto and Leni shielded their eyes, looking up to the fading blue sky, as the drone became a whine, higher in range as it drew closer. A fighter plane suddenly filled Otto's vision, the nose cone painted a bright scarlet. It was not of a type that Otto had ever seen before and it was heading straight towards them, no more than a hundred feet above the water. He glimpsed a pilot in white leather flying helmet and gloves, his mouth open and his teeth bared. The pilot raised a hand and waved, just as the downdraft hit the sail and rocked the dinghy from side to side.

For a moment, time slowed and shifted and Otto was once more back on the beach in Dunkirk with bullets chasing him across the sand and into the sea. He panicked.

"Otto, no!" screamed Leni.

But he was already over the side of the boat and plunging into the lake. The shock of the icy water knocked all the air from his chest. He kicked for the surface and saw that the dinghy was already thirty feet away. He began to swim after it, but it was going too fast. The wind had caught the sail. He could see Leni had scooted to the stern and was gripping the tiller. But she was obviously frightened. Too late he remembered she hadn't much enjoyed the sailing lessons.

"Pull the tiller towards you until the boat goes into the wind," he shouted, pushing himself to swim even faster.

To his relief, Leni did as he said. The bow came around and the sail emptied of wind and started flapping. Leni sat down, waiting for Otto to catch up. As he reached the little boat he grabbed hold of the side and began pulling himself on board. Unfortunately, it was just at that moment that Leni stood up to help him in, leaning over to grab his arm. The dinghy capsized, throwing her into the water beside Otto. The mast and sail sank below the surface, and the hull turned turtle.

Leni coughed and spluttered. "The packs!" she screamed.

Taking a deep breath, Otto dived under the water. He could see the packs just below him, gradually sinking to the bottom of the lake. A very deep lake, he remembered quite suddenly. He tried not to think about Dunkirk, or the feeling of the rope slipping from his hand. He dived after the nearest pack and grabbed it. For a moment he felt it drag him down like an anchor, then he kicked with all his strength towards the surface, pulling the bag behind him, until his free hand found the edge of the boat. His head emerged from the water, and he sucked at the air. Then Leni burst up beside him, making him shout out with surprise.

"Got the other pack," she gasped. "Can you swim to the beach?"

Otto nodded. Holding the pack with one arm, he kicked for the shore.

A few minutes later they struggled up onto the beach, lugging their waterlogged packs along the dark, silty earth and onto the large stones.

"I'm sorry, Leni." Otto sat down.

The upturned dinghy had drifted in after them and was banging against the rocks in the shallows.

"I don't understand. Why did you jump off the boat like that?" She was staring at him with a look of concern.

"It's just . . . well, the plane reminded me of something . . . Something that happened to me."

Leni nodded, seeming to realize that he didn't want to talk about it. "Well, that pilot was absolutely crazy. Can you believe he actually waved and smiled?"

Otto got to his feet. "We'd better not stay out here in the open," he said. The island was small and not so densely wooded as Herreninsel. The outline of the convent's main buildings could be seen through the trees.

Leni picked up her pack. "You're right. We need to keep out of sight until nightfall. Head up there to the tree line. We still have enough daylight to dry our things out, with a bit of luck." Then she stopped. "Oh, no!" she wailed. "The rope, we've lost the rope."

"It's all right," said Otto.

"No, it's not! If you hadn't jumped like that we wouldn't be in this mess!"

"Look, I've said I'm sorry. I'll think of something, all right? You go up to the woods."

"Why, what are you going to do?" Leni asked, still fuming.

"Get rid of that dinghy."

He picked up the biggest stone he could carry and walked back to the boat, then raised it above his head and let it fall. The stone crashed straight through the wooden hull, leaving a large hole. Otto waded out into the water, pushing the boat in front of him, and watched as it filled with water and slowly sank below the surface.

15

OBERSCHLEISSHEIM AIRFIELD, MUNICH

Before the propeller blades had stopped turning, Reinhard Heydrich had already unstrapped and was out of the cockpit. He slid down the wing in his immaculate white flying suit to be greeted by the commander of the *Luftwaffe's* experimental flight wing.

"What do you think?"

"Incredible, Major. Just incredible. Flying this plane is just as you promised it would be, but more so." Heydrich was breathless in his enthusiasm. "I thank you for the honor."

"The honor is the Luftwaffe's, sir, that you should be one of the first to fly the 190."

"How many do you have now?"

"The first six were delivered this week. Another twelve by the end of the month. Once we have evaluated them, full production will commence."

"The sooner the better."

Heydrich pulled off his flying helmet and ran his hand through his cropped hair. He was nearly six feet tall, with fleshy lips and cold gray eyes. At the age of thirty-seven, he was already head of the RSHA — the *Reichssicherheitshauptamt*, or Reich Security Service — and the most feared man in Germany. He had the power to make any person disappear without a trace.

He took a long swig of water from the metal canteen the major handed to him.

"There is something else I would like to show you, sir, if you have time. It seems as though our factories have something new and exciting for us to test almost every week."

Heydrich nodded. "I always have time when it comes to new planes."

They walked back across the airfield towards the line of camouflaged hangars, but just as they reached the first of them, Heydrich's car, a black Mercedes limousine, sped towards them. It came to a sharp halt, and Heydrich's driver jumped out and ran across to them, leaving the engine running.

"Urgent message for you from the Führer, sir."

Heydrich sliced open the telex message and read its contents. He frowned. "You must excuse me, Major. I am required immediately at the Berghof."

"I understand. Perhaps I can be of assistance? Please follow me."

Heydrich waved his driver away and followed the major into the nearest hangar. In the middle of it sat a helicopter.

"This is a Flettner Kolibri," the major said, with obvious pride. "She's the latest model of the Hummingbird, sir. We're testing her for the *Kriegsmarine*. She's ten times more maneuverable than any of our planes. She can land on a Reichmark."

Heydrich stared. In this he could be at Hitler's mountain home in less than thirty minutes. How impressive that would seem. The Führer sends for him and he appears almost instantly, like an eagle swooping down from the sky.

"Have your men call the Führer's security control at the Berghof. Tell them to expect us. It wouldn't do for me to be shot down, would it?"

Ten minutes later, Heydrich was sitting in the open cockpit beside the pilot, the rotors spooling above them. The helicopter lifted off, rising straight up into the air. It hovered there for a moment, like its namesake, then wheeled about and headed south, slowly climbing into the sky.

Heydrich looked down at Munich. Through his goggles he could just make out, to the north of the city, the concentration camp the SS had built near the town of Dachau. Then it faded from view and he could see the new Autobahns to the south, gray ribbons heading in all directions. Truly, he thought, there was nothing the Reich could not achieve.

16

SO IT BEGINS

It was dark by the time Leni had finished drying out the contents of their packs, checking, then restowing them. The only damage had been to some of their German food rations. She had thrown them away and instead made soup with some Erbswurst pellets, mixing the resulting broth with a tin of beef in gravy. She gave the pot a stir. It didn't smell too bad.

The sudden sharp snap of a fallen tree branch sent Leni diving away from the small campfire, snatching up the pistol lying beside her pack. She froze and gave a single-note whistle. A moment later it was answered by a three-note response. Otto was back.

By the time she'd poured the soup into their enamel mugs, he was squatting down beside her, his face running with perspiration from the muggy summer night air. She handed him a mug.

"Smells pretty good," he said, sniffing at it.

"Yes, well, you can cook next time," said Leni. Otto was already shoveling the soup into his mouth. "So, what did you find?"

Otto stopped shoveling for a moment. "Good news. The walls are low enough to climb and the nuns have gone to bed." MacPherson had given them precise instructions regarding the convent's routine, and it seemed the nuns were following it to the letter. "It's just a short run from the main building to the jetty. You'll easily make your way there in the dark."

Leni nodded, relieved. "What about other people on the island?"

"There are a few villas and a small hotel farther along, just as MacPherson said, but I've seen no one around." Otto finished his soup and held out his mug for more. "The only problem is the rope."

"You think all I've been doing is the laundry and the cooking while you've been off snooping around?"

"You've thought of something?"

"Of course I have," said Leni, a little exasperated. She spread out MacPherson's map of the convent, the flames from the small fire giving them enough light to study it. "Here's the laundry room. If I can get two or three sheets from it, I can cut them up and make a rope."

"Good idea," acknowledged Otto. "I was thinking of something similar myself."

"Oh, really," said Leni, arching an eyebrow.

"Yes, but maybe it's a bit risky spending too much time there, on the ground floor."

"That's why I'm going to make the rope here, in this little store cupboard on the same landing as the girl." Leni pointed to it on the map.

"It's going to take you a while," Otto said. He looked at his watch. "I think we should go now."

Leni knew he was right. She checked her watch. It was just after ten o'clock. The moon was coming up. It was half full, giving a good light and saving their flashlights.

They quickly made their way through the trees to the walled vegetable garden at the north of the convent. Leni took off her pack.

"Ready?" asked Otto.

Leni nodded, swallowing. "I feel sick," she said.

"Me, too," said Otto. "I think it's your cooking."

Leni smiled tightly and took some deep breaths.

"I'll be waiting at the jetty," Otto went on. "We have to be off the island by three o'clock at the latest. First light is at four." He looked at the fluorescent hands of his watch. "I have ten-oh-seven."

Leni looked at her watch. "Check." She stood there for a moment. "Look, if there's a problem, I don't want you to . . . come and get me. Just make a run for it."

"There won't be a problem," he said firmly.

"But if there is . . ."

Otto answered by stepping towards her. For a moment Leni thought he was going to hug her, but he just laced his fingers, cupping his hands to give her a boost.

"You'll be fine," he said.

She stepped onto his hands and he lifted her up the side of the wall. She swung her legs over the top and landed heavily on the other side, feeling grateful now for the hours of practice on the dreaded wall at Wanborough Manor. Her pack landed next to her with a thud.

"Three o'clock," she heard Otto hiss.

Otto listened to Leni's fading footsteps on the gravel. When he could no longer hear them, he struck out down the path by the vegetable garden wall. Then he skirted the low walls of the main building and slipped past the gates, which were closed for the night but not, Otto noted, locked. The island's isolation clearly afforded enough security — or so the nuns must have thought. A paved path wide enough for a cart led in an almost-straight line through more woodland to the jetty.

There was no one about, just the sound of crickets in the short grass and an occasional bat flitting above him. Somewhere a dog barked. The jetty loomed ahead of him, stretching out into the lake. Fishing boats and launches were tied up along both sides. They scraped gently against each other, their cork fenders groaning quietly. The hotel at the water's edge was full of lights and the sound of music, but it was some way from the jetty.

Otto heard Admiral MacPherson's words in his ear as he stole along, checking each boat: *"You can't miss it, Otto, it's a twenty-five-foot launch, blue hull with white superstructure. Good for thirty knots, should get you back to Stock in twenty minutes."*

There it was. A small pennant with the Benedictine symbol was flying from a short flag post on the stern.

Otto jumped on board and made his way forward to the covered cockpit. There was a wooden wheel and, beside it, the red starter button for the engine, together with the throttle lever, and forward and reverse gear stick. He ran his fingers over the chrome fuel, temperature, and pressure gauges. A compass was mounted in front of the wheel. Only the key to the ignition was missing.

Otto set down his pack and burrowed inside it, removing a small leather case. He opened it out and selected a skeleton key from one of a dozen. He tried it in the lock, but it wouldn't fit, so he selected another and tried again. At least picking the ignition lock would give him something to do while he waited.

17

LENI INSIDE

Leni made it to the main building in a few minutes. She squatted down in the shadows, catching her breath, waiting for her heart to slow and listening all the while. But there was not a sound.

She stole along the west side of the building until she located the window of the girl's room on the fourth floor. She took off her pack and opened it, removing a small canvas holdall she had prepared earlier. It held all the equipment she would need. Then she took out the gray novice's robe and pulled it over her own clothes. It was still a bit damp and smelled of the woodsmoke. She tied it around her waist with a thick cord and wondered how anyone managed to wear such a thing all day during the summer.

She closed the pack and stashed it against the wall, directly underneath the girl's window. Then she turned and made her way back the way she had come, keeping close to the wall, her eyesight now well adjusted to the gloom. When she reached the northeast side of the building she found that the door to the kitchen was locked. She would have to go in through the main door of the chapel, which she had been told was never locked.

It was at that moment that she saw the small window to the larder was open. It had a thin mesh screen over it to keep out the flies and mosquitoes. Leni drew her knife and neatly cut the screen away. Then she pulled herself up and through the window.

Once inside, she hurried into the kitchen. The place was quiet and immaculately tidy. Rows of pots and pans hung around the wall on hooks, and the long oak table was scrubbed clean.

It was a short walk down a stone corridor to the laundry. There Leni quickly found a pile of freshly laundered sheets, folded but waiting to be ironed and starched. She grabbed four.

Ten minutes later, she was padding silently down another stone corridor on the third floor of the building in her socks. She held her shoes in one hand, the small canvas holdall in the other, and the sheets tucked under the same arm. She halted at the end of the corridor, as she had on the first two floors, and listened. Still nothing. She took the staircase on the right-hand side. The convent was a warren. For a moment or two she wondered if she was going in the right direction and felt a flash of panic, then she pushed the thought aside and kept going. The stone floor was cold through her socks. As she reached the top of the stairs, a blinding white light snapped on.

"Who is that? And why are you not in your room?" The woman's voice was hard, indignant, the flashlight beam flashing along the walls and floor, seeking her out.

Leni turned tail and fled back down the stairs. She heard the clatter of shoes on the stones behind her.

"Come back at once!" the woman ordered.

Leni reached the bottom of the staircase and looked about frantically. In the gloom she could just make out a wooden door set into the wall opposite. She dashed across and pulled it open. It was a tiny cupboard, filled with a collection of mops and pails. As the flashlight beam cut through the darkness behind her, she managed to squeeze inside and pull the door shut. Through a crack in the door's panels she saw the light flashing up and down the empty corridor. She held her breath, wedged her shoes under her left arm, then used her right hand to slide her knife out from the sheath strapped to her leg. Her hand was shaking so badly she struggled to grip it. She sucked in her breath and held it. Would she actually kill a nun? Or anyone, for that matter? She fought to suppress the scream that threatened to burst from her mouth. Then the footsteps receded down the corridor and she remembered to breathe again, gasping for air.

She sat inside the cupboard for five full minutes, then

gingerly opened the door and stepped out. The icy stone floor was now pleasantly cooling. Her whole body was burning and sweat was running down her back. She ran back up the staircase, as silent as a ghost.

She found the storeroom on the fourth floor just where the map had positioned it. She stepped inside the small, windowless space and for the next twenty minutes or so, using her knife, carefully shredded the bedsheets into long strips that she knotted together. It seemed to take forever and by the time she'd finished she was perspiring even more, but when the convent's clock struck midnight she was ready. She slung the homemade rope over her shoulder and stepped into the corridor. As she passed each door she checked the small wooden nameplate beside it, painted in simple Gothic script with the name of the occupant: Sister Ellen, Sister Agnes, Sister Rosa . . . At last she found what she was looking for.

Outside the door at the end, the nameplate was blank. The girl with no name.

Leni pressed her ear to the door and listened. She couldn't hear anything through the inch of oak. Perhaps there was no one inside after all. Perhaps this whole thing was a wild-goose chase. Perhaps she could stop now and just run back to Otto and go home.

She knew that wasn't an option. She eased the iron doorring counterclockwise, and felt the latch lift on the inside. She stepped in.

It was a small, narrow cell. There was a mullioned window at the end, a table and chair beneath it. A small wardrobe was on the right and a single cot bed on the left.

Asleep in the bed was a young girl. Angelika. She lay on her back, her brown hair splayed out around her head. She had broad regular features with full cheeks. Leni knew she was nine, but she looked younger as she slept.

Leni shivered. The sweat was now clammy under her clothes. But it wasn't just that, she realized. It was the room itself, so cold and spartan, that made her shiver. There was nothing to suggest it was a little girl's room — no teddy or dolls, no toys, no colorful pictures on the wall like in Leni's old bedroom in Vienna. She'd even had her own gramophone player. Here, there were just a few prayer books on the table beneath the window.

Leni was about to gently wake the girl when she heard footsteps in the corridor. She stood absolutely still, listening. The footsteps came closer and closer and closer. Then they stopped. Right outside the door.

Leni threw herself under the bed, pushing aside a chamber pot, just as the door opened and a flashlight beam cut through the darkness. Leni squeezed herself against the wall under the bed and watched a pair of black shoes march across the room and stop directly in front of her face. The bedsprings creaked as the nun shook the sleeping girl roughly.

"You may fool the others, young lady, but you don't fool me, I know you're not really asleep!" It was the same nun who had chased after Leni, her voice harsh and cross.

The girl sat up sleepily. "I don't understand, Sister Margareta." She spoke with a soft Bavarian accent. "What are you talking about?"

"I'm talking about little girls sneaking around after lights out. In the kitchens again, weren't you, you greedy little pig!"

"No, I wasn't, I swear to God."

"How dare you take the Lord's name in vain? A whole bottle of milk, emptied just like that." She was filled with righteous indignation.

Leni's mind was racing, on the edge of panic. She had to do something, and fast. Before Sister Margareta ruined everything.

"I think the mother superior should hear about this . . ."

Oh, no . . . she wasn't going to march her downstairs now, was she?

"Please, I haven't done anything wrong." The girl was pleading now.

"Oh, spare me your lies! And no breakfast for you. No breakfast for little thieves. Do you hear me?"

As quietly as she could, Leni put her hand into her holdall and found the metal flask. She unscrewed the top and carefully poured some of the clear liquid inside onto a thick gauze pad. It was ether mixed with chloroform.

"May the Lord forgive your wickedness. Come along now!" The nun's feet suddenly stopped moving. "What's that strange smell?"

Leni made her move, sliding out of the bed in one fluid movement.

Sister Margareta stared down at her in utter shock. "What mischief is this?" she gasped.

Leni leaped to her feet and threw herself against the nun, slamming her against the opposite wall. At the same time, she clamped the drug-soaked pad over her nose and mouth.

Sister Margareta was short and slight, not much bigger than Leni and certainly not as strong. The nun struggled, trying to pull the pad away, but within twenty seconds she slid to the ground unconscious. Leni rushed to the door, closing it carefully. Then she snapped off Sister Margareta's flashlight, plunging the room back into semidarkness.

Angelika had shrunk back into the corner of the bed, her arms around her knees. She had gone very pale, and her breathing was shallow. But she hadn't screamed. That was good. Leni put her finger to her lips, and the girl nodded.

"Please don't scream, Angelika," Leni whispered.

Angelika stared. "How do you know my name?" she whispered back.

"I'll explain everything in a minute, but first I have to fix Sister Margareta."

Leni took a moment to think. Everything she was doing was new to her and no amount of training could help. She made a short list in her head: *nun, rope, escape.* Then she took out her knife, lifted the homemade rope over her head and dropped it on the floor. She found one end of it and cut off a few short lengths.

"Will you help me?" she asked the girl.

Angelika stared at Leni uncertainly, then glanced down at her tormentor on the stone floor. She scrambled off the bed.

"What do you want me to do?" she said.

"Lift her feet for me, please."

The girl hesitated, then lifted Sister Margareta's feet off the ground. Leni quickly tied the nun's ankles together, removed the pad from the nun's mouth and rolled her over so she was lying on her stomach. She pulled her arms behind her back and tied them together, too. Then she and Angelika rolled her onto her back again, and Leni fashioned a gag with a strip of sheet.

Angelika watched Leni work. "We're in a lot of trouble," she said.

"No, it's going to be all right," soothed Leni. "Help me get her into the bed, Angelika."

With a supreme effort they managed to heave the nun off the ground, with Leni at the shoulders and Angelika at the feet, and half dragged, half lifted her onto the bed. Leni pulled the blanket up over her head.

"You're strong," she said, and saw the girl smile in the darkness.

"Who are you?" Angelika asked.

"My name is Leni. Leni Fischer."

"Oh," said Angelika, then seemed to realize it was a silly question. "What are you doing here?" That was a better one.

Leni climbed up onto the table, then leaned forward and opened the window. It was a good twenty yards down. She hoped she had enough rope. She looked back at the girl staring up at her from the floor.

"What's it look like? I've come to rescue you."

"Rescue me?"

Leni made a loop at one end of the rope and then carefully placed it over the iron handle of the window's lock. She played out the rest of the rope to the ground below, and gave a tug on the loop to check it was secure.

"That's right. Well, not exactly rescue you, but get you away from here. Get you to Switzerland."

"Why?" said Angelika. She sounded very confused, as well she might.

"Well . . ." Leni didn't want to get bogged down with explanations. Any moment now, the door could open, and they'd be captured. The consequences of that didn't bear thinking about. "Look, please trust me. It's for your own good, I promise."

The girl was frowning now. Leni felt a terrible panic rising in her chest.

"I know this is all strange and a shock, but I'm really here to help you. Please say you'll come with me."

The seconds were turning into minutes, and time was running out. Leni tried to keep her voice level.

"I promise I'll explain everything more clearly, but right now we need to go."

Angelika finally reacted to the urgency in Leni's voice and glanced towards the door, clearly thinking about angry nuns.

"Now. We have a boat waiting."

Leni could see the girl was struggling to make a decision. She weighed the anesthetic-soaked pad she was still holding in her hand. Any more delay and she'd be forced to drug the girl and try to lower her down on the rope. That would be a nightmare.

Angelika looked at Leni, then at Sister Margareta lying in the bed, and finally at the stone floor, the bare walls. "I don't want to stay here. I hate it," she said simply.

"Then take my hand, Angelika, take it now."

Angelika reached out and Leni pulled her up onto the table. Angelika grasped the rope.

"You think you can climb down?"

Angelika swung her legs out over the window ledge. "Climbing trees is all I get to do around here. It got me three days in detention last month," she said, and with that she dropped out of the window. Leni looked at the pad in her hand, hesitated for a moment, then moved swiftly back to the nun.

She pulled the blanket back from her face and placed the pad over the nun's nose and mouth. It would definitely keep her out till the morning. She ran back to the window.

Outside, at the bottom, Angelika was waiting for Leni as she dropped the last few feet to the ground. She grabbed the homemade rope and flicked it, setting off a rolling motion that traveled upwards. After a minute or so, she felt the rope free itself of the window catch and fall into a pile beside her. She scooped it up, looping it into a coil and swinging it over her head. All set.

"I bet you know this place like the back of your hand?" she said to the girl.

Angelika smiled at her in the moonlight. "Specially at night," she whispered back. "When I'm thirsty."

"But you didn't drink that milk," Leni said.

"No, not this time," said Angelika, then she frowned. "But how do you know?"

"Because I did!" said Leni.

Angelika's smile became even wider then, and she grasped Leni's hand.

18

As soon as Otto saw the flashlight beam flash three times he felt he could breathe again. Leni had done it. She'd got Angelika, and she was on her way to the jetty. He responded with four flashes and almost immediately received two in return. That was the sequence they had agreed over their supper. If someone had got her, she would have flashed four times and Otto didn't really know what he would have done. Made a run for it or tried to rescue her? He liked to think he'd have tried to rescue her, but . . . Well, he didn't need to think about that now. It was just after midnight, according to the convent's clock and his own watch. They were ahead of schedule.

Five minutes later he made out Leni and the figure of a young girl hurrying down the jetty, their feet thrumming on the wooden boards. He made his way quickly to the stern of the boat. They were puffing hard, but they were there. That was all that mattered.

"We ran the whole way," Leni said, gasping for breath.

He felt her shaking as he helped her climb aboard. Then he held out his hand to the younger girl as she stepped down into the boat. So this was the child. She was smaller than he had imagined, her brown hair bouncing on her shoulders. She looked like a typical Bavarian country girl. Why was she so important? He put the question to the back of his mind. As far as he was concerned, he had a job to do. And the job was to deliver this girl to MacPherson in Switzerland pronto.

"I'm Otto, by the way," he said.

"Angelika. Pleased to meet you." She gave a little curtsy.

He laughed. He supposed she'd been taught to greet people like that by the nuns. "And me you," he said, bowing formally. "Have a seat. Make yourself comfortable on our luxury yacht." He grinned at her, then glanced back at Leni. "I was getting worried," he whispered. "You've been gone a long time. Did it go all right?"

Leni nodded, catching her breath. "Yes . . . sort of . . . mostly." She peeled off her pack and dropped it on the deck.

"She knocked out Sister Margareta," Angelika said breathlessly, glancing at Leni with something like admiration.

"What?" said Otto.

"I know!" replied Angelika. "Can you believe it?"

"It's nothing . . ." Leni's breathing was still ragged.

"She tied her up and stuffed her in the bed." Angelika giggled nervously. "It was . . ." She searched for the right word. ". . . spectacular!"

"Sounds like it," muttered Otto.

"Can we just get out of here?" said Leni.

Otto nodded and untied the stern rope.

The boat floated free of its mooring. Otto wasn't sure which way the current in the lake would take them, but, as luck would have it, they started to drift north, away from the buildings. They all sat quietly for a few minutes until he could see the outline of the convent bell tower against the night sky and judged they were a few hundred yards from the island. Then he turned the skeleton key in the ignition, listened for a moment to the fuel pumps whirring, and stabbed his thumb down on the starter button. The engines turned and fired. The sound was like a gunshot in the silence of the night, but it would be fainter by the time it reached the convent.

He threw the throttle lever forward and the launch pulled away from the island, heading out across the lake towards Stock. The bow sliced through the water, its blue hull gleaming darkly, a thick white wake opening up behind them.

Leni leaned forward and pulled the bedsheet rope she had slung across her chest over her head. She stood up, got her balance, and flung it overboard. Then she sat back down and put her arm around Angelika in the well of the cabin. An occasional tuft of spray caught their faces.

"Are you feeling all right?" Leni asked the girl.

Angelika looked up at Leni and smiled. "I think so," she said. She squeezed Leni's hand. "I feel like I'm in a dream."

"I know what you mean," said Leni.

Otto prayed it wouldn't turn into a nightmare. He dropped the engines to a low idle a few hundred yards from the main jetty and aimed for a large paddle steamer moored there. When he was fifty yards away he cut the engines completely, letting the boat drift in. It bounced gently on the steamer's cork fenders. He couldn't believe it. He'd finally managed a good landing. If only the manor's instructor could have seen it!

He let the girls climb off, then jumped onto the jetty and released the rope. What they needed now was for the current to hide their trail by catching the boat and taking it out onto the water.

There were still a good few hours of darkness left and the village was deserted. They made their way to the small stone church Otto had spotted the day before. It was the only building that would definitely be unlocked and empty at this time of night.

Once inside, Otto led them to the vestry at the side of the altar and they crowded into the little room. He slid the bolt shut on the door, then struck a match and lit the wall lantern. Leni stripped off her novice's habit and indicated for Angelika to follow suit.

"What are you doing?" Angelika asked as Otto rummaged through one of the packs before retrieving some smaller clothes.

"These are for you; they should fit fine," he said.

Leni started to help Angelika dress. Like Leni, she would be wearing the summer uniform of the Bund Deutscher Mädel, the League of German Girls.

Otto stepped across to her with a tube of what looked like oil paint. "We also need to dye our hair a different color, Angelika."

"Why?" Angelika frowned.

"It'll help us get to Switzerland faster, that's all. Stand still, please." He squirted a dollop out of the tube and started to rub it into her hair. Leni finished buttoning her dress and took over from Otto. He squeezed some of the paste into his own hair.

"Is it like a disguise or something?" asked Angelika. "Like dressing up?"

"That's right," said Leni. "We're going to pretend to be a family, traveling across Bavaria together."

"A family?" Angelika stared at them. "You mean, like you're my brother and sister?"

"Yes, your big brother and sister," said Otto, adding, "so we all need to look the same. If that's all right with you."

Angelika frowned. "But what's our name?"

"We're the Fischers from Salzburg. We'll tell you all about us as soon as we're on the road."

Leni finished rubbing the dye into Angelika's hair and quickly started on her own.

"I've always wanted a brother and sister."

"Well, now you've got them."

They waited twenty long minutes for the hair dye to act, then rinsed their hair under the tap as best they could. The water was freezing, and Leni yelped with shock. She rubbed Angelika's hair dry with her novice's robe, then did the same to her own before using a comb on them both. Otto combed his hair with his fingers. The three of them were now blond. Standing together in their uniforms they looked like poster children for the Third Reich.

Leni's voice was quiet but there was no mistaking the anger in it. "I hate these stupid clothes."

"Me, too." Otto touched her arm. "But let's try not to think about it." He handed Angelika a child's pair of tortoiseshell spectacles. "There's only clear glass in them."

Angelika took them tentatively from him and slipped them on. She blinked owlishly through them. "I love them! The nuns in the library wear glasses. Do I look like a librarian?"

Leni smiled approvingly. The transformation was remarkable.

"No one will recognize you now, little sister," she said.

Angelika frowned again. It was a lot for her to take in, but she was coping with it remarkably well so far. "Why shouldn't people recognize me? Is someone going to look for us?" she asked.

"The nuns. Just the nuns," said Leni hurriedly.

"Let's get moving, shall we? The sooner we go, the sooner we'll be in Switzerland." Otto was anxious now not to make her any more apprehensive. He took a step towards her.

She stepped away from him. "But what's in Switzerland? Why are we going there, really?" Angelika stuck out her jaw. Now that they were away from the convent, and she was in a new place with new people, she seemed to be realizing just what she'd done.

Leni shot a look at Otto. He nodded: They had to tell her something. Now was the time to give her MacPherson's story.

Leni took the girl's hand. "Because your parents are in Switzerland, Angelika."

The girl's eyes widened. "My parents? But . . . that's not possible! I don't know anything about my parents . . ."

Leni put her other arm around her. "Well, we're here to help you get to them. You're a very special child, and the people who've been keeping you in that place didn't want you to know the truth."

"But why?" the girl asked. She was starting to look confused, and, worse, her eyes were filling with tears.

"We don't know," said Otto. "Our job is to get you across the border in the next twenty-four hours before they realize what's happened and try to recapture you."

"Recapture me?"

Otto saw she was really alarmed now. He cursed his choice of words.

"Not *recapture* you, as such. But the nuns will be worried, quite naturally. They'll want to find you, make sure you're safe." He smiled as reassuringly as possible.

"I'm sorry. I know it's all a terrible shock," Leni added.

The three of them stood in silence. Leni bent down and tied Angelika's shoelaces tight with a double bow. Then she stood up and put her hands on the little girl's shoulders.

"How long have you been on that island?" she asked.

"Four years, three hundred and sixty-two days, and about thirty minutes. I was five when I arrived. And this Sunday," she added with a touch of pride, "it's my birthday. I'm going to be ten."

Admiral MacPherson hadn't told them she had a birthday coming up. Perhaps it wasn't relevant, thought Otto. But he wondered now what else had been kept from them.

"Well, you'll be able to have the most wonderful party with your parents, won't you?" said Leni brightly.

"Do you think so?" Angelika said anxiously. "I've never met them. No one ever told me a thing about them."

"We're sure of it, aren't we, Otto?" Leni and Angelika both looked at him.

Otto nodded as sincerely as he could. But all he knew for certain at that moment was that they should be getting away from this village as fast as they could. There was still no light in the sky but dawn would be here soon enough.

"But look," Leni said, "if you really don't want to come with us, it's fine."

Otto stared at Leni. What was she playing at?

"We'll drop you at the dock," Leni went on, "and you can explain everything to the mother superior in the morning."

"Leni, what —" Otto began.

"But if you choose to come with us now, we promise to do everything in our power to keep you safe and get you to Switzerland."

"And my parents are really there?" Angelika looked at Leni. "I could find out who they are?" The hope in her eyes was almost painful to see.

Otto wondered what Leni would say. Was she capable of telling this young girl such an awful lie?

"Yes," said Leni firmly, but she flinched slightly as she said it.

The church clock suddenly struck the hour, making them all jump. It seemed to jar the girl into making a decision.

"I'm sorry," said Angelika. "I am grateful that you've helped me get out of that place. Honestly, I am. It's just . . ." She hesitated. "I'll come with you."

Leni leaned forward and hugged her.

Otto quickly collected up all the evidence that they'd been there and dropped everything onto Leni and Angelika's discarded robes. Then he rolled them up and tied them into a ball.

"What are you going to do with that?" asked Leni.

"We'll drop it in a ditch on the way." He took a quick look around to make sure he hadn't missed anything. "Ready?"

The three bicycles were still where they had hidden them under a tarpaulin at the back of the boatyard.

"It's a couple of hours to Rosenheim," Otto said, wheeling his bike out towards the street. He glanced back. Angelika was standing still, holding the bike by the handlebars. "What's the matter, Angelika?"

The girl's eyes finally filled with tears. "I don't know how to ride this," she said.

Leni and Otto looked at each other in horror. They hadn't thought of this. They'd assumed every child could ride a bike.

"I asked the nuns once," Angelika went on, "but the mother superior refused. She said she didn't want me to injure myself in any way. She was always saying that, making sure I didn't do anything fun, like running and jumping and climbing."

Otto walked back to her. "It's all right, you can sit on the back of mine." His was an adult bike with a strong steel pannier over the back wheel. He helped Angelika on, then pushed the bike onto the street. It would slow them down. But he could only hope it wouldn't slow them too much.

He kicked up the pedal and placed his foot on it, a sudden sense of urgency gripping him.

"Hold tight!" he said, glancing back at Angelika sitting sidesaddle on the pannier.

"I will," she answered quietly.

He pushed the pedal down hard, trying not to wobble as he adjusted to the extra load on the back wheel, and soon started to build up some speed. Then Leni was beside him.

They exchanged a quick look between them. A mixture of relief and disbelief. They'd got the girl, but what in the world had they taken on?

19

A NASTY SURPRISE

The police boat was already waiting at the quayside as an unmarked Opel sedan drew up in the port of Stock. It was still early in the morning.

Heydrich had spent the night at the Berghof and had driven to Chiemsee just after seven. The journey had taken about forty minutes. He had chosen the most ordinary car he could find at the Berghof and ordered that it fly no pennants to identify it or himself as SS. He wished his visit to be unnoticed and had shed his black uniform and *Totenkopf* — death's head — cap in favor of a cream summer suit and Panama hat.

However, as soon as he walked down the jetty to the boat, every single person in the vicinity, the early-rising shopkeepers and fishermen, stared intently at him. A few obviously recognized him, but others just knew important Party members when they saw them. And this one was obviously very important. Not only that, but the local police chief, pale with anxiety, saluted smartly before Heydrich could stop him.

Heydrich climbed aboard, scowling. The boat pulled away from the harbor and set course for Fraueninsel.

There was no other traffic to slow their journey. A light swell made the bow bounce a little. Heydrich had overflown the lake only yesterday for pleasure, but now he was here for a very different reason.

He dismissed the hovering police chief and settled himself in the cabin, placing a brown manila envelope on the polished teak table in front of him. The Führer had only managed to speak to him for a few moments the night before, a private audience in Hitler's own sitting room. He had taken Heydrich's hand and shaken it firmly, looking straight into his eyes. "I have a special task that I wish to place only in your hands."

Heydrich had been deeply honored by the trust that was being bestowed on him. Calmly, the Führer had told him about a child, a girl, living on Fraueninsel, and how he believed his treacherous deputy, Rudolf Hess, might have betrayed her existence to the British. Accordingly, it was of the highest importance to him and to the Fatherland that she was moved to a new place of safety, that she must not be allowed to leave the Reich under any circumstances. Heydrich had assured the Führer that he would carry out the orders on his life.

The engine throbbed beneath his feet as he broke the seal on the envelope and took out the single sheet of paper on which his specific orders had been typed. He noted the signature at the bottom was Hitler's.

He quickly scanned the document. So, he was to fly the child to Schloss Fürstenstein. He knew the castle well. There was some talk about it being the Führer's official residence when the war was won. Once there, he would hand over the girl to the safekeeping of the staff. No record whatsoever was to be kept of this order.

Heydrich took out his cigarette lighter and sparked it alight. He let the yellow flame catch the corner of the page, and watched the paper turn to ash and float away.

Soon the engines slowed, and Heydrich saw the convent's long wooden jetty sliding into view. Minutes later he stepped off, the police chief again saluting smartly.

"Wait here," said Heydrich, then stopped as a middle-aged man in rough sailing clothes came hurrying along the jetty towards them.

"*Chef der Polizei!*" he called out. "How fortunate! We were just going to send word to you, sir. The convent's boat has been stolen. Last night. It is most extraordinary." He glanced at Heydrich but didn't recognize him.

The police chief was clearly mortified that a crime had been committed in his jurisdiction, and reported in the presence of his high-ranking visitor. "I'm sure there's a simple explanation, Klaus," he said to the man, taking him to one side. "Let us look into it."

Heydrich left them to it and marched briskly towards the convent where he threw an already flustered young nun into a panic by telling her to interrupt the mother superior's morning prayer and to have Angelika fetched immediately.

Ten minutes later he was walking lockstep with the mother superior towards Angelika's room. Angelika hadn't been at breakfast or at mass. The mother superior was looking worried — and this made him suddenly uneasy.

"I expect she's still in her room," the mother superior chattered. "It's hard to sleep on these hot summer nights, and sometimes the younger members of our community tend to linger in bed. And, of course, we are not prepared for your visit, sir. We expect Angelika to have one visitor on her birthday each year — Herr Hess . . ." She stopped, flushing, as if unsure whether this name could still be mentioned, then rushed on. "But that is not until Sunday, the twenty-second. I have it marked in red ink in my diary."

"I see," Heydrich said lightly, slowly turning the brim of his hat in his hands as they came to a stop outside a room with a blank nameplate.

"Well, here we are." She turned the latch on the door and pushed it open. Heydrich saw her sag with relief. Angelika appeared to be fast asleep, completely covered by her sheet. In fact, she was snoring quite loudly.

"Come along, you silly girl." The mother superior clapped her hands as she strode to the bed and whipped back the blanket. She froze.

Instead of a nine-year-old girl, they were looking at a nun, tied hand and foot and clearly unconscious. And the window was wide open.

"Do you have any explanation for this, Reverend Mother?" Heydrich's voice was low and quiet.

"I . . . don't understand. The girl must have taken leave of her senses. I mean, who would do such a thing?"

Heydrich nodded. "Who indeed?" He leaned forward and removed the anaesthetic pad from the nun's face. He sniffed it. "Chloroform."

The mother superior's eyes widened. "Do not worry; she'll be found. I'll have everyone search for her at once."

"Were you aware that the convent's launch was stolen last night?" Heydrich asked.

The mother superior's face took on a grayish hue.

"Perhaps you would escort me to your office, Reverend Mother? I need to make a telephone call."

"I'm afraid we do not have a telephone."

"What a pity. Nevertheless, there are matters that need to be discussed. Serious matters."

"Of course." The mother superior looked even more ashen as she stepped from the room and started down the corridor.

Her office was a large oak-paneled room, the walls lined with portraits of saints. The mullioned windows looked out across the lake.

The nun walked stiffly to her desk and sat down. Heydrich closed the door but remained standing. "I'm sure you understand the gravity of the situation, Mother Superior."

She looked utterly bewildered. "I'm at a loss to know why she would choose to run away . . ."

Heydrich shook his head slowly. "She didn't run away. And you know it." His voice was a monotone, the anger masked beneath a professional detachment. "Your one responsibility was to keep her safe, and you have singularly failed in that regard."

The mother superior nodded. It was all she could do.

"I will not detain you any longer. As you can imagine, time is now of the essence. There is just one piece of paperwork I require from you." He reached into his jacket and produced a fountain pen. "Do you have paper?"

She opened the central drawer in her desk and extracted a sheet of writing paper.

"You will write the following for me: 'It is with deep regret and shame . . .'" He paused as the mother superior began to write. "'. . . that I must admit to a gross and terrible failure on my part to safeguard the welfare of an innocent child. In so doing, I have disgraced myself, my Führer, my country, and . . .'"

Heydrich took particular relish in the next noun. "'. . . my Church. I have criminally abused the sacred duty that was entrusted to me. So it is with no regret that I must take the following action.'"

Heydrich paused and walked around the desk. He stood beside her, looking down at her neat Gothic script on the paper.

"Yes, that is sufficient. Sign it for me."

The mother superior frowned. "Is the letter finished?"

"Indeed it is. Sign it."

The mother superior added her name and title. She put the pen down and waited. "I don't understand," she said after a moment. "What action do you wish me to take?"

"This," said Heydrich, placing the muzzle of his service pistol on her right temple and pulling the trigger.

He dropped the gun onto the desk, blood already spilling across it, then reached down and picked up the woman's lifeless hand. He placed it on top of the pistol. Suicide, a cardinal sin. On no account could she be given a Christian burial. A terrible fate, if you believed in such nonsense.

Heydrich stepped out into the stone corridor. Nuns were already running towards him, as the sound of the shot, still faintly audible, rolled around the convent. He strode past them. There was much to do.

20

OTTO'S PLAN

Angelika didn't complain once as they made their way along the country roads, bumping over potholes in the darkness. Leni was impressed. She'd been half expecting some spoiled, whiney little girl, but instead Angelika sat quietly on the metal pannier, humming some tune known only to herself. Perhaps she was just happy to be traveling somewhere, anywhere, after five years of captivity. She'd been brave at the convent, too, Leni thought, and she felt an itch of curiosity to get to know the girl better. Then she remembered how MacPherson had told them not to become friends with the girl. He'd always referred to her just as the "package," as though she were an item you sent in the post.

Dawn broke as they got near to Rosenheim, red and orange streaks against the dark navy of the night sky, and by the time they reached the railway station it was daylight. They left the bicycles a short distance from the station, and Otto shot off to find some breakfast. Leni and Angelika tucked themselves into an alleyway by the side of the ticket office, which shielded them and also gave a good view of people coming and going.

Leni was just beginning to wonder where Otto was when he returned with pastries and his water bottle filled with warm milk. The town was waking up now and the streets were filling with people. The benches in front of the station were bathed in early-morning sunlight.

"Come on, let's sit on one of those benches." Leni took Angelika's hand.

"We should stay here, out of sight," said Otto, but the girls ignored him and settled themselves in the sunshine.

Otto followed them, sighing as he handed out the food. It had been so early that he had been first through the bakery's door and had managed to buy three doughnuts filled with plum jam. Angelika gazed at this unheard-of delicacy with a look of wonder for a full minute.

"What's wrong?" asked Otto as he wolfed his down.

"Nothing, nothing's wrong. It's just . . ." Words failed the girl and she nibbled at the edge, savoring the taste in her mouth before taking a bite so big that jam dribbled down her chin.

"Don't eat so fast," scolded Leni. "You'll get a tummy ache."

She realized she sounded like her mother, and for an instant felt a pang of homesickness. Her sisters were probably walking to school right now, their satchels slung over their shoulders.

"I don't care," said Angelika, stuffing the last piece of warm dough into her mouth. "It tastes so good!"

"I know," said Otto. "Much better than English food."

Leni glared at him. *What an idiot!* she thought. Otto shook his head apologetically. Fortunately Angelika was gulping the milk down and didn't seem to have noticed what he had said.

"Right, the Innsbruck train leaves in seven minutes," he said, hurriedly changing the subject. He dug into his trouser pocket and pulled out the train tickets, handing two of them to Leni. "I suggest we get on the train separately: you and Angelika first, and then me. We take seats apart. What do you think?"

"You're asking for my opinion?" asked Leni, realizing he was chastened by his mistake.

"I am."

"All right, I think you should go first and we'll follow. That way, if there's anything wrong you can warn us."

"What do you mean? What would be wrong?" Angelika was paying attention now.

"With the arrangements, the seating, that's all," Leni said.

"Agreed," said Otto. But it was his turn to glare at her now.

He rose from the bench and strode confidently into the station. It was already getting much busier, which was a good thing, thought Leni.

All three of them boarded the train without a hitch. They found seats in the same carriage but at opposite ends, sitting quietly as the rest of the train filled with travelers. Then, just as it was about to depart, Otto suddenly got up from his seat and walked down the aisle towards Leni and Angelika.

"Quickly, follow me," he hissed out of the corner of his mouth.

Leni looked at him, startled.

"Just do it!"

What was wrong? They scrambled after him. Otto stopped in the section between the two carriages.

"We're getting off."

"What?" said Leni.

Otto opened the carriage door on the opposite side to the platform. There was a drop of about six feet to the ground below. They heard the sharp blast of the platform guard's whistle.

"There's no time to explain. Here, I'll help you . . ." He took Angelika's hands and swung her out of the doorway. She dropped out of sight. Leni went next and then Otto dropped the packs down to her before jumping out himself. He reached up and pushed the carriage door shut. The train was just starting to move, the wheels squeaking and clanking, the train's engine snorting.

"Follow me . . ."

He ran along the side of the train, hugging close to it to avoid being seen by any passengers inside. On the parallel track was a long freight train, its engine pointing in the opposite direction. The wagon cars had open tops, covered with gray tarpaulins.

As they reached the end of the departing Innsbruck train, Otto crossed between the tracks to the freight train, and climbed up the short steel ladder bolted on to the end of the nearest wagon. He pulled back the tarpaulin and took a look inside. "It's all right, come up here . . ." He sat astride the wagon's edge and helped the other two to climb in. Then he dropped inside and pulled the tarpaulin over them. In the gloom Leni could see the wagon was loaded with wooden boxes.

She grabbed hold of his arm. "Otto!" she hissed. "What was that all about?"

There was another sharp blast of a whistle.

"I've never been on a train," said Angelika excitedly. "And now I've been on two!"

"And this will be even more of an adventure," Leni said to the girl soothingly, then raised her eyebrows at Otto, waiting for an explanation.

The wagon suddenly shunted backwards, knocking them off-balance. They all sat down on the wooden boxes.

"I'm sorry to spring it on you like that, but as I was sitting in the other train, I saw this one come in and I remembered what we were told to do."

"Er, would that be: Get on the Innsbruck train?" said Leni.

"No, not that. It was, 'Trust your gut.'"

Angelika frowned. "What does that mean?"

Leni ignored her. "Is that what this is? Your instinct?" She was feeling panicky and cross.

"That's right, don't you see? As soon as they discover she's gone, where's one of the first places they'll start looking?"

"You tell me." Leni now felt less sure of herself.

"Well, the roads obviously, but also the passenger trains. And the first one to leave Rosenheim is the one to Innsbruck. They'll check that, but they won't think about the cargo trains."

"Maybe so, but we don't even know where this one is going."

"It's got to be Munich. It's going north and that's the first city on the line. It has to stop there."

He pulled out the silk map of the area and spread it out on one of the wooden boxes.

Leni leaned over to look. "But we're going deeper into Germany."

"Only a little bit. And besides, they wouldn't expect us to do that, would they? We can change trains in Munich and get one going west to Kempten. With a bit of luck we might make the border even faster, by nightfall."

Leni followed his finger as he traced the route from Munich till it stopped at the Bodensee. It all looked so straightforward, so simple when you just drew a line across a map. Leni didn't know what to say. There was a logic to what Otto was proposing, and perhaps it was a clever thing to do, but it didn't feel right. She just couldn't put her finger on why. There was another shriek from the whistle and the wagon lurched forward, smacking into the one ahead. Another lurch and it was slowly moving.

It was too late for her to object now.

21

MUNICH MORNING

Otto woke as the train braked sharply, throwing him off the packing case he had slumped against. He was glad to be awake. He had been in the middle of the terrible recurring dream he'd been having ever since he'd arrived in England. In it he was swimming far out at sea at night. There were no stars and the water was black, too. The waves were breaking over his head, the spray stinging his eyes. He was with his family — his father, mother, and Karl — but then, one by one, they would disappear, slip away, until he found himself alone, treading water and calling out their names. He had the dream about once every month and it stayed with him for the rest of the day.

He got to his feet now and poked his head out of the tarpaulin. They were pulling into the city. Munich. Perhaps being here had triggered the dream again. He checked his father's watch. It was nearly eight. The journey had taken a little under two hours.

He ducked back down inside the wagon and roused Leni. She, in turn, shook Angelika awake.

"We need to jump out before the train gets into the sidings," Otto said. The train had slowed almost to a standstill.

The girls nodded. He helped them clamber up the side and swing their legs over, finding the steel ladder. They each climbed down and made the short jump onto the stony ground beside the tracks. Otto tossed Leni's pack down, then followed her with his own in his hand. It was the reason he missed his footing and fell, but he jumped to his feet quickly.

"I'm fine, I'm fine," he said, embarrassed.

Leni looked around. "What's the plan, then?" She had retrieved her own pack by now.

"Follow me," said Otto authoritatively.

They crossed the tracks, and hurried through a rail yard full of empty carriages and wagons and the sound of shunting engines. However, they didn't run into anyone and quickly reached a staircase cut into the brick embankment wall. They climbed the steps and found themselves standing on a Munich street.

"According to this . . ." Otto was studying his railway timetable. ". . . there's a passenger train leaving at noon for Kempten. We can change there and get the local line to Immenstadt and from there to Bregenz."

"You mean we've got to hang around Munich till twelve?" Leni frowned, and Otto could see she didn't like the idea. "Shouldn't we stay on the move?"

"It's a fast train to Kempten. What's the alternative? Get an earlier train and have to change a couple of times, or get a bus which takes ages. It's only the morning, and if I'm right this is the last place they'll be searching for us."

Otto was set on his plan. Leni shrugged, acquiescing, but she wasn't happy.

They were walking down the street now, passing shops just opening up for business.

"Can we go to the National Museum?" Angelika tugged at Otto's sleeve. "I saw it in a book in the convent."

"That's a great idea," said Otto, "or maybe one of the big parks. There's lots to see in Munich." For a moment he felt genuinely enthusiastic, then he glanced at Leni. Her face was still drawn.

"It's the best plan, really, you'll see." They found themselves on a corner, the streets leading off in four different directions. Otto looked around.

"I suppose you know where we are," said Leni, a little sarcastically.

"As a matter of fact, I do," he said, managing a tight smile. He wondered whether to tell her that Munich was a place he knew very well indeed, that it was in fact his hometown. A part of him felt reassured to be back in a place that was so familiar to him, but he also felt a sense of dread and fear in the pit of his stomach. It was only a year since he had escaped the Gestapo here.

Ten minutes later they had stowed their packs in lockers at the main station and purchased tickets for Bregenz. Now they had a few hours to kill. They jumped on a tram and went along Neuhauser and Kaufinger Strasse, past the Academy of Sciences, the Akademie der Wissenschaften. Otto stared at the building as they bumped past it, then found Leni looking at him. He examined the tram's floor instead.

His father had taught chemistry at the Akademie. Otto knew the place inside out. Many afternoons he'd go to meet his father after his lectures had finished. They would walk the five flights of stairs to his small laboratory at the top of the building, and his father would show him his latest experiments. Otto couldn't really understand them, but he loved all the equipment, the centrifuges, and the strange chemicals like thorium. Otto had thought that maybe one day he might be a Munich chemistry professor, too. Not anymore.

The tram's bell rang. They'd reached Marienplatz. They quickly changed lines, taking another tram to Ludwigstrasse. It was almost as if he'd never left. So much was the same. The shops were still full of goods, the people on the street were still well dressed, and the city still smelled of fresh-baked bread, coffee, exhaust fumes, and a sour soupy smell Otto always put down to the sauerkraut. But here and there were boarded-up businesses with Jewish stars painted over the boards, even more sandbags and swastikas. He remembered that terrible night in November three years ago. The Nazi supporters had all come out onto the street late in the evening. Roving gangs, armed with bricks and staves, had smashed all the windows of the Jewish shops and businesses, and their owners had been dragged out, some in their nightclothes, and beaten on the pavement. Then they'd been tossed into waiting Nazi trucks and driven away. People had called it *Kristallnacht* — the Night of Broken Glass — because there was so much broken glass all over the pavements the next day. His mother had cried; he remembered that, too. Then everything had changed. People had become afraid. He glanced at Leni. She had been so lucky to get out. And so brave, he thought, to come back.

They got off near the Hofgarten.

"Now can we get an ice cream?" asked Angelika.

"Just give me a minute," said Leni. Otto found she was staring at him sternly. "Can I speak to you?"

"What about?"

Leni took his arm and pulled him to one side. "What's going on, Otto?"

"What do you mean?" Otto decided he'd have to brazen it out.

"Don't treat me like a fool. This is your home, isn't it?" Leni's blue eyes dared him to deny it.

Otto was tempted, but he didn't want to lie to her. "So what if it is?" he admitted defensively.

Leni shook her head. "That's why we're here." She started to pace around. "I *knew* getting that train didn't feel right. What have you done?" She checked they were still out of earshot of Angelika.

"Look, yes, I admit this is where I'm from," Otto said a little crossly. "It's got nothing to do with us being here, though." He was lying now. But he couldn't go back. "It's the right thing to do, traveling this way." That was true. He could see Angelika was straining to hear the conversation.

"Then why are you trying to ditch us till we catch the train?" Leni planted her hands on her hips. She could see straight through him and out the other side, thought Otto. It was annoying.

He paused, wondering whether to confide in her. He decided against it. "There's just . . . something I need to do. I'll be as quick as I can. It's nothing to worry about, I swear. Meet me at the tram station in the Promenadeplatz in two hours. We'll all go to the train station together."

Leni looked at him, her eyes serious. "I'm trusting you, Otto. Don't let me down or do anything stupid."

"Don't worry, I won't."

But that was a lie, too.

22

MANHUNT

As soon as the police boat had raced back to Stock, Heydrich had ordered every house, building, and structure in the village to be searched from top to bottom. Nothing had come to light. He had then traveled to Prien am Chiemsee in the Opel to coordinate the initial operation and to issue general orders to Munich regarding the security of the border and troop deployment. It was clear to him the girl had been snatched by foreign agents. It was also logical, as the Führer had said, that this affair led back to Hess's recent treachery and his flight to Scotland. Therefore those foreign agents were almost certainly British or British-trained.

At Prien, his adjutant and driver had arrived with his six-wheeled Mercedes and his personal effects. He had quickly changed into his SS uniform, strapping on another Walther pistol, and jumped into the limousine. His first duty was to inform the Führer, in person, at the Berghof.

As his car roared along the road, the siren blasting out, Heydrich pondered the potential escape routes open to the abductors. The Swiss border was 161 miles as the crow flew. It would take less than a day by car or train to reach it, although crossing the border itself might be more difficult. Whoever had taken the child had already been moving since the small hours. It was essential to get roadblocks on all routes twenty miles or more from the border. Heydrich assumed that they would be traveling by car. *Probably a man and woman,* he thought.

The car's radio telephone rang and he snatched it up. "This is Heydrich."

"There are reports in the village of a boat engine being heard at around two A.M." It was the police chief from Stock. He still sounded anxious, eager to please. "And the convent's launch has been found drifting on the east side of the lake, out of fuel."

"They must have let it go. Any reports of a car engine?"

"No. However, a child's bike was found at the back of the church. It was reported stolen yesterday afternoon along with two adult bicycles."

"Is that all?"

"For the moment, sir."

Heydrich hung up, thinking hard. They must have cycled out. To Rosenheim, most probably. They would have had a car waiting there for them, or else used the mainline railway. The quickest way to the border from there was south through Innsbruck. He had to get ahead of them, meet them on the way. He picked up the telephone and reached Gestapo headquarters in Munich.

"This is Heydrich. Give me General Müller."

He waited to be connected to the Gestapo chief. He knew he could trust Müller to carry out his orders discreetly and to the letter. Besides, there was no way this operation could be kept top secret anymore. Finally he heard Müller's voice at the end of the line.

"Müller, have three extra companies of SS mountain troops sent down here in addition to the four going south. And have the train station at Rosenheim searched and its staff questioned. I'm looking for three people — two adults and a girl." He had a final thought. "Call the commander at the Oberschlessheim Airfield. Tell him I will need the Flettner helicopter at the Berghof at once. "

He slammed the phone down. He felt slightly more satisfied knowing he was beginning to throw a vast dragnet across the country. Whatever it took, he would get this girl back. But first he had to get to the Berghof and tell the Führer the terrible news. And that wasn't all. Hitler had said the child must not leave the Reich under any circumstances. Heydrich needed to be certain of what that really meant. He leaned forward in his seat.

"Faster! Go faster!" he yelled at his driver.

23

ADMIRALTY ARCH

MacPherson was sitting at his desk at the Admiralty. He glanced for the umpteenth time at the clock on the wall. It was almost twenty-seven hours since he had stood on the damp grass at the edge of the runway and watched the Mosquito return from Germany. Since then, a long terrible silence. The lack of news made him short-tempered with everyone.

He got up from his chair and looked out of the window. St. James's Park was dotted with sandbagged anti-aircraft batteries, which were fighting for space with rows of deck chairs. To his left was the entrance to the newly constructed bunker that was the prime minister's command headquarters, deep below street level. Not even a squadron of bombers dropping their payload right on top of it would penetrate that stronghold. The PM would no doubt be calling him soon for the latest news.

Unfortunately it didn't look as though he would have anything to tell him.

Of course, MacPherson understood it would be very difficult to get reports back on such a mission. It had been agreed right from the start that the children would not attempt to make any contact with London themselves. It was not safe or practical for them to carry radio equipment, and anyway there had not been time to train them. Sending telegrams to safe addresses in Switzerland was also out of the question, the essence of the mission being speed and secrecy. Besides, any postmaster in the Reich would immediately be suspicious of a young person doing such a thing, and almost certainly the Gestapo read every such document.

MacPherson sat down again, still disgruntled, and contemplated a small bronze figurine on his desk. It was a dancing faun, the emblem of the London Controlling Section, symbolizing secretive dealings and disinformation.

There was a knock on the door and a young woman dressed in a Wrens uniform brought in breakfast on a metal tray.

"Kippers and toast, sir." She cleared a space on his desk and set the food down. There was a steaming cup of tea in an enamel mug.

"Thank you." He realized he was famished.

Then she handed him a telegram. It was from Bletchley Park.

He waited until she had left the room and closed the door, before ripping open the envelope and scanning the contents.

The boys up at Bletchley had intercepted and decoded a Gestapo order to all SS units along the Reich's borders with Switzerland in Bavaria and Austria. The border was to be sealed with immediate effect and all posts and crossing points were to be put on full alert. Extra Waffen-SS units were also being dispatched.

Otto and Leni had got the girl. They'd bloody done it.

MacPherson slammed his fist onto the desk, and the breakfast on the tray jumped.

He reached for the phone. "Get me a car. And have Signals send a message to our contact in Geneva. Message reads: 'Eagle arrives tonight. Kestrels on the wing.'"

Four hours later, the blue Hudson raced along the harbor road that ringed the naval dockyards at Plymouth. Above the car loomed the slate-gray hulls of battleships and cruisers, the gangplanks packed with sailors embarking. Dock cranes swung in and out, loaded with provisions and ammunition. There were more ships anchored out in the harbor. Up in the sky were lines of barrage balloons, silver and gray, the first line of defense against German dive-bombers.

The Hudson came to a halt outside a large hangar with a concrete slipway leading down into the water. MacPherson was out of the car in an instant and hurrying into the hangar. There he was greeted by a young officer from the Fleet Air Arm service, the navy's own air force. He was sporting a neat mustache and puffing on a pipe. MacPherson took it as a cue to fish out his own.

"Strictly no smoking, but the CO doesn't seem to mind." The pilot smiled and thrust out a hand. "Commander Bracken. I believe I'm your taxi driver for the night."

MacPherson shook hands, then stepped past him and stared at the seaplane that was going to carry them to Switzerland. As a navy man, he'd have preferred to travel by sea. But that was impossible for this trip, and the plane looked sturdy and well built, with a powerful single engine and a double cockpit covered with a sliding canopy. A hatch in the rear cockpit led down to a cabin fashioned inside the plane's large central float. In America the aircraft was used as an executive taxi for admirals. MacPherson had persuaded the prime minister to have it sent over from America for just such a purpose as tonight's. It was perfect for the job. The indoor cabin would have plenty of room for Otto, Leni, and the girl.

A dozen technicians were still working on the plane. Some were fitting extra fuel tanks, while others were repainting the fuselage and wings, changing them from light gray to a night-flying matte black. The plane would carry no markings.

"The Grumman Duck. Not a bad old bird. But a tad slow. So unfortunately," Commander Bracken took his pipe from his mouth, "she's also known as 'The Sitting Duck.'" He nonchalantly tapped out the bowl of his pipe on the edge of the wingtip. "But we won't let that one worry us, sir."

"No, we won't," said MacPherson gruffly.

"Any idea where we're going, sir?"

MacPherson frowned at the pilot. "All in good time, Commander. Remember: 'Loose Lips Sink Ships.' And 'tad slow' aeroplanes, too."

24

JAEGERSTRASSE

Otto stood at the top of the staircase on the third floor of the apartment building. He was racked with indecision.

He had already spent an hour sitting on a bench on the opposite side of the street, debating whether or not to go in and, inevitably, reliving that terrible day just over a year ago when he'd got back early from school, complaining of a stomach-ache. His father had come home early, too — quite by chance, a cancelled meeting — but his mother and Karl weren't there. His father had suggested a game of chess. Just as Otto had put him into check there had been a loud hammering on the door.

"Who is it?" his father had called out, getting to his feet.

"Gestapo! Open up!"

"One moment!" His father had grabbed Otto and pulled him up.

"Open the door!" A fist banged again on the door.

"I am not dressed — give me a moment," his father had shouted in reply, knowing that would not stop the men. He talked fast as he hustled Otto through the apartment to his study, the sound of boots kicking the door fracturing their conversation.

"The time has come, Otto."

"No —"

"We've talked about this . . . You know what you have to do . . . You have everything."

His father had pulled open the top drawer of his bureau and thrust an envelope into Otto's hands.

"Passports and Reichmarks and French francs, enough for all of you. You have your identity card?"

Otto had nodded and his father had hugged him tight for a moment, kissing him on both cheeks. The hammering of the door grew louder.

"I am coming!" he shouted back, then looked at Otto. "Wait five minutes and then go."

Calmly his father had closed the study door behind him as he walked to the front door and opened it. "Now what is all this about?"

Through a crack in the study door, Otto saw three men step into the hallway, the first one in a suit, the others in black Gestapo uniforms.

"Herr *Doktor*, you are under arrest for undermining the war effort."

A terrible jolt of fear had run through Otto as he heard those words. He had read somewhere that the crime of "undermining the war effort" had been designated a capital one. And with that his father had been marched away. The men had not even bothered to check the apartment. Perhaps they had thought he was still at school.

After they had left, Otto had waited five minutes, as his father had instructed, in a state of blind panic. Then he had run out of the apartment building and crossed the street to sit on the bench opposite. He stayed there for some time, wondering what to do, before taking the tram to his school, only to discover that his mother had picked Karl up half an hour before. He had frantically run through the city, following their usual route home, but they were nowhere to be seen. And so he had returned to the bench and waited for them, the tears never far from his eyes.

A taxi had pulled up and his mother and brother had got out, a series of department-store packages in their arms. He had jumped up and been on the point of shouting to them when four Gestapo men had climbed out of a plain black car parked near the entrance. He had watched dumbfounded as the men had quickly crowded around them, taking their packages, grabbing their arms, pushing them into the back of the car. Karl had started crying.

He had stood in the street and watched the Gestapo take his family into oblivion.

Now he was standing outside their front door once more. He glanced up and down the corridor one last time. There were three apartment doors on the third floor, and all were firmly closed. It was very quiet. He took a final breath, gathering his courage. He'd got this far, he told himself. He must go on, take the chance. He slipped off his heavy walking boots and kneeled down, easing back the skirting where it met the doorframe. Behind was the front door key, just as it always had been. He stood up and slid it into the lock, wondering if it would work. It did. He took a breath and gently pushed the door open, his boots in his hand.

A tall, handsome man with graying hair was standing in front of him. He was dressed in green suit trousers and a matching waistcoat, his tie loosened. He threw open his arms. Papa!

For a second, Otto allowed himself to imagine the scene. But there was no one to greet him. The hallway was empty.

He eased the door shut and listened intently.

"Hello . . ." he called out softly, then a little louder. Nothing.

Everything seemed just as it had been the day he left the apartment. Except it wasn't. The coats hanging on the rack were neither his mother's nor his father's. In the kitchen, the smell of breakfast permeated the air, coffee and fresh bread. The table and chairs were different. So was the crockery piled in the sink and the pictures on the wall. Another family was living here now. He felt his heart begin to race a little faster. He was an intruder.

He hurried to inspect the other rooms. Their old sofa and armchairs were gone, but his parents' bed was still there. In his room, the twin beds had been pushed to the wall and a child's crib sat in their place. In the dining room the long table and chairs that had been his grandfather's were still in use, but the watercolor his mother had painted had been replaced with a large portrait of Hitler. There was a glass cabinet filled with bronze and silver sporting awards.

Otto stared. He felt a tightening in his chest, an unstoppable urge to rip the Führer's picture down, to smash the cabinet, to throw the possessions of these interlopers out of the window into the street below. He felt the tears spring in his eyes. He'd known his father wouldn't be here. But in some corner of his heart he'd hoped that somehow his mother and brother might be. He would have hugged them and told them what he was doing, and they would each have known that they were all still alive.

He wiped his nose and his eyes, pulled himself together. It was time to get out of this place. It wasn't his home anymore. It was nothing.

The phone rang in the hallway and Otto jumped. It was like an alarm going off in his brain. He must have been insane to think of coming back here. *Get out, get out now!* he told himself.

The phone continued to ring as Otto raced to the front door, bending down to pick up his boots. As he reached to turn the handle, the ringing stopped. In the brief moment of silence that followed, he heard footsteps on the stairs and voices outside. A man and a woman were arguing. The footsteps and voices stopped right outside the apartment door. Otto spun around and ran back down the hall into the dining room, throwing himself under the table. The beaded edge of the linen cloth stopped a few inches from the floor.

He heard the lock turn and the front door swing open. Something was wheeled into the hallway. The door closed.

"If it's important, they will ring back, Heinz."

"Yes, yes."

The man strode into the dining room. Otto could see his brown shoes, polished to a high sheen. This was bad, he thought, as he listened to the man turn the pages of the newspaper that lay on the table. Really bad. He told himself to keep calm. The front door was only a few feet away. He just had to sit tight.

25

MISSING

Otto was not the only one trapped in a nightmare situation. Somehow Leni had managed to lose Angelika. It had been only half an hour but it felt like an eternity.

Everything had been fine until then. The two of them had taken Otto's advice and walked to the Englischer Garten, and Angelika had finally got her wish for an ice cream. The girl had sworn that she had never had one before, but then said actually, she just couldn't remember. Maybe she had.

After that, they'd jumped on a tram and ridden down Prinzregentenstrasse to the National Museum. Leni, increasingly anxious about sticking out, had decided they would blend in with all the other schoolchildren touring the museum. She realized she was anxious not because of Angelika but because of herself. She half expected someone to point and shout "Jew!" at any moment. Somehow she kept a smile fixed on her face and tried to answer Angelika's questions about the city, the shops, the fountains, and statues.

Angelika had been interested in the exhibits at the museum but also, Leni thought, a little distracted. She put it down to her seeing so many new things. It was a lot for such a sheltered child to take in. They'd tagged along discreetly with another party of children while Leni kept a careful eye on the time and fretted about what Otto might be doing. Everything seemed to be just about all right until Leni turned her back on Angelika for a minute. When she looked around, the girl was gone. Leni had felt her stomach somersault.

She had hurried forward to the next couple of galleries in case Angelika had gone ahead, but could not see her, so had doubled back to the earlier ones. No sign of her. Not only that but, she realized, it was going to be impossible for her to recognize Angelika from any distance. Not for the first time, Leni cursed her poor eyesight.

She raced back to the toilets, hoping Angelika had taken herself there, but the stalls were empty of any nine-year-old girls. To search the whole museum would take hours, and she dared not ask any of the attendants and so set in motion an official search party. The questions that would be asked — names, addresses, parents. No, she had to find her herself, and fast. She peered really hard, trying to sharpen her vision, but Angelika was nowhere to be seen in the crowds of visitors swirling past her.

Leni got back to the main entrance, hoping that if Angelika was also looking for her, she might make her way there as well. She felt the tears well up inside, but fought to stop them spilling. Again, it would only attract attention. As she stood there, her mind racing, she tried to think what Angelika might be doing, why she would have left her. They had been getting along fine, having a lovely time. Surely she hadn't got nervous about the whole thing and handed herself in to the authorities? It was a possibility, in which case a police car might come screaming up to the museum at any moment to arrest her.

Then something else flashed through her mind. On the tram journey along Prinzregentenstrasse, they'd passed a building festooned with large Nazi banners hanging from the windows. Angelika had stared intently at it. "That place, I know it," she had murmured. Leni had dismissed it at the time, but now . . .

She ran as fast as she could down the street. She could get to the building and back to the museum in a few minutes if she really sprinted. As she reached Prinzregentenstrasse, out of breath, she looked frantically around. The pavements were filled with shoppers hurrying to and from the daily food market known as Viktualienmarkt in the main square, and Leni had to bob and weave around them. She stared around, squinting furiously. Just as she was about to give up and return to the museum, she caught sight of a flash of blonde hair on the opposite side of the street. Leni ran straight across the street. A car swerved past her, its horn blasting a rebuke.

It was Angelika. She was standing right outside the building with the Nazi banners, gazing up. Leni almost collapsed with relief.

"Angelika!" She didn't mind how loud she shouted her name. She wanted her to stay there, right there, rooted to the spot.

The girl waved at her. "Leni!"

Leni was by her side now. She wanted to give her such a telling-off, but knew better than to make a scene or upset the girl. Especially outside a building plastered with swastikas. Of all the places she could have chosen to visit . . . Briefly she wondered what the building was, and what the Nazis inside would think if they realized a British agent and this important girl were right outside. She bit her lip and instead gave her a weak smile. "What are you doing here? You gave me such a fright . . ."

Angelika looked up at her, saw how red in the face she was. "I'm sorry, I didn't think. I just wanted to come back and have a look at this house."

"Why?" asked Leni. She took the girl's hand and started to lead her away.

"I'm not sure," she replied.

"Don't ever do something like that again," said Leni. "Promise me."

"Ow!" said Angelika. "You're hurting my hand."

Leni realized how hard she was gripping and relaxed her hold.

"I'm sorry," she said. "I was worried."

Angelika nodded. "I'm sorry, too."

Leni checked her watch. It was late. They needed to get to the station. "Let's take a cab," she said. There was no way she was going to let this girl out of her sight from now on. She managed to hail a passing taxi and helped Angelika in. As it pulled away, the girl stared out of the back window.

"At Christmas time, a long time ago, I went in there, I'm sure of it. There was a party," she said. "I wonder if my parents were there, too. I wish I could remember."

Leni stared at her, then back at the building, decorated with swastikas. The question that had been in the back of her mind from the first day came to the fore once more: Who was this girl? It was quickly replaced by another question: Where the hell was Otto?

26

ESCAPE

Otto hadn't moved a millimeter or a muscle for the last ten minutes. The brown shoes hadn't moved, either, as the man continued to turn the newspaper pages on top of the table. Then, just as Otto was beginning to despair, the phone rang again, the shrill bell making his heart skip. The man hurried from the dining room to answer it. Otto got ready to spring out and race for the door. Then a tiny hand lifted the edge of the cloth, raising it up a little.

A baby girl, perhaps two years old, with blonde curly hair and chubby cheeks, stared curiously at Otto. He put his finger to his lips.

"Mutti!" the girl cried. She had a loud voice for such a small person.

Otto prepared himself for the worst. His pack was at the

station, and without a knife or his pistol the situation would be hopeless.

"What are you doing, *Liebchen*?" A woman's shoes appeared by the baby.

"Mutti . . ." The baby let go of the cloth and took a step towards Otto.

"No, no, not under there." The mother bent down and scooped her baby up.

"That was the office. Something big has come up." The man had come back. "All personnel have been ordered to report immediately."

"But, Heinz, it's your day off."

"It's from the top, Heydrich himself. Get me a clean shirt and see if my boots are polished. Come on, Helga, hurry up."

Otto shook his head. Of all the people who could have moved into his house, it had to be a Gestapo officer.

The three of them left the room, and Otto heard them walking down the corridor to his parents' bedroom. This was his chance. He took a firm grip of his boots and moved. In a couple of steps he was by the front door. They were talking in the bedroom.

Otto eased open the door and slipped out into the corridor, sliding on the linoleum in his socks. He left the front door ajar, not wanting to risk the sound that closing it would make. He pulled on his boots, lacing them as fast as he could. It only took a dozen seconds.

"Mutti!"

Otto looked up. The baby was standing on the threshold of the open front door, looking right at him. Then the mother appeared, and her mouth dropped open with shock.

"Heinz!" she shrieked.

Otto didn't wait to see Heinz. He sprinted to the stairs and flew down, taking the steps three at a time. As he hit the first landing, the woman's second shriek pierced the stairwell and he lost his footing on the polished stone. He fell headlong, rolling over and over until the next landing broke his fall, and lay there, momentarily stunned. Then the man's head appeared at the top of the stairs, staring down. Fear surged inside Otto. He pulled himself up and starting running down the steps again, ignoring the pain in his ankle.

"Hey, you, *halt!*"

Otto didn't look back, though he heard the man's boots clattering on the steps above him. Then he was in the entrance hall, his head down, praying no one was coming in or out at that moment.

Luck was against him. A big man in gray overalls was standing by the front door, talking to the postman. It was Günter, the building's caretaker, a simple man who had been gassed in the Great War.

"*Halt!*" The other man's voice echoed down the stairs.

Günter looked back from the doorway towards Otto. He was bound to recognize him. They used to swap cigarette cards. But Otto couldn't take the chance that Günter would be kind to him now. There was only one course open to him. He swerved away from the front door, and into Günter's apartment, throwing the bolt on the door.

Otto saw immediately that nothing had changed in the sparsely furnished two-room studio, apart from the inevitable addition of the Führer's portrait on the wall. He wrenched open the small window above the washbasin and wriggled through. Then he was in the alleyway by the side of the building, dashing towards Jaegerstrasse at the front. At the end of it, he turned left into Fürstenstrasse.

Fortunately the streets were packed with morning shoppers and service personnel on leave. Otto ducked between them, trying to blend in. Surely the man wouldn't pursue him this far?

Unfortunately Heinz was Gestapo and therefore not the type to give up. Half-dressed in his uniform, black trousers and boots and a collarless white shirt, he was running straight after Otto.

Otto sprinted into Ludwigstrasse. A passing omnibus and car blasted their horns at him. At the end of the street he glanced back again. The man had no intention of losing him and was in fact gaining. Otto ran into Maffeistrasse and then Promenadeplatz. But any hopes of losing the man in the wider boulevard were dashed by the presence of soldiers sitting outside the beer halls, drinking great mugs of beer. Otto would stick out a mile. His only option was to duck into one of the alleys by the side of a beer hall and hide behind the wooden beer crates and barrels. After running past the first two halls, he found a suitable alleyway and ducked in.

He reached the end where all the spent bottles and barrels were kept, and managed to wedge himself in out of sight. He crouched there, desperately trying to catch his breath, his ankle on fire. He looked at his watch. He was supposed to be meeting Leni and Angelika at the station right now.

Then came the sound of splintering wood and breaking glass. Otto peeped out from his hiding hole. The man was walking slowly down the alley, pulling over the wooden crates, shattering the bottles. Otto could smell the sweet malted aroma of the dregs.

"I think it would be best for you, young man, if you were to give yourself up now, with no further struggle."

The voice was cold and official now, and all the more menacing for that.

Otto cursed the fact once again that his weapons were at the station. His hands shaking, he gently withdrew an empty bottle from a crate and grasped it firmly around its neck. Then he stood up and stepped out from his hiding place.

The man was twenty feet from him, his feet planted wide.

"I am an inspector with the Gestapo, and you, young man, are under arrest."

Sweat was pouring down Otto's face. He slammed the end of the bottle again the brick wall, leaving a jagged shard in his hand.

The Gestapo officer shook his head. "You do realize that your life is now over."

Otto realized it only too well. "Stay back!" he said.

"I've had enough of this." The man strode towards him. Otto waited until he was almost with an arm's grasp of him, then sidestepped to the right and slashed the broken bottle at the man's left side.

"You little — !" The man glanced with fury at his shirtsleeve, sliced open below the elbow, blood spreading through the white cotton.

Otto jabbed again, but this time he was not so lucky. The man caught Otto's wrist in his hand and slammed his hand against a crate. *Bang, bang, bang.* The bottle dropped from Otto's hand. The man transferred his fist to the neck of Otto's shirt, grasping it tight so he could lift Otto off the ground.

"We shall make a very special example of you," he said, his lip curling.

Then Otto saw a blur of brown behind the man, heard the sickening thud of the impact, and saw a beer bottle exploding from the back of the man's head. The man's eyes went glassy and he let go of Otto. He took a step back and dropped to his knees, before crumpling to the ground.

Leni was standing directly behind him, still holding the neck of the bottle in her hand. He stared at her incredulously.

"How . . . ?"

"We were in a taxi, on our way to the station, we saw you running down the street . . ." Leni struggled to get the words out. Otto nodded, his heart still hammering. He was finding it hard to catch his breath.

Angelika was a few feet behind her, her eyes wide.

Otto waved and smiled weakly. "It's all right, Angelika. He was a bad man, that's all."

Angelika walked slowly forward and stared down at him. Otto couldn't tell what she was thinking, whether she was frightened or upset. She seemed almost detached.

"Is he dead?" she asked.

Otto shook his head. "No, no. He'll be fine."

"Are you all right?" she said.

"I'm fine, too. Don't worry." He dragged himself to his feet.

"I don't like this place," she said.

"Me neither," said Otto. "Let's go." He took her hand. It felt hot and clammy.

He wanted to look at Leni, but right now he felt he couldn't meet her eye.

27

KEMPTEN EXPRESS

They had just minutes to retrieve their packs. They clambered aboard the train as the platform guard blew his whistle and the train pulled out of the station. They managed to find a six-seater compartment to themselves and within five minutes of departure the train guard had come and punched their tickets. Now they could sit back and relax — at least for the next hour. Not that Leni was in the mood to do any such thing. She sat opposite Otto, glaring at him.

"How many more times do you want me to apologize?" Otto muttered. They'd pulled the blinds down on the side windows and door, hoping this might deter anyone from joining them in the compartment.

"A few more times," Leni said acidly.

"All right, I'm sorry. I don't know what came over me. It was just . . . we were there in Munich and I thought —"

"No, Otto, you didn't think. You just chose to please yourself, regardless of the risks." Leni knew he had been up to something, but she'd never have believed he could have done something so stupid and dangerous.

"What's Otto done wrong, Leni?" Angelika was sucking on a candy.

"He hasn't done anything wrong," said Leni.

Angelika looked confused. "Then why are you cross with him?"

"All right, he did something silly, a bit like you leaving me in the museum."

"Oh," said Angelika. She looked at Otto. "So we're both in trouble."

"What are you talking about?" asked Otto.

"Don't change the subject," countered Leni.

"Who's changing the subject? What happened at the museum, Leni?"

"All right, Angelika went missing for a little bit, but it was fine. So don't even try to equate that with what you did."

"I wasn't going to." Otto folded his arms and looked out the window.

The train had got up a good head of steam and was well out of the suburbs of the city. It clattered along, past fields filled with ripening corn, orchards, and small-holdings just beginning to fill up with the season's bean, tomato, pepper, and zucchini plants. Farther on were fields of hops and vineyards beginning to leaf. Only the gray-and-green military trucks towing field guns in long convoys on the dusty roads spoiled the rural landscape.

Angelika rested her head against Leni's shoulder, and closed her eyes. They'd been on their feet since the early hours with just a few snatched minutes of sleep on the freight train.

"Well, what happened?" Otto arched his eyebrows in Angelika's direction.

"That wasn't my fault," said Leni defensively.

"If you say so."

"Oh, let's just drop the whole thing," said Leni, feeling there was nothing more to be gained.

"Fine by me," said Otto.

The three of them sat in silence for a while, the heat building. Leni felt Angelika gradually relax against her and her head become heavier on her shoulder. When she was sure that the girl was asleep, she whispered, "You made us come to Munich just so you could see if your family was still there."

Otto shook his head. "Of course not. Going to Munich was the right thing to do."

She said nothing, deciding to let him stew. She knew she was right.

"If it had been in Vienna, wouldn't you have wanted to visit your home?" he said eventually.

"I knew it," said Leni quietly.

"Well, wouldn't you? I bet you would."

"Don't you dare say that to me. I wouldn't take any risks that would endanger my life or yours. And you should do the same. How else can we trust each other?"

Otto's face was flushed, his forehead beaded with sweat. Leni suddenly realized he was on the verge of tears.

"You're right, Leni, it was stupid, it was selfish, and it was pointless. They're gone, they're never coming back, and I'm never going to —" His voice broke and he stopped.

"It's all right, it's all right," Leni said, feeling terrible. She hadn't meant to upset him like this.

Otto shook his head. His mouth was set. "I promise it won't happen again," he said, struggling to control his voice.

Leni wanted to reach over and take his hand, but she didn't want to disturb Angelika. "I know, I know," she said.

Otto blew out his cheeks and stared out the window. Leni decided to change the subject as quickly as possible.

"I haven't told you why Angelika ran away."

"Why did she?" Otto looked back at her.

"She saw this house on the way to the museum and then went back to look at it."

"What kind of house?"

"Just a building, but it was covered in swastikas and banners."

"What street was it on?"

"Prinzregentenstrasse."

"Was it an office building? The Gestapo headquarters are on Prinzregentenstrasse." Otto was looking interested now.

"No, it looked like an apartment building."

Otto's eyes widened. "Then it's Hitler's personal residence in Munich. That's the only other place of importance on that street."

Leni felt her heart thump. "She said she'd been inside, when she was very little, at Christmastime."

"Do you believe her?"

"Why would she lie?"

The two of them sat quietly for a moment.

"Who is she?" Leni asked at length.

"I don't know, and I don't want to know. Our job is to get her out of here in one piece as quickly as possible, not to start being detectives."

"But you must be curious."

"No. Curiosity is bad for you," he said, but Leni could see he was.

The door to the compartment slid open. A middle-aged woman in a dark wool suit stood in the doorway.

"Is anyone sitting there?" She pointed with her umbrella to the empty seat beside Leni.

"No, it's free," said Otto, standing like a well-brought-up young man. "May I help you with that?"

"No, thank you, I am perfectly capable." The woman lifted

a small leather valise onto the rack above the seat and sat down next to Leni.

Otto and Leni looked at each other. Around the woman's neck on a piece of black ribbon was a Mother's Medal. A small blue-and-white enamel cross with the swastika in the middle, it was awarded to mothers on a special day in May. But more important, as far as Otto and Leni were concerned, she was wearing a dark blue cuff on her left sleeve. It bore the title *Reichsfrauenschaft*, identifying the woman as a national staff member of the Nazi Party. They were sharing the compartment with a professional busybody.

The woman settled in for a minute or two, then slowly cast her eyes over Otto, Leni, and the still-sleeping Angelika.

"So tell me," she began. "What are three children doing all alone on a train?" She didn't wait for an answer. "Don't tell me . . . you're running away from home." And she smiled at them conspiratorially.

28

DISCOVERY

From the helicopter, Heydrich could see the farmer sitting in his hay cart and looking as though he was about to have a heart attack when the Flettner dropped down into his field. The field was already full of army vehicles, and black-uniformed SS troops had fanned out in search formation.

Once on the ground, Heydrich jumped out of the helicopter and marched across to the farmer, whose eyes were still wide with shock.

"Show me," he said.

Five minutes later, they were beneath the tree, staring up at the severed lines and shredded parachute canopy. A junior officer ran towards him with Otto's dirt-covered flying suit and helmet. Heydrich examined them carefully. American-made but issued to the RAF. As he'd thought: British agents.

"Order your men to search the whole area." He turned to the farmer. "The Reich is grateful. I will notify your local leader of your good service."

The farmer raised his arm in salute.

Heydrich made his way back out of the woods. Both his Mercedes and a detachment of troops for his personal use had arrived.

"So now we know where they came from and where they landed," he said to the junior officers that had gathered around him. "I suspect there is more than one operative. Logic would suggest a man and a woman, so that they can travel as a family. The question is, where are they now?"

At that point, a young lieutenant raced across the field towards them on a motorbike. He skidded to a halt beside the briefing party and ran across to Heydrich.

"Sir, the photographic prints that you requested from the Berghof."

Heydrich flipped open the envelope and looked at the thick sheaf of photographs of the girl. They were all the same, the most up-to-date picture of her, taken the previous year, fifty copies still damp from the processing. She was a pleasant-looking child, round-faced and smiling, her hair in pigtails like his own daughter. She was wearing traditional Bavarian dress. The photograph had been taken against a plain white background, most likely the convent's walls.

"Distribute these to the officers. This is the girl we are looking for."

"Sir! SS General Müller from Innsbruck." His driver was holding up the limousine's phone. Heydrich strode across, took the handset.

"Müller? I hope you have some positive news?"

"What I am about to propose sounds incredible, but I ask you to consider it carefully." Müller's voice was calm and collected, denoting his police background. The radio line was bad, but Heydrich was keen to hear what this bloodhound of an investigator had to say.

"Go on."

"We've taken statements from every conceivable person in Rosenheim, Prien, and Stock. Yes, there were tourist couples visiting Herreninsel yesterday, but no one sticks out. Furthermore, there were no tickets purchased at any of the surrounding railway stations by a couple with a child."

"So what? They could have taken a car, a series of cars."

"And yet none has been reported stolen in the last twenty-four hours, and no one can remember an unknown couple arriving in one in any of those places."

"They could have hidden it up a lane or a farm road?"

"Perhaps, but here is another possibility. Railway employees at Prien remember a teenage boy and girl buying tickets yesterday for Stock. Unknown teenagers. There was an altercation with some youths from a local club of the NSFK. Then at Stock, a girl and boy of similar descriptions bought tickets to visit the palace on Herreninsel. It was in the afternoon, the last tour of the day. The ferry crew can't recall them coming back. There is a Hitler-Jugend summer sailing camp in Stock, but all the children are accounted for. But a girl did go into the local chandlers and buy twenty yards of rope."

"Go on." Heydrich was listening intently, catching the edge of excitement in Müller's clipped voice. They hadn't found the rope that had been used to climb out of the convent window. *Probably sitting on the bottom of the lake*, he thought.

"This morning, the ticket seller at Rosenheim station sold three tickets to Innsbruck to a young man probably aged around fifteen or so. The first available departure of the morning."

"And do their descriptions match those of the previous day?"

"More or less, sir."

Heydrich drummed his fingers on the car. "And what do the railway people at Innsbruck tell you?"

"It would seem that they got off before Innsbruck. The ticket collector here is positive three children of these descriptions did not come past the barrier."

Heydrich could feel the hairs on his neck prickling. The day before, flying low between the two islands, he'd buzzed a little sailing dinghy. It had had a red sail, he recalled. And there had been two teenagers, a girl and a boy, in the boat. Late afternoon, early evening. Could it have been them?

"Herr Reichsführer," continued Müller, "I realize what I am proposing seems unlikely —"

"How many stops did the Innsbruck train make?" Heydrich interrupted.

"About half a dozen, sir — it was the slow train."

"Question every person at those stations. Someone must have seen something."

Heydrich tossed the receiver back to his radio operator and made his way back to the waiting officers.

"Show me those overalls again."

One of the officers held up Otto's flying suit.

"On the small side, wouldn't you say?" Heydrich said thoughtfully.

It seemed too unlikely. But when one considered it further, there was the most devilish cunning to such a strategy. Three children traveling together, when logic dictated that two adults would have taken the child. England had its fair share of displaced German children whose parents had either fled with them or had them sent abroad. It was risky, dangerous, a wild gamble on the part of the British. And yet . . . why not? As a child Heydrich had read Sherlock Holmes. The detective's famous axiom came to mind now: "When you have eliminated the impossible, whatever remains, however improbable, must be the truth."

He looked at his officers. They were waiting expectantly. Yes, he was inclined to believe Müller.

"Send word to all units that we are now looking for three children: a teenage girl and boy, and the child."

29

TOO MANY QUESTIONS

"Yes, that's right, I remember your school very well," beamed the matronly mother in the railway carriage. "The headmaster was a Herr Schuler when I was there. Do you know him?"

Otto nodded, even though he hadn't the slightest idea who Herr Schuler was. The woman had not stopped asking them questions from the moment she had sat down. He exchanged another quick glance with Leni. She, too, was being subjected to all manner of queries. It felt more and more like an interrogation.

The woman had started by asking them where they were going, and had been satisfied with their story about their visit to their godmother in Bregenz. Then she had asked them where they were from.

"Salzburg," Otto had said confidently.

"Salzburg? How interesting," the woman had replied.

She had herself spent a couple of years in the city training to be a teacher. Of course, now she had left that behind and worked for the Party, but she had happy memories of the city and proceeded to question them about it in great detail. Her knowledge appeared to be encyclopedic, but so far Otto and Leni seemed to be holding their own. Just.

"Now, tell me this," she continued, looking first at Leni and then at Otto. "I recall there were two lovely old bakeries by the school, Joseph's and . . . what was the name of the other? Let me think . . . Schekter's, that was it." She smiled. "Which was your favorite?"

Otto frowned, appearing to think about it. "Well, they were both good."

"Come along, young man, you must have had a preference."

Otto mentally flipped a coin. "Schekter's."

The woman smiled again. "Ah, yes, I do believe their *strudl* was the best."

"If you'll excuse us, *meine Frau*, we must be getting off at the next station." Otto looked at Leni hard. He was getting nervous now of this woman; there was something snakelike about her.

"Yes, we must," Leni hurriedly backed him up, and gave Angelika a gentle shake. Sleepily, the little girl opened her eyes.

"But you are traveling to Bregenz. You don't need to change until Kempten," the woman said.

"That's right, but . . ." Otto racked his brains for a reason.

"A friend of our family's lives at the next stop," Leni jumped in.

"And we have a gift from our mother for her," Otto finished.

Angelika was now fully awake and listening in, her forehead creased in a frown.

The woman looked at Leni. "You know, young lady, I am sure you have a Viennese accent."

"Really? You must be mistaken," said Leni. "Come along," she said to Angelika, "we're getting off."

"And what is your name?" the woman asked Angelika.

Leni and Otto shot each other another anxious glance.

"Caroline," Leni said, just as the little girl opened her mouth. "Her name is Caroline." She prayed Angelika wouldn't contradict her.

Otto stood up and pulled the packs down off the rack. He slipped his over his shoulders. He could feel the tension rising.

"Young man, wait."

"We have to go, madam, please."

The woman suddenly got up and stepped in front of the compartment door, blocking their path. The three children froze.

"What is she doing?" said Angelika, turning to Otto, then Leni, in confusion.

"What am I doing?" The woman's voice was cold. "I'll tell you what I am doing. I am ordering you to sit down and remain seated while I call the guard."

This was bad.

"I don't understand," said Leni. Otto could see she was fighting rising panic. "What have we done wrong?"

"You don't understand?" The woman was clearly starting to enjoy the situation now. "Well, *I* don't understand, either. I don't understand how you could prefer Schekter's to Joseph's when no such bakeries exist." She smiled back at them triumphantly.

There was a long moment of silence. Then Otto lunged forward, shoving the woman away from the door with all his strength. She was taken by surprise and fell heavily onto the seat. Otto pulled the door open, and Leni and Angelika dived out after him into the corridor.

"How dare you touch me like that!" The woman was struggling to get back on her feet. She grasped the doorframe with her hand for support.

Otto grabbed the handle and slammed the door back on her fingers. He heard her howl with pain as he raced after the others. He reached them in the interconnecting partition between two carriages. The steel floor plates were sliding under their feet.

Otto glanced around the wall of the partition. There was

the woman! She was stumbling down the corridor after them, clutching her injured hand.

"Young man, stop at once!" she called out. "Guard!"

"What do we do?" Leni said.

"Jump," replied Otto.

"What about her?"

Otto unslung his pack and plunged his hand inside. He found his pistol and the silencer.

"Stop!" The woman was getting closer.

He started to screw the silencer on the end of the barrel, but his hands were shaking too much.

"Let me," said Leni. He handed the parts to her, and she deftly assembled them. "Don't look," she said to Angelika, and then handed him the gun. He nodded briefly to her. There was no time, no alternative. He stepped back into the corridor. The woman was less than thirty feet away.

"There you . . ." Her voice died as he raised the pistol and pointed it at her chest. She stopped dead. Otto's finger closed around the trigger, felt the pressure build. Then the woman's face turned gray, her knees buckled, and she crumpled to the ground.

"She fainted," Otto said. "She fainted." He turned back to the others. "She fainted," he said again. He hadn't had to shoot her.

"Then let's go," said Leni, looking as relieved as he felt.

Otto immediately pulled down the door's sliding glass window and leaned out to grasp the handle on the outside. He twisted it, and the door swung open, slamming into the outside of the carriage. Wind rushed into the partition. The train seemed to be moving faster than ever.

Leni stepped forward, threw the packs out, and jumped. Otto didn't waste a second. He grabbed Angelika around the waist, swung her out, and dropped her like a stick off a bridge. He went last.

He landed with a tremendous thud on the embankment. The lush thick grass broke his fall but didn't slow it, and he was rolling uncontrollably down the steep slope until he reached the others at the bottom, all in a tangled heap. The train chugged on. He waited until it was out of sight and then pulled himself up, helping the others. Angelika was crying softly, and Leni was rubbing the little girl's back.

"Is she all right?"

"Just winded, I think. Nothing broken."

"It's not that," sobbed Angelika. "Everything's ruined now, isn't it? That woman will tell the police and then they'll take me back to the convent and we'll never get to Switzerland and I'll never see my parents."

Otto squatted down beside her. "You're wrong, Angelika. Everything's going to be fine," he said, gently but firmly.

"Really?" She looked doubtful but he could see she wanted desperately to believe him.

Otto nodded emphatically. "I promise."

Angelika leaned forward and hugged him.

For a moment he was at a loss, then he hugged her back.

Yes, he had promised. And he would make it so.

30

HITCHING SOUTH

"Right, get ready . . ." Leni shouted down the road to Otto. She and Angelika were crouched behind the hedgerow. Through the thick foliage she could make out the civilian truck trundling towards her. It was a Czech-built Skoda. She found herself smiling at it, remembering that her brother Jacob had had a red toy one made out of tin. The truck was the first piece of traffic actually heading in the right direction since they'd started walking over an hour ago. They were still a good twenty miles east of Kempten.

Otto lay down by the side of the road. Sure enough, the truck pulled to a halt, and a rough-looking driver got out. "Mother?" she heard Otto say. She grinned. He was a good actor!

"I'm not your mother." The driver gave Otto a tap in the ribs with his boot. "What's wrong with you, young man? Are you drunk?"

"No, no . . . I think I must have fainted from the heat. I've been walking all morning." He got to his feet shakily. "Where are you going?" The driver turned away from his truck and mopped the back of his neck with a grubby-looking necker-chief. It was very hot.

"Now!" Leni hissed to Angelika, and together they ran to the back of the truck.

"South," Otto said.

Safely stowed with Angelika in the back of the truck, Leni crossed her fingers that the driver was going south, too.

"All right, jump in. I'm heading that way myself."

Otto pulled himself and his pack up into the cab, and slammed the door.

At last, thought Leni. They were back on the road, and heading to the border.

The truck bed was full of agricultural tools, including a dozen new scythes, tied together in a fat bundle.

"Can I ask you a question, Leni?" Angelika whispered, although the chance of the driver hearing her above the sound of the engine was next to zero.

Leni nodded.

"Am I really going to meet my parents?"

Leni looked at her. She suddenly seemed even younger and more vulnerable than her nine years.

"Why do you ask that?" she said, trying to deflect the

question. Whatever the truth was, she had no intention of straying from MacPherson's script.

"I didn't think so," said Angelika.

"I didn't say you weren't. I haven't met them myself, but I've been told they're waiting in Switzerland for you." That was true.

"Really?" Angelika couldn't hide the doubt in her voice.

Leni nodded as convincingly as she could.

"I can't believe it," said Angelika. "I used to wish so much they would come and see me, take me away from the convent, but in the end I decided they never would. Ever."

"Let me ask you a question now," Leni said. "That building in Munich, the one you knew. That's the Führer's personal apartment. Are you sure you went there?"

"The Führer?" Angelika was clearly surprised by this. "Yes, I mean, I remember it. Being taken there. I don't know how old I was. It was Christmas, I do remember that. There was a tree and gifts and lots of other children, and we all sang carols."

"Who took you there?"

"A nanny, I think. I can't remember her name. And Uncle Rudi was there."

"Uncle Rudi?" Leni felt they were getting somewhere.

"He's the man who visits me with the chocolates on my birthday."

"What does he look like?"

"Like a grown-up." Angelika shrugged. "He's got black hair."

So do half the men in Bavaria, thought Leni.

"He's very friendly when he visits, but it's only for an hour. He never said anything about my parents."

"Did you ask him?"

Angelika shook her head. "He said I was a very special girl, just like the mother superior did."

"Did you ask him why he came to see you?"

"I did, but he used to smile and laugh and say he was like Saint Nicholas, just visiting to give me a present."

They sat in silence in the hot stuffy air, the truck rattling and bouncing.

"Where are your parents?" Angelika asked.

"Oh, they're in Salzburg," Leni said casually.

"That's nice," Angelika said after a long pause. "It's hard being alone sometimes."

Leni took her hand. "I know. And I promise you that, whatever happens, you won't be alone. You'll always have me and Otto as your friends."

"Promise?"

Leni nodded, and this time she truly meant it.

"Are you really brother and sister?" asked Angelika.

Leni was taken aback, but the girl was looking at her so intently she knew there was no point in lying.

"Well, no, actually, we're not. But promise me you'll keep that a secret."

Angelika smiled. "Of course I will, and . . . well, I've never told anyone this, there was no one to tell, but now you're my friend, I can tell you. Can you keep a secret, too, Leni?" Angelika leaned closer to her.

"Yes, of course."

"Cross your heart, hope to die?" Angelika was solemn.

Leni crossed her heart and muttered the words.

"You see, I've thought about it a lot, and maybe my parents don't exist."

"Of course they exist." Leni smiled. "Everyone has parents, Angelika. We may not know who they are or where they are sometimes but they exist. Otherwise *you* couldn't exist, could you?"

"Not necessarily," replied Angelika.

Leni stared at her. "I don't understand. What do you mean?"

"I'm saying you don't have to have parents. Not if you're an angel." The girl said it quietly but with complete seriousness.

Leni thought she must have misheard. "Pardon?" she said.

Angelika was looking at her sincerely, almost serenely. "That's right. Perhaps I'm an angel. Every Sunday I walk with the Reverend Mother, just the two of us, around the island. And she says that I'm special, that I have to be protected from the outside world . . . I think that's why Sister Margareta doesn't like me. She doesn't like it that I'm special. The Reverend Mother said one day it'll all be explained to me, when I'm older. So that's why I think I must be an angel. Because they're special, aren't they?"

Leni looked at this girl. At that moment she felt so protective of her, of her innocence. "Well," she said gently, "it's a possibility . . ."

"Then you believe me?" Angelika face lit up.

"I'd like to," Leni said simply.

Angelika smiled broadly. "I'm so glad I told you. I thought you might think it was a stupid idea."

"Of course not," said Leni. "Why don't you tell me all about it?"

31

PICKING UP THE SCENT

Heydrich sipped his coffee and continued to study the large-scale map spread out on the rough table. He had stopped at a roadside inn about an hour from Munich. In the middle of the yard behind the inn, his helicopter was being refueled by a tanker truck under the watchful eye of the pilot.

The rest of his men were resting by their vehicles, eating lunch. His driver was talking into the radio, keeping abreast of the hunt.

As he studied the infinite number of roads, tracks, and mountain paths leading towards the border, he realized finding these three children was going to be like finding the proverbial three needles in a haystack. He was desperate to get back to the chase. Unfortunately he had to wait. Bormann had called him an hour earlier from the Berghof to tell him of Hitler's express wish that another person be brought in to help.

The gentleman in question was now on his way from Berlin to join them. His name was Ludwig Straniak, and he was a mystic and astrologer, part of the SS's Institute for Occult Warfare. More important for this case, he was apparently an expert in radiaesthesia. This meant that he had the ability to find a person merely with the aid of a map and a pendulum. Heydrich was skeptical, but if the Führer believed in it, then naturally he would follow orders. He watched as the radio operator pulled off his headphones, climbed out of the Mercedes, and ran over to him.

"Something unexpected has arisen, sir. Perhaps it's significant. Headquarters just had a report from the Gestapo office in Kempten."

Heydrich searched the map carefully before stabbing the location of the town with his forefinger, northwest of his current position.

"Go on."

"They were called out by the local policeman to a village east of there. A stop on the railway line. A woman was claiming to have been assaulted by three children on the Munich-to-Kempten train."

Heydrich looked up sharply.

"Not only that. The woman was convinced that the children were lying about where they were from. They claimed to live in Salzburg, but she's sure that was not true."

"What were the ages of the children?"

"A boy of fourteen or fifteen, a girl a little younger, and another girl of about nine or ten."

"Descriptions?"

"Blond hair, all of them. Dressed in Hitler-Jugend and BDM uniforms."

They must have dyed the child's hair.

"What trains left Rosenheim for Munich this morning?"

The operator checked his notebook. "There were no passenger trains till ten A.M., but a freight train went through at the same time as the Innsbruck train was leaving."

"Has the woman seen the picture of the girl?"

"Not yet, sir, I have sent a dispatch rider with it. He'll be there within the hour."

Heydrich was walking towards the helicopter. He stopped as he heard, and then saw, a BMW sedan racing down the road towards them with two SS outriders in front, sirens on.

"Don't wait for the rider to get there. Let's assume it's them. They'll be heading towards the Swiss border. Tell the Innsbruck group to swing south towards the mountains and cover the roads south and west of, say, Oberstdorf. Order the other groups to go north of that. Hopefully, with the help of our special weapon, we will have them in our grasp before nightfall."

"Special weapon, sir?" asked the operator.

The BMW screeched to a halt in a swirl of dust beside Heydrich. Sitting in the backseat, looking a little shaken by the speed of the journey, was a spectacled, bearded man in a gray summer suit. He had the air of a distracted teacher, down to his soup-stained tie, and climbed out unsteadily, squinting at the sunshine. He dug into his suit pocket and retrieved a pair of clip-on shades that he fixed over his spectacles.

"Our secret weapon," said Heydrich with a sneer. "Herr Straniak, from the Institute for Occult Warfare."

The radio operator looked at Straniak skeptically.

Heydrich stepped towards the man, offering his hand in greeting. "I understand the Führer holds much store in your gifts."

Straniank nodded. Then something strange happened, which Heydrich would come to remember at the very end of his life. As their hands touched, the mystic stepped back, pulling his hand free. He had gone a little pale.

"Is everything all right?" Heydrich stared at the man, startled by his apparent rudeness.

"Y-yes, of course," Straniak stammered. Then he appeared to recover. "Forgive me, I am a little tired from the journey."

Heydrich nodded, but he was unconvinced by the explanation. He had clearly seen an unmistakable look of fear and alarm in Straniak's eyes. There were rumors that some of these mystics had psychic powers and were able to see the future. Ridiculous boasts, so far as he was concerned. He put the man's reaction to his handshake to the back of his mind. "I understand. But I am afraid we must get moving once again.

Please . . ." Heydrich indicated the helicopter. "I'll explain everything as we fly north."

Straniak looked alarmed. "We are not traveling in that contraption, surely?"

"Indeed we are. I assure you, it is entirely safe. Follow us to Kempten, quick as you can!" he said to his operator, then to Straniak, "Get your things. There is no time to lose."

32

A BRIEF RESPITE

When he estimated they were around twenty miles in a direct line from the Swiss border, Otto asked the truck driver to let him off at a deserted road junction. This was where they needed to head west. They had decided to walk, following minor roads, to avoid being seen or having contact with anyone.

The driver drove off with a wave out of the window. Otto stood alone for a moment, then Leni and Angelika emerged from the dry roadside ditch they had jumped into when the truck had pulled to a halt.

They started walking along the side of the road, constantly alert to the sound of vehicles, but it was still the lunch hour and they met nothing on their way. After about half an hour Angelika skipped ahead. It gave Leni the opportunity she'd been looking for to talk to Otto.

"Her uncle Rudi, the one that visits her every year on her birthday."

"What about him?" said Otto.

"Who do you think he might be?"

Otto shrugged. He didn't want to think about such matters. He was wholly focused on getting them across the border alive. "Look, maybe we should just —" he began.

"Well, I think he's Hess, Rudolf Hess."

Otto stared at her. "You do?"

"Well, his name obviously — Rudi, Rudolf — and Hess does have black hair, and we know he flew to England last month. And then we're suddenly recruited to come over here. I think it's all connected."

"I suppose it's possible." But it all sounded a bit unlikely to him.

Angelika turned and called back to them. She was standing on a wooden bridge. "Look!" she shouted. "A river!"

Otto and Leni caught up with her and looked down. They were tired and hot and sweaty. The bubbling water below looked incredibly inviting in the sweltering afternoon sun. A silver fish darted out from the bank.

"Can't we stop and have a swim, please?" It was Angelika who voiced what the other two were thinking.

"We should keep moving," said Otto unconvincingly. "The border isn't far now."

"Just for ten minutes, Otto." Leni looked flushed and weary.

"It's dangerous, Leni, we'll be exposed." But he was starting to waver.

"There's no one around. Come on!" she said.

Otto looked around. It did seem quiet. And they were a safe distance from the town. "All right," he said. "But ten minutes only."

The three of them slid down the side of the bank and stashed their packs under the bridge. Angelika was squealing with delight. "No noise!" scolded Otto, pulling off his walking boots and socks. Within seconds Leni and Angelika had stripped down to their underwear and were wading out into the middle of the narrow river.

Once they got used to the shock of the icy water it was delicious. Nothing like the sea at Dunkirk, or the muddy ditch at the manor, or the lake. Perhaps what had happened at the Chiemsee had helped him to overcome his fear. Otto took a deep breath, then dived and swam down, touching one of the stones on the riverbed before kicking for the surface. He laughed when he saw Leni and Angelika splashing each other.

He swam around some more and then hauled himself up onto the grass bank to dry off. He closed his eyes, felt the heat of the sun on his body. He lay like that, the sound of the girls splashing and laughing in the background, and let his mind drift. It was so nice to just stop moving for a few moments, to relax and lie still. He propped his hands behind his head and looked around.

They were almost in the foothills of the Tyrol. If they could skirt the mountains all the way to the Bodensee it was probably only twenty-five miles away. Then all they had to do was find the motor launch that MacPherson had arranged to have placed on the German side for them. Once darkness fell they would cross the Bodensee and the border, and rendezvous with MacPherson on the Swiss side of the lake. It seemed tantalizingly close, yet impossibly far away.

"Would you help me?" Leni called out, and he looked around at her. She was by the edge of the bank, holding out her right arm. Otto got up and stepped down to her. He grasped her hand and pulled her up. She came out of the water in a fluid movement, and Otto found her cold, wet body pressed up against his own sun-warmed skin. He suddenly wanted to kiss her, really kiss her, like in the movies.

Then she let go of his hand. "Thanks," she said, and stepped past him. He stood there for a moment, quite still.

"What about me?" Angelika was staring up at him from the river.

He grabbed hold of her hand and hauled her out. When he turned around, Leni had slipped her skirt and shirt back on, and she was wringing out her ponytail. She caught his eye and smiled. It was a different kind of smile to any she'd given him before, thought Otto.

As he walked across to the underside of the bridge to retrieve their packs, he found himself smiling, too — just as he heard the sound of approaching vehicles.

"Quick! Under here!" he shouted.

Leni grabbed Angelika's hand and they ran to join him. In less than a minute, the first vehicle was rolling over the bridge. The wooden supports creaked and groaned. Otto leaned out just enough to see a gray army Kübelwagen full of SS troops, with their distinctive black helmets, silver skulls on the side. Then came a troop-carrying truck.

"Are they looking for us?" Leni whispered.

He felt her warm breath on his ear, droplets of water from her ponytail spotting his shirt sleeve.

"Yes," he said, turning his face to hers.

Her face, her lips, were only millimeters from his. Her mouth was slightly open, her breathing fast.

"We're in so much trouble," Angelika whispered.

All sorts of trouble, thought Otto.

33

HIDING OUT

They had been walking for several hours and the three of them were exhausted. So exhausted that Leni and Angelika were lying flat out just inside the tree line, away from the road. Otto had gone ahead to reconnoiter a tiny hamlet to see if there was somewhere they could rest and hide till nightfall. Then they would strike out for the border and the lake and, God willing, safety.

They had decided to travel all night because it was not getting dark, really dark, until after ten o'clock. And then there were the roadblocks. They had nearly walked straight into the first one after their swim in the river. It was made up of the vehicles they had seen crossing the bridge. The truck had been parked across the center of the road and the Kübelwagens in line behind it. The troops were stopping and searching every vehicle extremely thoroughly. People were being turned out of their cars, hoods and trunks inspected, identity cards perused. Children in particular were being carefully scrutinized. Fortunately Otto, Leni, and Angelika had managed to get off the road before they were seen. They gave the soldiers a very wide berth.

When they had met another roadblock just a few miles on, they had decided to leave the road entirely and instead follow alongside it in the nearby woods. It was the old mountain road, known as the Alpenstrasse, and it took them west towards the border, zigzagging through the foothills and valleys. But the going was tough. The rough paths trodden down by locals suddenly gave out and they had to climb over fallen trees and thick spreads of ferns. Every time they stopped for a rest, Leni and Otto would scan the road with their binoculars and, sure enough, there would be more roadblocks, or military vehicles filled with troops heading west for the border. They'd both exchanged anxious glances but said nothing, conscious of the need not to alarm Angelika. But it was clear that there was an organized search. And that someone knew where they were heading. The woman on the train had no doubt alerted the authorities, who had put two and two together.

Leni opened her eyes now and sat up, feeling better for the rest. Why wasn't Otto back? It was funny: They barely knew each other, but she missed his presence keenly. The way he had held her at the river, the look in his eye, the hotness of his breath against her cheek, had made her feel as though something incredibly exciting was about to happen. She put it out of her mind. She wished she'd been able to talk to him more about Angelika, but there hadn't been the opportunity. Perhaps later. She knew one thing for sure: All these troops racing to find them meant Angelika was someone very important.

Leni leaned over and nudged the girl awake.

She opened her eyes, stretched, and yawned. "I'm hungry," she said.

"Here, drink some water." Leni handed her the water bottle. She wanted to keep what little food they had left till the evening.

"Isn't Otto back?" Angelika asked.

Leni shook her head.

"He's all right though, isn't he?"

"He's fine. He'll be back soon."

"If anything happened to him, I don't know what I'd do."

"You like him, don't you?" said Leni softly.

"Yes," she replied matter-of-factly. "And so do you."

Leni felt herself blushing. "No, I don't," she protested.

"Well, he likes you," she said. "Do you think he likes me?"

Leni nodded. "Of course he does."

"Has he told you?" Angelika was looking at her hopefully.

"Well, not in words, but I can see he does. He's very protective."

Angelika smiled. "He is, isn't he?" She glanced at Leni. "I mean, I know you are, too."

But it's not the same, is it? thought Leni. She used to wish she had older brothers, but now she didn't care. All she wished was that Jacob and Isaac were safe somewhere and that she'd see them again one day.

There was a sudden sound of footsteps and Leni pulled Angelika down. She reached into her backpack and put her hand on her pistol, putting her finger to her lips to indicate silence. The footsteps stopped. Then a single-note whistle rang out. Leni smiled with relief and whistled the three-note response. Moments later Otto was squatting down beside them.

"We have to be quick. There's a cow barn about half a mile from the village. It's empty. We can approach it from the woods without being seen. It'll be a perfect place to hide out until it's dark. Then we can carry on."

Angelika sighed. She looked worn out. "I'm so tired. Can't we just wait here?"

Otto looked at her. "How about if I give you a piggy-back ride?"

"A piggyback ride?" Angelika was smiling now. "What's that?"

"You've never heard of a piggyback ride?" said Otto, and Angelika shook her head. "It's simple, silly, you jump onto my back . . ." He kneeled down and took off his pack, handing it to Leni.

"Thanks a lot," she said. She'd drawn the short straw.

Angelika jumped onto Otto's back.

"You're as light as a feather," Otto said as they set off.

The barn did look ideal. It was set at the top of a field looking down on the small hamlet. The cows were up on the high pasture at this time of year, so it was empty. Best of all, it was only one hundred feet or so from the woods, with the doors at the back.

They crept in and wedged the doors firmly shut using a thick piece of timber.

"Let's get up into the hayloft," Otto said, pointing to a ladder.

They clambered up, Otto pulling the ladder up after them, then scrambled over mounds of straw to the front of the barn. From there, they could watch the hamlet through cracks in the shutters.

Angelika lay down in the hay and closed her eyes. She looked flushed.

"Go to sleep," said Leni. "We have a long walk tonight." She hoped the little girl would be asleep soon. She was desperate to talk to Otto about her. He was by the shutters, staring out. She crawled over and sat next to him.

"By my reckoning we're only about fifteen miles from the Bodensee," he said. "If we set off after dark we could probably make it in seven hours."

Leni did the mental arithmetic. "And then what? Lie low for the whole of tomorrow?"

"Yes, once we've located the boat. It's moored in an inlet

just south of Bregenz. We can approach it from the hills above. As soon as it's dark we cross the lake to the rendezvous point. It's our best bet. Admiral MacPherson said he would wait for as long as it takes."

"All right." Leni pulled her knees up to her chin. "They're closing in on us, aren't they?" Time, she felt, was running out.

"If we keep off the roads, we've got a good chance," Otto replied, not answering the question.

He took out the binoculars and peered towards the hamlet. There were about six houses on one road, a tiny church at one end, and a small inn in the middle of the houses. A farm track led from the hamlet to the barn, across a meadow.

"I think she's asleep, don't you?" Leni said.

Otto glanced at Angelika and nodded. "Why? What is it?" he asked.

Leni realized her heart was beating faster. "I've been thinking about her, about who she could be. If Hess is her so-called uncle, who do you think is her father?"

They both looked at the sleeping Angelika. The late-afternoon sun had cut through a hole in the roof, bathing her in a mote-filled shaft of light. Although her cheeks were flushed from the heat, her face was relaxed and her expression calm. It made her look so peaceful, even ethereal.

"Oh, come on, you're not saying..." Otto sounded incredulous.

"Yes, I am. That's exactly what I'm saying."

"Hitler?" Otto said the word so softly.

"Yes. I think that's why the Germans all want her so badly. That's why the British want her, too."

Otto looked at her, appalled. Then, very slowly, he nodded. For the first time, Leni could see he was afraid.

She went on. "Angelika has spent half her life living in a convent, cut off from the outside world. She has no parents. At least, no one she remembers. The mother superior tells her every week how special she is, how they must look after her. And Hitler's deputy comes to visit her every year on her birthday."

"And she remembered being at Hitler's house in Munich. She must have been sent away to the convent before she could ask questions . . . or before questions could be asked about her." He put his head in his hands. "Angelika was right — we're really in a lot of trouble."

"Don't you think I know that?"

"They're never going to let us get away." Otto was struggling to control his panic.

"Stop it, Otto," Leni said firmly.

"It's Hitler's child, Leni. His daughter. What are we going to do?"

"I don't know . . . I'm thinking."

They sat there in the stifling heat. Silence.

"Seems to me we've got only two options," Otto said after a while.

"Which are?"

"We leave her here with a note for her to walk to the hamlet. We take off now, make for the border. We can make up some story for MacPherson."

Leni shook her head. It was the surest way for the two of them to survive, but she hated the idea — and she knew Otto did, too. "No. How do we know what the Nazis will do to her? They might lock her up forever, or worse."

"That's not our problem."

"Isn't it?" Leni looked at him, hard. "Do you really want to do that? Cut and run?"

Otto glanced over at Angelika, who stirred slightly in her sleep, a lock of blonde hair falling across her face. Leni could see him twisting inside, wrestling with it all. Finally he looked back at her. "Then we complete the mission, get her over the border tonight. Hand her over to MacPherson," he said.

"And what's *he* going to do with her?"

"I don't know and I don't care. Leni, those are our orders." Otto tried to close off further discussion.

"And what about her? Do we tell her who she is?"

Leni and Otto looked at her again, then at each other. She was no longer just a girl to them. She was their little sister now. A reminder of the younger siblings they had both lost.

"She thinks she's meeting her parents in Switzerland," Leni said slowly, remembering the girl's hope. "Let's leave it like that."

She could only imagine what a bombshell the truth might be to the girl. Angelika hadn't chosen to be born, to be the child of that man.

34

STRANIAK DIVINES

They were in the helicopter heading west when Straniak began shouting and gesticulating wildly for the pilot to land. They descended rapidly and found a level spot in the middle of a valley where two rivers converged at roughly right angles.

Straniak hopped out and rushed towards the meeting point of the rivers. Sticking out of the ground was a series of boulders, no doubt washed down at some point from the mountains above. One in particular, a large slab of granite, had attracted his attention. He stood next to the stone for thirty minutes or so and then hurried to a nearby yew tree. Breaking off a low branch, he fashioned a Y-shaped dowsing twig and started to walk in tight circles around the slab, holding the twig with the tips of his fingers.

Heydrich watched with growing irritation.

"Herr Straniak, I don't wish to hurry you but we are losing the light."

"We have three more hours of light today," Straniak replied, and he continued his circling.

"Not for safe flying."

Straniak closed his eyes and sighed deeply. "I will be as quick as I can."

"Can I assist you?" Heydrich asked.

"Silence would be helpful."

Heydrich wanted to strike this silly man for his arrogance, but he held himself in check. There would be plenty of time to teach him respect once the girl had been found. He shifted his weight and felt the perspiration running down his back, soaking his shirt. Straniak had better prove his worth if he valued his neck.

"I think you will find my presence valuable in your search," Straniak murmured.

Was he a mind reader, too?

Before Heydrich could say anything more, Straniak continued. "We are standing directly on a very strong ley line."

"And that is good?" Heydrich had only a vague idea what a ley line was. Mystical pseudoscience, as far as he was concerned.

"Very good for tracing psychic energy." Straniak leaned down and opened his brown attaché case, extracting a number of items. First he spread out a map of the area, and dropped a gold coin over their current location. Then he placed the original photograph of the girl on the map. Finally he picked out a small brass pendulum attached to a fine black silk thread. This was his great expertise, the reason the German Navy had given him an entire department in Berlin: to seek out Allied battleships and cruisers on the naval charts of the world's oceans.

Very delicately he held the pendulum over the photograph with his thumb and forefinger. After a few seconds, seemingly of its own volition, it began to turn, spinning slowly around, the revolutions gradually getting faster and faster. The pendulum became just a golden blur, the sunlight bouncing off it in tiny blinding flashes.

Now Straniak began to trace the pendulum over the map in a neat, mathematical grid. Heydrich watched, transfixed. If nothing else, the display was the most remarkable trick. The pendulum kept moving west across the map towards the Bodensee, crisscrossing north to south in a wide arc.

Quite suddenly, the pendulum stopped spinning, rooted over a particular spot, a slight vibration emanating from it.

"That is where the child is," said Straniak quietly.

Heydrich scrambled forward, dropping to his knees to read the name of the place on the map. It was a tiny hamlet near the village of Weiler. If Straniak was right, he had truly found the needles in the haystack.

35

HEYDRICH ARRIVES

Otto stared up at the strange flying machine as it appeared over the hamlet with its peculiar *thud-thudding* noise. It was not like a normal plane with wings, but instead seemed to hover in the air by some sort of spinning blade. He had never seen anything like it before. He watched with growing unease as it flew in a wide arc over the place. He could see three people in the open cockpit, all wearing leather flying caps and goggles. He felt his heart start to thump. Then as quickly as it had appeared the machine shot away, the sound of the engine fading against the mountains.

Otto immediately roused Leni and Angelika. The little girl protested at being woken. She seemed very tired now — there were deep shadows beneath her eyes.

"What's wrong, Otto?" Leni mumbled.

"Some sort of a flying machine came over. I think it was looking for us." He tried to sound calm.

"What do you mean?" Leni sat up, fully awake now.

"Just get ready to go." Otto kept his voice clipped, but his stomach was dancing with nerves. "It may be nothing."

"Of course it's nothing. How would anyone know we were here?" Leni was trying to sound calm, too, but Otto could see she knew it was serious.

He went back to the shutters, and lay on his stomach, scanning the village through the crack in the shutters with his binoculars. After ten minutes he'd seen nothing. Perhaps he'd overreacted? Then his heart skipped a beat. There. At the back of the village. Movement. He moved the binoculars. There it was again. His breathing stopped. It was a soldier, an Alpine soldier in camouflage gear, the broken green-and-brown mountain pattern that blended him into the scenery so effectively. And another . . . and another. They were crawling across the fields on the far side of the village. Scores of them.

He ran to the ladder and slid down it. The girls were by the back door.

"Soldiers. Go!" He raised his voice as loud as he dared. He lifted the timber barricade and pushed open the door. It was a straight dash to the woods behind.

"Come with us, Otto!" Leni grabbed his arm, her fingers digging into his flesh. She looked scared.

"No, this is the only way." He pulled himself free. "I can hold them here. You get a good start. Stay in the woods as much as you can. You can find your way with the map and compass, the way we were trained. You'll make the border, Leni."

"And then what?"

"Get to the boat, of course, like we discussed. Head for the rendezvous point. MacPherson will be there to take the girl."

"Who's MacPherson?" said Angelika. Her question was tinged with panic.

"A friend of your parents," Otto lied quickly. He wanted to be rid of them now.

"Why are you looking at me like that?" said Angelika.

"Like what?" snapped Otto. He didn't have time for this.

"Like you're angry with me? What have I done?" Angelika looked as if she might cry.

"I'm sorry," Otto said quickly. What had she done? Nothing. This wasn't her fault. He'd signed up for this mission knowing deep down it would probably get him killed. He had no right to be angry with her. She didn't have the slightest idea who she was. She was just a little girl lost who had put her trust in him and Leni. He suddenly felt very responsible for her.

"You must go, Angelika, now." He leaned forward and hugged her tightly, and she hugged him back.

Then Leni took Angelika's hand, and they were away, running for the trees.

Otto closed the heavy door and secured it with the timber. He took a last look through the gap in the door and saw the girls make it safely into the woods. Every minute from now on would count.

Then he realized he hadn't checked the door at the front of the building. He grabbed a pitchfork resting against the wall. It would do the job. He had almost reached the door when it swung open.

Otto dived into one of the milking stalls and held his breath. The door swung shut and he heard footsteps, which stopped abruptly. Whoever it was had also stepped into one of the stalls. Otto rested the pitchfork against the wall and, agonizingly slowly, dropped down to his knees and leaned forward to look under the gap.

A soldier was standing in the stall nearest the door. Otto could see his army boots, then a pair of army camouflage trousers dropped around his ankles, followed by his underpants. Otto stood back up before the man squatted down, but he knew what he was doing and the unpleasant sounds that followed confirmed it. *Just finish it and get out,* thought Otto. *Get out!* There was the sound of clothes being rearranged and then footsteps. Otto waited for the sound of the door, but it didn't come. He tightened his grip on the pitchfork, pressed himself harder into the wall, and once again held his breath. The footsteps got closer and closer to Otto. Then they stopped. In the silence Otto could hear the other man's breathing, he was that close. Otto's chest was on fire, his throat constricting, he couldn't hold his breath anymore. With a sudden gasp he sucked in air, and in an instant the soldier was standing in the entrance to the stall.

He was holding a Schmeisser submachine gun by its pistol grip, and it was pointing straight at Otto. They looked at each for a second, both stunned by the other's appearance. The soldier was not much older than Otto.

He opened his mouth, perhaps to shout to his comrades or give Otto an order, but Otto's pitchfork thudded into his chest before any sound could come out. He fell backwards.

Otto stood, frozen with shock, the enormity of what he had done hot in his mouth and his chest. His ears were ringing. The soldier wasn't moving and Otto understood in an instant that one of the fork's prongs must have pierced his heart. He rushed forward and pulled the pitchfork out. It came out horribly smoothly. Before he knew it he had doubled over, vomiting violently, a thick spurt of sour-tasting liquid. He was sick two, three more times, his eyes watering. He spat to clear the residue.

Then he turned back to the body. The soldier was definitely dead, a thick pool of blood expanding under his back. "I'm sorry, I'm sorry," Otto found himself saying, as if that would somehow help.

Then slowly he bent down and pulled the machine gun over the soldier's head. He had to yank it quite hard and he thought he might be sick again. His hands were shaking uncontrollably but he managed to get the gun free. It felt heavy and cold. He slid the safety catch on and leaned down again. He noticed the SS lightning bolt patches on the soldier's collar, but he studiously avoided looking at the face. He unclipped the leather bandoliers on the soldier's belt and pulled out the magazines. The grenades, too. He stuffed them inside the front of his shirt. They were not like the neat pineapple-shaped ones he and Leni had been issued with, but small metal tins attached to a short handle. The blood was pillowing behind the soldier's head now. Otto felt another heave in his stomach and stumbled away, fighting not to be sick again.

He climbed back up into the hayloft and dragged the ladder up behind him. He couldn't stop shaking. He wanted to cry. But his eyes were dry. So was his mouth. There was a pounding of his heart and a buzzing in his head. He'd just killed someone. But it didn't seem real. None of it seemed real.

He threw the machine gun down by the window and picked up the binoculars, breathing fast. He had to jam the end of the glasses against the shutters to keep them steady. The thought of Leni and Angelika, well into the woods by now, flashed through his head. It helped calm him a little. Maybe they'd be over the border by dawn. He could hold out till then.

Sweat was running down his face, stinging his eyes. He blinked it away and watched the proceedings unfold.

The troops were swarming all over the hamlet now. The occupants of the houses were being herded out of their dwellings, other troops pouring in to search them. There were trucks and Kübelwagen and motorbike-sidecar combinations. And a huge six-wheeled Mercedes limousine parked in the center. A soldier was attaching a large speaker to a post on the running board. Moments later the strange flying machine returned and dropped straight down at the right-hand side of the village. Otto watched as three men climbed down from it: the pilot, a man in a black SS uniform, and a third in a gray civilian suit. They walked across to confer with the men in the limousine.

Otto's hands had stopped shaking. He picked up the submachine gun, checked the magazine was full, and racked the slide, slotting a bullet into the breech. Then he looked through the shutter again. Half a dozen soldiers were walking up the track towards the barn. One was calling out a name: "Schmidt!" Otto knew it must be the dead soldier. Perhaps he'd asked his sergeant's permission. Otto cursed his bad luck.

There was a sudden whine of feedback from a public address system.

"Children, listen to me carefully . . ."

The voice cut through the late-evening air. Otto grabbed the binoculars again. The SS officer from the helicopter was standing in the limousine, holding a microphone. "My name is Reinhard Heydrich. I am chief of the Reich's security services."

Heydrich! Otto felt another wave of panic and fear engulf him. Every person in Germany knew who Heydrich was. He could hardly believe that the most feared of all the SS leaders was here in this tiny place searching for him.

"I know that you are here, children. The game is up."

The soldiers were fifty feet from the barn. Otto had no choice. He slid the selector to auto and squeezed the trigger. He aimed high, the gun bucking, empty bullet casings flying past his face, until he'd emptied the magazine.

He peered out. The soldiers had scattered, and were now firing wildly back, bullets thudding into the thick wooden walls. Otto dived down.

"Cease fire!" yelled Heydrich over the public address, and the firing stopped. Otto sat back up and watched as a searchlight attached to the windshield of the limousine was switched on and the beam suddenly swung around and pointed directly at the barn. He quickly changed the magazine.

"That was a foolish thing to do. We now know exactly where you are. The area is surrounded. You are surrounded. The situation is hopeless."

Otto thought about firing again, but before he did Heydrich continued: "Now then, I understand you are merely children acting under orders from the British authorities, but you must stop this foolishness immediately and surrender. Surrender, and you will be treated fairly and properly according to the laws of the Reich."

What laws are they? thought Otto with a surge of blind fury. *The same ones that dragged my father out of his home, and rounded up my mother and brother?*

He jammed the muzzle of the gun through a gap and fired, kept firing until the magazine was empty once more.

He saw Heydrich and others dive for cover as the bullets slammed into the side of the limousine, one of them exploding the searchlight.

Otto stayed crunched up against the shutters in the hay-loft. He could see troops spreading out around the barn. A half-track armored vehicle drove up from the hamlet and stopped about a hundred yards away from him. Its heavy machine gun, which poked through a steel shield, slowly rotated and elevated until it was pointing straight at him. Its engine quietly rumbled. It seemed to have a life of its own.

Otto couldn't drag his eyes away. It was utterly terrifying and mesmerizing at the same time. He toyed with the idea of shooting off a burst at the vehicle but knew it was pointless; the bullets would simply bounce off its armor. He felt his pistol digging into his stomach and pulled it out of his waistband, setting it on the straw next to the machine gun. What were they doing? Why hadn't they attacked? He struggled to keep his composure. His stomach was burning with hunger but he knew he couldn't swallow a thing for fear of retching. It was getting darker. Maybe that's what they were waiting for. Yes, that was probably it. He gripped the gun tighter, trying to stop the fear overwhelming him.

Darkness came. And with it more heavy engines revving and the sound of harsh orders barked out. Otto continued to watch the hamlet, but now he could see nothing except the lights from the vehicles and a few from the houses. Then a replacement searchlight was switched on and shafts of white light cut through the innumerable cracks and gaps in the barn. Otto scrambled back, afraid that an eagle-eyed marksman might try a shot.

"I am sure we can resolve this matter peacefully." Heydrich was addressing him again through the loudspeaker.

"We'll shoot the girl!" Otto bellowed back at the top of his voice.

How weak and reedy his adolescent voice sounded compared to Heydrich's harsh voice of authority. He almost expected to hear laughter from the massed troops facing him. But there was only silence.

"I swear, come any closer, try anything, and we'll kill her!" It was his last throw of the dice and Otto knew all it would win him was a little more time. But every second, every minute that he gained was another step, another few feet closer to safety for Leni and Angelika.

"Young man," came Heydrich's voice once more, "I am aware that children are capable of doing very stupid things, but please do not do anything foolish. Let me come up alone and speak to you personally."

Otto watched Heydrich step out into the spotlight's glare and begin to walk towards the barn.

"You see, I am unarmed!" Heydrich shouted. He held up his hands, palms forward. "I just want us to talk about this whole situation."

Otto knew he was being drawn in, but he couldn't help but reply. "We don't want to talk."

"You must realize the situation has gone against you now. We must find a peaceful solution. You mustn't harm the little girl." He sounded so reasonable, thought Otto, so calm.

Heydrich had nearly reached the front of the building.

"That's far enough." Otto's voice quavered.

"Young man, please be reasonable now. You're not going to shoot me. You're not going to shoot anybody."

"Stop!" Otto yelled, but there was no conviction in his voice. He squeezed the trigger before he even realized it.

The Schmeisser jumped in his hand. A plume of dirt shot up in front of Heydrich's right foot, showering his face with fine grit. Otto considered shouting an apology but that was just ridiculous.

"Hold your fire, all of you!" Heydrich shouted.

Otto stared down at Heydrich, his black uniform framed in the white light of the searchlight. He looked like the Grim Reaper come to collect another soul. Slowly Heydrich raised his arm. What the hell was he doing? wondered Otto. He felt dizzy with confusion and nausea and fear. It was as if the whole world was falling apart around him. He just wanted everything to stop . . .

Heydrich dropped his arm. *"Angreifen!"*

Attack! Before Otto could react, there was a terrible explosion, and the wooden shutter he was hiding behind was torn off the wall, hurling him across the hayloft. Smoke began to fill the air — thick, white, impenetrable smoke — followed by another deafening *boom-boom*.

Otto pulled himself to his feet. His ears were ringing but he couldn't hear anything else. The smoke filled the loft so completely that he was not only deaf but blind. It was like being in a cloud. He couldn't tell up from down, left from right. He stumbled forward and a pair of hands grabbed him. A fist drove into his stomach and he doubled over, then something hard hit him on the side of his head. And white turned to black.

36

INTERROGATION

Otto drifted in and out of consciousness as he lay on a cold steel floor that was moving. He must be in a vehicle. Sometime later, it might only have been seconds, it pulled to a halt.

"Get him out," he heard Heydrich bark.

Otto was hauled up and held upright by a pair of soldiers. It was just as well; he had no strength in his legs. He watched through a haze as other officers joined Heydrich. They must be telling him there was no sign of the girls in the barn.

"Take two companies into the woods behind the barn. Send another company to the west side of the woods to join up with the others. If you need more troops, call them in. Even if they left a couple of hours ago, they can't have got too far away."

"What about you, sir?" asked one officer.

"Leave me my Mercedes, six men, and two motorcycle units as messengers. That will be sufficient for the night."

Heydrich turned to Otto, surveyed him for a moment. "Take him to the inn and clean him up. As soon as I find out from this youth where the others are heading, I will contact you. Now be off!"

The third man from the flying machine hurried across.

"I will have them clear a room in the inn for you, Herr Straniak," Otto heard Heydrich say. "Perhaps you can tell me the whereabouts of the other children faster than that young man is going to. Though I doubt it."

At that moment Otto realized he was going to be interrogated by the most feared man in the Third Reich.

The soldiers dragged him into what must be the inn, through a corridor to a back room, and dumped him onto a hard chair. He closed his eyes from the sudden glare of the electric lights. Someone tied his torso to the chair with rope. His ankles were bound in a similar fashion.

"Well, that's better."

Otto slowly raised his head. Heydrich was sitting on the edge of a table in front of him. The place was empty except for a few tables and chairs, and a bar along one wall. On the walls were pictures of skiers and climbers and prize cows.

Heydrich was staring at him with a mixture of malice and curiosity.

"You have some color back in your cheeks. I was worried."

Otto noticed that Heydrich's eyes were too close together for his long face. It was unnerving.

"What is your name?" Heydrich's voice was slightly higher than normal, too. He hadn't noticed that when he was speaking through the loudspeaker.

"Otto Fischer," said Otto.

"Otto?" Heydrich's voice was laced with sarcasm. "You know, I don't believe I've ever interrogated a child before," he said casually.

Otto looked Heydrich straight in the eye. "I'm not a child."

"No, that's right. You are almost an adult and I must treat you as such." He tapped his finger against his chin a couple of times. "So, Otto Fischer, perhaps you'd like to explain to me what's been going on."

"I'm visiting my godmother in Bregenz." Otto was glad his head had stopped throbbing, but his tongue felt huge and puffy.

"Your godmother." Heydrich nodded. "Let me guess, this would be your fairy godmother?"

Otto shook his head.

"Oh, I see. She's real, is she?"

Otto nodded this time.

Heydrich got off the edge of the table and pulled a chair closer to Otto. He turned it around and sat with his legs on either side, his arms resting on its back.

"You are an interesting young man. The British secret service was indeed lucky to find you. And on such short notice. I shall be interested to discover who you and your colleague really are. But wait . . ."

He got up, as though he'd suddenly remembered some-thing, and walked across to the small bar. There was a rack of wine bottles behind it and a single brass beer tap jutting out from the bar top.

"You must be dying of thirst."

Heydrich selected a tall glass and set it on the counter. Then he reached underneath the bar and lifted up a block of ice the size of a shoe box. He turned to the back of the bar and found the implement he was looking for. An ice pick. A steel needle seven inches long, pointed at one end and with a round grooved handle at the other.

"You know, I used to love this drink when I was your age."

He began to stab at the block of ice, splitting off small shards before scooping them up and dropping them in a tall glass. When the ice fragments had reached the rim he added a generous measure of orange syrup.

"Now, this is the secret." Heydrich glanced conspiratorially at Otto, then popped the porcelain stopper on a bottle, filling the glass up. "Sparkling lemonade, not soda water."

He carried it back and set it down in front of Otto. Otto looked at the glass in front of him, the ice floating on the top, the bubbles rising to the surface. He had never wanted a drink more in his life.

"Now then," Heydrich continued, "it will be so much easier and quicker for both of us if you tell me where your col-league and the girl are heading."

Otto said nothing.

"Quickly now, and then you can have a drink. You can drink all you want."

Otto pressed his lips together and remained silent.

"Cat got your tongue?" Heydrich let the silence build between them. "Are you a Jew?"

Otto hesitated. "Yes," he said.

Heydrich stared at him for a moment. Then he laughed — a short, hard, humorless laugh. He picked up the glass and took a sip. "That tastes very good." He glanced back at Otto "You are no Jew. You are a German — good, strong Aryan stock. From Bavaria, if I'm not mistaken. I wonder, Munich?"

Otto nodded. There was no harm in admitting he was from Munich, he thought.

"A beautiful city. Well then, a fine German boy like you should be serving the Fatherland, not betraying it. Please, I ask you, one German to another, consider where your duty lies, to whom you owe your loyalty. Help me, help the Führer. Help Germany."

Otto looked down at his feet. They had taken his family, he kept saying to himself. They were not Germans. They were Nazis. Nazis, Nazis. He didn't see the blow coming. Heydrich hit him hard across the face. The pain exploded across his skull. He cried out.

"Enough. I have tried to be reasonable. Where are the two girls? Where are they going?"

Otto shook his head, his eyes watering from the pain. Then he realized he was crying. "I don't know."

"Liar." Heydrich hit him on the other cheek, full force. "We can do this all night."

"I swear, I don't know." But Otto could feel his will giving way already. If Heydrich broke him now, would Leni and Angelika still have enough time to get to the border?

Heydrich leaned forward and pulled Otto's chair right up to the side of the table. He undid the rope around his right wrist, took hold of his hand, and slammed it down on the tabletop. He dropped the ice pick he was still holding next to it. "Last chance before I take a less gentle approach. Where are they going to cross the border into Switzerland?"

Otto closed his eyes. Tears were running down his cheeks, which were burning from Heydrich's blows. "I haven't a clue," he sobbed.

There was a rap on the door.

"What is it?" asked Heydrich sharply, still holding Otto's hand on the table.

"Herr Straniak wishes to speak with you, sir." A soldier was standing in the doorway.

"I will come immediately." Heydrich straightened up. "Just in case you get any ideas about leaving . . ." In one quick, sudden movement, he rammed the ice pick through Otto's hand, pinning it to the table.

Otto let out an anguished howl. The pain was agonizing, sending bright white stars across his vision. He felt instantly sick.

Heydrich walked across to the bar and picked something up. He tossed the object across and it landed on the table, spinning around till it stopped by Otto. It was a steel corkscrew.

"Do you have any idea what it feels like if one of these is inserted into an elbow or a knee joint?" he asked.

Otto, gulping for air, was unable to respond.

"I'll take that as a negative," Heydrich said. "But unless you answer my questions, you are going to find out."

The door was slammed shut and a key turned in the lock.

Otto knew he was in shock. But there was only one thing he could do. His other hand was still tied to the arm of the chair. He leaned forward and closed his teeth around the handle of the ice pick. He bit into the wood and pulled and pulled and pulled. But Heydrich had driven the spike through his hand and right into the oak table. He closed his eyes from the pain, sobbing again, trying to get his breath. He knew that he wouldn't be able to hold out when Heydrich came back.

He heard something. He opened his eyes, stared around. Someone was knocking on the back window. And then he saw a face. As he tried to make it out, a fist wrapped in cloth punched through the glass and turned the window catch.

"Leni?" Otto whispered. His voice cracked and he thought he would start crying again, but this time with happiness.

Leni pulled herself through the narrow window and crossed the room in a couple of strides.

"Don't say anything. We have about one minute." Then she saw his pinioned hand and winced. "Oh, God." A pool of blood was forming under it.

"Pull it out," whimpered Otto.

She took a breath. "This is going to hurt, but you can't make any noise, understand?"

Otto nodded dully. She unwrapped the cloth from her hand, shook it hard to make sure it was free from any glass shards, then stuffed it in Otto's mouth. Then she put two hands around the ice pick and yanked. At the second attempt she got it out. She was right: It was agonizingly painful. Otto yelled, the veins standing out on his neck, but the cloth muffled the sound. She sliced through the ropes around his torso, ankles, and his other wrist, and helped him to his feet.

"Leni . . . you came back," began Otto weakly. He was still in shock. "You came back for me." He wanted to hug her, kiss her in gratitude.

"Don't talk . . . we have to move fast." She helped him towards the window. A telltale trail of blood spotted their progress. "You'd have done the same for me. Besides, it's the last thing they'll be expecting. Quickly now!"

Otto wrapped the cloth around his injured hand and, with Leni's help, managed somehow to pull himself through the window and drop down to the ground outside.

They leaned against the back wall of the inn.

"Where's Angelika?" he asked.

"Right here." Angelika appeared out of the shadows, her face etched with worry. Otto managed a smile and hugged her.

"Your hand!" she gasped. The blood was soaking through the cloth.

"Don't worry, Angelika, it's not too bad," Leni said as she tightened the cloth and tied it in a knot.

"How did you get past the soldiers?" he said.

"That's just it, there's only about half a dozen soldiers out there at the most. It was easy to slip around to the back of the inn in the dark. I guessed this was the only place they could hold you." Leni was talking fast. She pulled some grenades from her pack.

Otto's hand throbbed. He tried to forget the pain. "What's the plan?" he asked.

"We have to get away, of course." She handed him a grenade. "Can you handle that?"

He nodded.

"Right, this is what we're going to do . . ."

37

GETAWAY

After leaving Otto, Heydrich had marched down the corridor to the front of the inn. The terrified-looking innkeeper told him that Straniak was in a small bedroom on the second floor, and Heydrich had hurried upstairs.

"Please, just one moment, I am double-checking the reading. It is strange."

Heydrich waited as Straniak's pendulum did its work. He glanced at his watch, wondering how far the other two children had got. "I can get this information out of the boy faster. He is at breaking point already."

"The boy will lie, you mark my words."

As before, the pendulum stopped dead.

"So, where are they?" Heydrich hurried forward.

Straniak was frowning, uncertain. "I don't understand . . . it must be a mistake."

"What do you mean?"

"The girl is here. Right here, in the village."

"What are you talking . . . ?" said Heydrich. Then the light-bulb went off and he was out of the room and running for the stairs. He reached the ground floor and tore back along the corridor, fumbled for the key to the back room, jammed it back in the door, and wrenched it open. The boy was gone. Spots of blood led to the small window, which was wide open, the pane smashed.

Heydrich picked up the glass of orange lemonade and hurled it at the wall. Then he ripped his pistol from his holster.

"Guards!" he roared, and raced towards the front door. "Guards . . ."

A deafening explosion drowned out his voice, the pressure wave blowing the door in and lifting him off his feet, slamming him against the wall. The floor was covered in shattered glass, the curtains on fire.

He staggered to his feet as staccato machine-gun fire cut through the night. More explosions shook the building. He made his way to the front door, his pistol still in his hand. His ears were ringing.

Straniak was staggering down the stairs from the second floor, his nose bleeding, his wire-rimmed glasses cracked. "Help me," he croaked.

Heydrich couldn't hear what he was saying, but he didn't

care anyway. He pushed Straniak aside and stepped over the shattered door.

In the main street, flames were lighting up the darkness, throwing shadows against the wooden houses. His Mercedes was upside down, engulfed in flames. A couple of soldiers were lying in the street, clearly dead. The handful of other troops he had kept with him were running about, some vainly attempting to extinguish the flames with buckets of water from the village well.

"Find them!" Heydrich shrieked, spittle flying from his mouth, just as the fuel tank on the Mercedes exploded in a massive orange fireball, blowing three of the soldiers through the air like rag dolls. Heydrich was lifted up once again and dashed down onto the hard stone cobbles. He lay there for a moment or two, the wind completely knocked out of him, a sharp pain in his chest each time he tried to breathe. He hoped nothing was broken.

Then came the roar of an approaching vehicle. It was one of the BMW R75 motorcycle combinations he had kept back, and it was traveling towards him at fifty miles an hour. Heydrich had one second to roll out of the way before it plowed straight into him. As he moved he caught a glimpse of a girl, no more than fourteen, sitting astride the motorbike, her head down over the handlebars. He squeezed off two shots before she was lost in the darkness.

38

AFTERMATH

Leni caught up with Otto and Angelika at the end of the hamlet. She skidded to a halt, revving the engine to make sure she didn't stall it. Angelika and Otto threw themselves into the sidecar, and Leni kicked it into gear. They raced away from the hamlet and Heydrich, heading east.

"You're going in the wrong direction!" shouted Otto above the din of the engine.

"No! We have to go this way," she shouted back. "The search patrols went west; we'd run straight into them."

Leni kept her eyes on the narrow lane. It would join the main road in a couple of miles. Behind them came the sound of the other motorbike combination. She glanced around. There it was, about half a mile back.

"Faster!" Otto shouted, pushing Angelika down and, with his good hand, grabbing hold of the machine gun fixed on the sidecar. He swung the gun around so that it was pointing backwards. Leni tried to keep the bike steady so that he could line up the forward sight with the headlight of the pursuing bike.

Someone on the other bike had had the same idea.

Tracer rounds pulsed towards them — fierce, phosphorous beads of fire. Trying to ignore the pain in his hand, Otto squeezed the trigger and the sidecar's machine gun chattered back, flame shooting from the muzzle.

But the bullets kept coming, and Leni decided to take evasive action, swinging the bike from side to side, even though this made things more difficult for Otto. He fired again. Behind them, the headlights of the motorbike swerved violently and smashed into the side of the road. Seconds later the fuel tank caught, a bright yellow ball of flame erupting skywards.

"Yes!" Otto shouted in triumph.

"Nice shooting," yelled Leni. She slowed the bike as they reached the junction to turn right onto the main road. "How long do you think we've got?"

"Not long. We need to get as far away from here as fast as we can, and then dump the bike." Otto helped Angelika up from the floor of the sidecar.

"It's all right, Angelika, we're safe now," Leni shouted.

Angelika nodded uncertainly, but she was staring at the blood-soaked handkerchief wrapped around Otto's hand, her eyes full of anxiety. "Does it hurt very much?"

"It's not so bad." But now that the adrenaline of the chase was fading, it was pretty bad. He leaned back in the seat and closed his eyes. Angelika leaned against him.

Leni looked at her passengers anxiously. Otto was obviously in a lot of pain. And she could only imagine how Angelika must be feeling right now, after the gunfire and the explosions. Leni turned onto the main road, and kept up the speed on the motorbike. The wind whipped at her face but she didn't feel the cold. Her mind was now occupied with a looming dilemma.

She knew she should carry out the mission's orders and deliver the girl to MacPherson. At the same time, she had a growing feeling that it was the wrong thing to do. She had misgivings about his intentions. Nothing good was in store for Angelika, that was for sure. Her childhood, her whole life, would be destroyed, her innocence ripped away. She'd become a bargaining chip, perhaps, or a propaganda tool. And she would forever be known as Hitler's daughter. It was not a fate Leni would wish on anyone. Whatever her orders were, her heart was telling her something different.

She kept these thoughts spinning through her head until they reached another junction. They'd seen nothing on the road. Luck had been with them so far. She stopped to check the map. It was time for them to start going west again, and make for the border and the Bodensee. Otto woke with a start and looked around blearily. He'd either been asleep or had passed out. Angelika was still curled up against him.

"Feeling better?" Leni asked, cutting the engine.

He managed a weak smile back. "I feel fine," he croaked unconvincingly, his voice still raspy from his ordeal. "Where are we?"

"Here." Leni spread out the map on the front of the sidecar and pointed.

Otto leaned forward and studied it. "Right," he said. "That's not too bad."

"Why don't you see what supplies we've got?"

He nodded. "Come on, sleepyhead." He gave Angelika a gentle shove.

"Are we nearly there?" she asked, rubbing her eyes.

"Nearly." Leni folded the map up before she could look.

Otto and Angelika climbed out and stretched. "Let's see what food we can find," Otto said, opening up one of the metal panniers on the sidecar. Angelika dived into the other one.

"Look!" she said, holding up half a loaf of bread and a fat length of pepper salami.

Even better than field rations, Leni thought. She was starving. None of them had eaten anything for hours.

"Well done, Angelika," she said, and started to check through her own pack. She still had the maps, flares, flashlight, and first-aid kit, plus her knife and the PPK. She also had one last grenade. Otto and Angelika sat quietly on the ground, chewing on the salami and bread. He offered some to Leni but she shook her head. His pack had obviously been lost, or perhaps was sitting back at the inn.

She opened up the first-aid kit and took Otto's hand gently. He winced and clenched his teeth as Leni removed his makeshift bandage. She unscrewed the top on a small bottle of iodine and, without warning, poured some into the wound in the palm of his hand. Otto bellowed with the pain.

"I'm sorry, but it's for your own good," said Leni a little crossly as she applied a dressing and began to bind it tightly with a fresh bandage.

Otto blew out his cheeks, then breathed deeply. "That's what my mother used to say."

"That's what all mothers say," Leni said. She finished and went back to the map.

"I wonder if my mother will say that," said Angelika.

Otto and Leni glanced at each other, then away.

"I'm sure she will," said Leni, but she felt bad for the lie. "Well, which way shall we go?"

"Let's head south into the mountains. Once we get to the tree line we'll dump the motorbike and then walk due west for the Swiss border."

Leni considered Otto's suggestion. "We'd reach the woods at the southern tip of the Bodensee."

"Exactly. We can find the boat and get to the rendezvous point on the water by dawn."

The wind was beginning to build and large clouds were scudding across the night sky. But the air still felt heavy and humid.

"Summer storm from the north," said Otto, glancing up.

"I have to *go*," Angelika announced, getting to her feet.

"All right, but be quick. There's some bushes over there," said Leni, and the girl hurried away.

Leni waited a moment or two. "We can't hand her over to MacPherson," she blurted.

Otto looked at her, hard. "And why not?"

"I don't trust him. I don't trust what he'll do with her."

"That's not for us to decide." Otto kept his voice low. "We have our orders; we agreed to carry them out."

"I don't care. Why can't we decide?" countered Leni.

"Because we can't, Leni. Think about who she is. Just think about that for a moment."

"That's exactly what I'm doing! And you should, too. Everybody wants her for that reason: to use her, exploit her, harm her. Well, forget who her father is and think about who she is for one moment. She's just a nine-year-old girl who doesn't know anything. We have to do what's right for her. We have to protect her from them all."

"You make it sound so simple."

"Well, maybe that's because it is."

"How do you know what's right?" Otto was getting cross, but Leni was just as stubborn.

"Tell me I'm wrong, then," she said, flipping the debate. "Tell me she'll be fine with MacPherson. Tell me he's only got her best interests at heart." She waited for Otto to deny it.

After a moment he let out a long sigh. "You're not wrong, Leni." He leaned down and pulled off his right boot. "Give me your knife."

Leni handed her knife over and watched as he pried off the heel of his boot. "What are you doing?"

Something dropped out of the hollowed-out heel into his hand. Leni could see in the moonlight it was a small glass vial filled with a clear liquid.

"What is it?" she asked quickly.

"Cyanide. It's a cyanide ampoule. It kills in less than a minute."

Leni looked at it, horrified. "Why do you have it?"

"Why do you think?"

"For Angelika?" Leni felt sick.

"MacPherson told me I was to give it to her if things got really bad. He handed it to me the afternoon we left, when you went upstairs to write a letter. Under no circumstances was she to fall back into enemy hands. Those were his words, and he said they were an order from the very top."

"You mean the prime minister?"

"I don't know, I suppose so."

"Oh my God," Leni said, her face very pale.

Otto shook his head. "I wanted to tell you earlier, but he gave me another order. That you were not to know. He said you'd get too emotional, that it was up to men to make the tough decisions. Or something like that."

"And what decision have you made?" Leni looked at him intently, at the vial still resting in his palm.

After a moment or two, Otto closed his fist and hurled it out into the darkness.

"The right one."

Leni smiled with relief and for a second she wanted to hug him.

"Yes, you have. You'll see, it's for the best."

"Maybe," replied Otto tentatively.

Leni stepped towards him until they were almost touching. "Thank you," she said softly.

Otto touched her arm. "I should be thanking you, for coming back to save me."

Angelika trotted back to them, saw them standing close together. "Is everything all right?" she asked.

"Of course," said Leni. "But Otto wants to say thank you." She turned to him. "It was Angelika who insisted we come back for you."

"You did?" said Otto, staring at her.

Angelika shrugged self-consciously, then nodded.

"Why did you do that?"

Angelika looked back at Otto pensively. "I didn't want you to die." She said it quietly but firmly.

Otto stepped forward and hugged the girl. "Thank you, with all my heart," he said.

Leni felt as though she might cry.

39

LOSING TIME

Heydrich paced up and down outside the village inn, trying to keep his anger and frustration in check. Almost two hours had elapsed since the children had escaped and he still hadn't been able to communicate with the other units. The girl had taken one motorcycle combination; the other had crashed in pursuit of the children, it seemed; and it was impossible for the Flettner to fly at night. His shortwave radio had been comprehensively ruined along with his prized Mercedes, and the girl had taken the precaution of cutting the lines of the only telephone in the hamlet, the one at the inn. They had been well trained, that was for sure. His only option had been to send one of the soldiers west on the innkeeper's horse to catch up with his SS units and alert them to the news.

He glanced across at his remaining soldiers, still dowsing the fires, before he stepped back inside the shattered inn and went in search of Straniak. As he made his way towards the back room he looked at his watch for the fifth time in so many minutes. Every minute that was lost would make his job harder. They had to be near the mountains now, and if they left the roads and headed into them it was going to be a very difficult undertaking to flush them out. The only consolation was that the Flettner had not been damaged and Straniak was just about in one piece. It was not over yet by any means, Heydrich resolved.

He found Straniak skulking in the back room, suffering from nothing more serious than a bloody nose. He had wedged cotton gauze up his nose to staunch the bleeding, and there was a bandage holding his glasses together. He was holding his pendulum over the map once more, but it appeared to be swinging aimlessly.

Heydrich walked behind the bar, selected a clean glass, and poured himself a beer. He drained it in a single draft. "I trust you will have something for me soon," he said.

Straniak looked cross. "It's impossible!" he complained. "There is a terrible ringing in my ears, all my senses are damaged. My work, if it is to be successful, requires absolute calm and peace."

Heydrich walked over to Straniak. He leaned down slowly, grasped the top of Straniak's shirt, and pulled him up from his seat.

"I understand that, and I want you to understand something, too," he whispered. His face was inches from Straniak's.

"We are undertaking a personal — and I stress the word *personal* — mission for the Führer himself. Your failure to provide me with information will be a taken as an act of treachery to the Reich. And I have no need to explain how we deal with traitors."

Heydrich let him go, and Straniak massaged his neck.

"Forgive me," he said hoarsely. "The explosion must have clouded my judgment. I am honored to be able to help the Führer and I will redouble my efforts." He pulled the cotton plugs from his nose and saluted stiffly. "*Heil* Hitler!"

Heydrich let him go back to his work, and strode towards the front door to await the arrival of his men. As he reached the door he noticed the innkeeper's dog, some sort of Bavarian hound, sniffing at the boy's backpack, which they had retrieved from the barn. There was probably some food in it, thought Heydrich.

Then he had another thought. A good one.

40

MacPherson shifted uncomfortably in his seat. In spite of the loud drone of the Grumman's engine he had managed a few minutes of fitful sleep here and there. But he was wide awake now. They must be getting close to the Bodensee. He glanced up through the clear canopy of the cockpit, but could make nothing out in the blackness.

Then the plane suddenly banked, and MacPherson could see the outline of the lake. Commander Bracken straightened up and cut the engine. In the ensuing silence MacPherson could hear nothing but the wind whistling through the struts and wires, but he felt the plane gently slip down in a long, shallow glide. This way, it was hoped, they would be able to land on the water without raising any alarm from either the German or the Swiss authorities.

Minutes later and the pilot set the plane's central float down on the surface of the lake, sending up a great wave. The spray slammed into MacPherson's canopy. But at least they were down in one piece. Before takeoff, MacPherson had instructed Bracken where to land, and it looked as though he'd managed it perfectly. Ahead of them was a large villa set back in the trees, its lights blazing from the ground floor and, more important, a launch racing towards them from a large boat-house by the lake's edge.

MacPherson had unstrapped and slid back the canopy by the time the boat pulled alongside. He slotted the little metal ladder into the lugs on the side of the fuselage, and climbed down. The boat was riding up and down gently beside the plane. MacPherson jumped onto it. He had never been so happy to be out of the air and on the water.

A young woman with blonde hair was standing at the launch's wheel. She was wearing short Alpine trousers and a thick woolen shirt. In the moonlight, MacPherson could see the butt of a pistol poking out from her calfskin shoulder holster.

"Hello, Admiral. Safe trip?" Her voice was low and cool. She flicked her cigarette away into the darkness.

"Yes. Thanks for meeting us, Durand."

The woman expertly attached a towline to the steel eye on the front of the plane. Then she brought the engines up and the line snapped taut.

"There's plenty of room in the boathouse for the plane. No one will be any the wiser you're here."

"Well, if it all goes to plan, we'll be gone in a few hours," said MacPherson.

It was a little after midnight and they had to be away before three. Otherwise it would be too light and they would have to wait for the following night to make the flight. He was desperate to set eyes on this girl and even more desperate to get her back to London. What a prize she would be.

With the plane safely moored and the boathouse doors firmly locked, MacPherson and Durand took their seats in the launch once more. Bracken had been left inside the boathouse with some sandwiches and coffee. MacPherson had given him strict instructions to contact his office every thirty minutes on the radio in case of new information. The boathouse had a speedboat if he needed to get to MacPherson for just such a reason.

"All right, take me to the rendezvous point," MacPherson said.

The woman spun the wheel and flung the launch out across the water. As the lake itself was neutral territory, boats were constantly crossing it from the Third Reich and Switzerland, and they passed quite a few in the darkness, their running lights just visible.

They were heading for a little swimming platform a few miles out from Bregenz. Durand had selected it as an ideal rendezvous point. The two of them rode in silence. MacPherson was happy merely to smoke his pipe and feel the cool air against his face.

"Admiral," the woman said hesitantly, "may I ask who these children are?"

"No," MacPherson replied firmly, "you may not ask."

The silence returned.

41

BACK ON THEIR TRAIL

It was two in the morning when they reached the end of the road. Literally. Leni had driven the bike up a small mountain track as far it would go. Fortunately they had not met any road-blocks or patrols. Perhaps the German forces were still being concentrated at the border, Otto thought.

With Otto and Angelika pushing the sidecar, they managed to run the bike into a small gully and out of sight. They snapped some low-hanging branches from the fir trees around them, and used them to brush the tire marks from the track leading back to the road.

Otto then led them off the road and squatted down with the map.

"Seems to me we're about here." He pointed to a spot well south of Weiler, south, too, of the Bodensee. "If we want to reach the rendezvous point we need to go north." He pointed again, this time to a place on the southeast corner of the lake. The border was clearly marked.

"You're right." Leni nodded. "But that's not what we want to do, is it?"

Angelika, who was listening intently, frowned. "Why don't we?"

Otto could see Leni was still just as determined that they should decide the girl's fate rather than MacPherson. He was not sure that breaching orders was wise, either. But they could have this discussion again once they'd crossed the border into Switzerland. Heading straight west now would be much quicker. It would mean the border was at least twelve miles closer.

"Excuse me, I did ask a question," Angelika piped up again.

"Because the frontier here . . ." Leni marked the spot with her finger, reading Otto's mind. ". . . is much closer. Once we're in Switzerland we can make our way to where we're meant to meet."

Angelika nodded, satisfied by Leni's logic. Otto folded the map away quickly. They started walking up through the foothills. It would be first light in a couple of hours and then they would have to keep out of sight, but for the moment they made good progress through the woods.

Otto walked ahead of the two girls, picking a path. He thought about Angelika, about what Leni wanted to do.

Leni was certainly right that no one had the girl's best interests at heart. For the British she would be used ruthlessly to win the war. But then, as MacPherson had said, their job was to carry out the mission and not concern themselves with anything else. Was that right? How could that be right? If he thought that way, he would be no different from the Nazis who had taken his family. They had just been obeying orders, but what they had done was wrong. Deeply wrong. What finally settled the matter for Otto was Angelika herself. She had made Leni go back and rescue him. He owed her his life. He would do all he could to protect hers. He looked back at the two girls.

"Come on, let's see if we can go a little faster," he said, almost cheerfully.

"Can I have a piggyback ride?" asked Angelika.

"Hop on!"

He felt Angelika jump up, and then she was wrapping her arms around his neck, her legs around his waist.

The sun came up to a colder morning. Large clouds were passing over the mountain's peaks and the wind had continued to stiffen from the north. They all felt the chill in the air, getting colder still as they climbed higher. The going was getting harder. Otto had to drop Angelika from his back and instead helped her over the fallen tree trunks and large boulders. She grasped his good hand firmly, humming a tune. After a few moments, Otto recognized it.

"That's 'Blood Red Roses,' isn't it?" It was a very popular romantic song, always on the radio.

Angelika shrugged. "Is it?"

"Where did you hear that?" he asked. "At the convent?"

Angelika shook her head. "No, it's just always been in my head." She thought for a moment. "Perhaps my mother sang it to me when I was a baby."

Otto could see the prospect of actually meeting her parents was now becoming more real to Angelika. He felt bad knowing that there would be no family reunion on the other side.

They walked for another half an hour before stopping for a break. It was then that they heard the distant sounds. The baying of dogs.

Otto scanned the valley below with binoculars. A large pack of hounds was racing in their direction, foot soldiers running to keep up. Behind them were special Alpine jeeps, their rear wheels converted to caterpillar tracks. Otto immediately recognized Heydrich in the lead vehicle. Somehow or other he had managed to pick up their trail.

"It's as though they know where we are," said Leni, panicking.

Otto felt his stomach sink as he put two and two together. "My pack back at the village. It's given them my scent."

There was no possibility of rest now. They had to keep moving if they were to make it to the border.

Leni refilled the water bottle from a mountain spring. She'd also found the last of the candy and shared them out. They needed all the energy they could get.

Otto squinted through the binoculars again, saw Heydrich staring up, almost directly at him. He estimated the distance at no more than nine miles. He felt the fear rising. A part of him had begun to believe they had slipped the net, but now it was tightening again. He glanced at the girls. Both of them looked exhausted.

"We have to go." He stuffed the binoculars into the remaining pack and hefted it onto his shoulders.

"They'll have to follow on foot eventually and we've got a good start," Leni said, but her face was white. She must also have realized that their position was almost hopeless against such a determined enemy.

A fox gets a head start but he still ends up being torn to shreds by the hounds, Otto thought.

Angelika gave a sob, then another. "They're going to catch us, aren't they?" She seemed on the edge of terror.

Leni grabbed her and shook her. "Listen to me, Angelika, no one's going to catch us!" The harshness in her voice made Angelika stop crying.

"Leni's right. We're fast and clever and we've got you, Angelika, to help us." Otto looked at her sternly. "Now come on!"

"Do you really think that?" asked Angelika.

"Of course he does," said Leni.

"Take my hand." Otto held out his good hand for Angelika and together they set off, climbing as fast they could, higher into the mountains.

Ten minutes later and they were already panting for breath. Leni looked back down into the valley. The dogs and vehicles were still heading their way.

"They're gaining on us," she said flatly.

"Quiet," said Otto in reply, and suddenly dropped down to the ground. The other two copied him and edged up to where he was. "Look!" he said.

About three hundred yards ahead and a little below them was a large clearing in the trees. Mountain pasture led down to the valley. A circle of tents was pitched in the center of the clearing around a large communal fire. A flag was flying from a handmade pole. On it was a winged man, Icarus, with a swastika at his feet: the emblem of the NSFK, just like the one painted on the side of the truck back at Prien am Chiemsee. And there, just above the tents, was a glider. It was staked to the ground at the top of the clearing, ready to skim down the hill and soar up into the sky.

"It's a gliding club, like the one we met in Prien," Otto said. "There are lots of them in the mountains at this time of year."

Leni followed his gaze. "We couldn't. I mean . . ." she began.

"Look down there." Otto pointed to the dogs and the vehicles making their relentless progress towards them. "What do you suggest we do?"

"But we don't know how to fly."

"I do, I mean, I read a book on it once at school."

"You read a book?" Leni was looking skeptically at him.

"We could make the border in ten minutes — maybe less. Come on, Leni, we've run out of options and you know it."

The baying of the hounds was louder now, the sound of the vehicles, too. The whole place would be alive in the next couple of minutes. It was now or never. Otto looked around the encampment. It was still quiet. But that would change in a trice. Angelika pushed in between them.

"How would you like to go flying, Angelika?" asked Leni.

Angelika gazed at Otto, eyes wide with wonder. "Really?" she said.

Otto looked back at her for a moment. Was he mad taking such a young girl on a flimsy glider? *But better a mad flight ending in disaster than a bullet in the back of the head*, he thought.

Leni began emptying the contents of her pack. Otto passed her the gun and grenade, with two spare clips of ammunition. He stuffed the compass and map into his pockets, and slung the binoculars around his neck. He handed the water bottle and a whistle attached to a strong black cord to Angelika. She smiled, hung the bottle across her body and the whistle around her neck. He could hear the sound of the hounds getting louder. Any minute now they would rouse people in the camp.

"Quick on your feet. We don't have any time left. Give me your knife, Leni."

She passed it to him and Otto sprinted for the glider. It was a two-seater with the wing behind the open cockpit. A rope had been tied to the metal skid at the tail of the plane, and the other end was staked to the ground. The glider itself was sitting on a four-wheeled launching cart, which was pointing downhill.

Otto started sawing at the rope with his knife just as Leni and Angelika arrived and the first shot rang out. It was a pistol round. A neat hole appeared in the canvas tail fin just above Otto's head.

Luckily the lip of the cockpit was only waist height. The girls clambered straight in, Angelika sitting between Leni's legs.

The next gunfire was semiautomatic. Chunks of turf kicked up around Otto as he struggled to sever the rope. He kept sawing. Dazed and confused gliding students were spewing out of their tents in vests and undershorts.

The vehicles were about half a mile down the hill, their engines screaming as they bounced over the bumpy ground. The dogs were making better progress, leaping ahead, sensing their quarry was near.

With a final desperate slash, Otto severed the rope. He sprinted to the cockpit, put his hand against the side of it, and pushed as hard as he could. The glider immediately started to roll forward on its landing cart, and Otto had to scramble to pull himself inside. He jammed himself in the canvas seat next to Leni. The glider shot past the tents, the wingtip uprooting one, trailing it along before it blew away as they gathered speed.

Out of the corner of his eye, Otto saw a boy leap onto a bike and cycle towards them. The glider was accelerating quickly, but the boy was clearly determined to stop it. As he came alongside the cockpit Otto stared in astonishment.

"Him!" he yelled. "It's him!"

It was that thug from Prien, Rudi. The boy was staring at them, equally astonished. Leni shunted Angelika forward, twisted around, and pointed her pistol at the boy's head. "Bang!" she yelled at the top of her voice. The boy's eyes widened in fright. Then the front wheel of his bicycle hit a tree stump and he shot over the handlebars and went somersaulting down the hill, followed by the bicycle.

Angelika let out a shrill scream of warning and Otto turned back. One of the dogs had reached them. It raced along beside the cockpit and leaped into the air, its fangs bared. Otto felt a pressure wave as a bullet went past his face and hit the dog squarely in the jaw. The hound flew back, blood spurting. Otto stared at Leni in shock. The muzzle of her pistol was seeping smoke. She looked stunned at what she'd just done.

"Are you all right?" he yelled. She made no reply.

The glider was now traveling very fast and so were the army jeeps. They were facing a head-on collision. Otto could quite clearly see Heydrich in the lead vehicle, bringing his

Schmeisser up to bear on them. Otto wrenched the control stick back just as the machine gun spat flame, and the glider swooped up into the air, the rear metal skid clipping the top of the car's windshield. The launching cart bounced past Heydrich's jeep and crashed into the one behind. Bullets seemed to fill the air but the glider was climbing fast. Otto glanced back and caught sight of Heydrich, his submachine gun cradled in his arms, firing wildly up at them. A line of bullet holes chewed through the wing above Otto's head.

Leni had the grenade in her hand ready to drop it, but Otto yelled, "No, save it, save it!" She nodded.

Another sharp updraft of wind caught the light wooden craft and threw it upwards like a paper dart, shooting it higher into the morning sky. They all screamed. Otto felt the bottom of his stomach falling through his feet. Up, up, up they rose, until Leni yelled something and tugged Otto's arm. Out to their left was the blue-gray expanse of the Bodensee. Somewhere on the southern tip, MacPherson was sitting on a boat, waiting patiently for them. For a moment the sun glinted off the surface, making it shine like silver, then a dark cloud rolled in.

"We're really flying," shouted Angelika. Otto stared at the instruments fitted on the dashboard. Altimeter, compass, airspeed indicator. He tried to remember what he'd picked up from the book he'd read. Gingerly he pushed at the rudder pedals and the glider started to bank to the left. But the wind kept pushing them south. *It shouldn't matter*, thought Otto, a mental picture of the map in his head. They might end up crossing the border near the town of Davos, which was a long way from the lake but still in Switzerland. Then all they had to worry about was how to land. And what to do with Angelika.

42

INTERCEPT

They were completely lost. That was the only thing Otto was sure of. Since takeoff, the wind had got stronger and the clouds darker, and the glider had climbed higher and higher. The altimeter was at nine thousand feet and all of them were shaking with cold. The glider was being buffeted by crosswinds and Otto had to battle all the time to try to keep it level. Luckily they'd managed to strap themselves in and as there were three of them, they were wedged in tight in the open cockpit. But that was small compensation.

What made it truly frightening was being in the clouds. They were encased in thick, freezing fog and completely blind. Leni was shouting something at Otto but the roar of the wind made it impossible to hear. He clung to the control stick, his feet on the rudder pedals, flying by instinct. He knew that at any moment they could fly into the side of the rock face and be splattered across it. Angelika, squashed in front of Leni, had tucked her head into her knees.

Leni kept shouting above the howling slipstream. Otto finally distinguished her words. "We have to land!"

"Don't you think I know that?" he yelled back.

Suddenly another updraft sent them shooting straight up and then they burst through the top of the clouds into the blinding blue above. It was like going from night to day. The glider bumped along the top of the clouds like a speedboat on a choppy sea. For a moment everything seemed perfect. The glider was slicing through the air now, the only sound the wind whistling through the gliders' wires. And then Otto looked ahead. A mountain peak was right in front of them and approaching fast.

Angelika shouted, "It's Piz Buin!"

"What are you talking about?" Leni cried.

"It is in the Silvretta range, ten thousand feet high with a glacier on the south side," she recited at the top of her voice, like a talking encyclopedia.

"So what?" yelled Otto back, failing to see what she was so excited about.

"Look at the cross on the top, look!"

Leni and Otto stared at the summit of the mountain. Just visible was a wooden cross driven into the rock.

"It marks the border! Once you get on the other side —"

"We're nearly free!" Leni interrupted. She screamed with excitement.

"Are you sure?" said Otto, suddenly doubtful. Patches of flinty gray rock were pockmarking the snowcapped peak.

"Yes! My favorite book in the library. It was about the Alps. I can recognize all the different mountains, I swear."

Otto looked across to Leni. Maybe it was the wind, but her eyes were streaming.

He watched the peak coming closer, knowing they'd have to somehow get over it and crash-land on the southern side. He had absolutely no idea how to do that. Perhaps the mountain would be forgiving, he thought, then realized how silly that sounded. He leaned forward to check the instruments. Still heading due south. If he could just keep it steady, just keep control. He glanced out to the left. Heard something. An engine perhaps. Surely not. He looked all around.

"Do you hear that?" he yelled.

"There!" shrieked Angelika, but this time she wasn't pointing to the mountains.

A wingtip peeked through the cloud cover to their left. For a moment, Otto hoped they were all imagining it, then it flicked up again. The top of it was white, the underside a very pale blue. On both sides were the black-and-white crosses of the Luftwaffe. Otto felt a terrible quickening in his belly. It couldn't be . . .

The plane exploded up through the clouds. Leni and Angelika screamed. Otto yelled just as loudly. The plane was a Fieseler Stork, a light, incredibly agile reconnaissance plane, ideal for mountain flying.

Otto forced himself to look at the cockpit. Just as he feared, Heydrich was staring back at him from the pilot's seat. Behind him were the strange man with the glasses he had seen at the inn and an SS officer. The SS officer was pointing a submachine gun at them. The glider was already filled with holes, one short burst and it would be a flying colander. The machine gun coughed into life. But the bullets went high.

Heydrich jabbed his thumb, indicating for them to go down.

"It's a warning shot!" Otto shouted. "He wants us to go down."

"Well, he can forget that." Leni pulled the pistol from her waistband, leaned across Otto, and fired six shots. With her eyesight, she was unlikely to hit a single thing.

"Are you crazy?" Otto yelled.

The muzzle of the officer's submachine gun spewed flame just as Otto threw the stick forward and they shot down into the cloud. Down and down, like an elevator with snapped cables.

Otto had about five seconds to react as they broke through the cloud base.

The first thing he could see was that the glider was heading straight at a sheer wall of ice. But to the right of it was a U-shaped opening between Piz Buin and the next peak. Beyond that lay Switzerland.

He kicked his feet on the rudder pedals and pulled the stick to the right. Leni had wrapped her arms around Angelika and hunched forward, braced for the fatal impact. The glider was on its side, losing altitude rapidly and sliding across to the gap.

"We won't make it," shouted Leni, and struggled to grab the stick.

Otto shoved her back and kept hold. The glider's wing was now practically vertical to the ground. At the last possible moment, the craft almost touching the frozen snow, they shot through the gap and Otto wrenched the stick back, leveling the glider out and dropping down onto the southern side of the mountain. There was a glacier about one hundred feet below them and Otto took the risk, dropping the nose even steeper, till they were diving for the snow.

"Here we go, here we go!" he shouted at the girls, and Leni curled herself even more tightly around Angelika. Seconds later, they slammed down onto the glacier, bounced up into the air briefly, then crunched back down again. The glider's left wing tipped down, the edge slicing into the ice. With a terrible rending sound it was torn off and the glider started to spin down the mountainside. After a few dizzying revolutions, the right wing caught a rocky outcrop and was ripped away, too. Now they were heading straight downhill, gathering speed, bulleting along like a bobsled. They all held on for dear life, but just when it seemed they would be airborne again without wings, the sheer slope flattened into a plateau and the remains of the glider bumped to a halt.

The three of them sat in silence, their hair and eyebrows encrusted with snow. Slowly Angelika leaned across Leni and scooped a handful from the side of the glider.

"Snow," she said, and gingerly took a mouthful. She chomped on it, letting the melted water dribble out from the sides of her mouth. "Delicious!" she said, and she laughed.

Leni laughed, too, and unbuckled her seatbelt. "See? You can fly," she said, giving Otto a prod.

He was sitting stock-still, his hand welded to the control stick. "We did it, we did it," he said.

Leni helped Angelika out of the cockpit. Behind them the summit of Piz Buin was now shrouded with clouds. They had landed on the south side and were facing west, the sun behind them. A long snowfield, peppered with ridges and ravines, led down to the tree line. Beyond that, maybe six miles away, Leni could make out two villages. If Angelika was right, then at this very moment they were safely over the border.

"We're in Switzerland!" She yelled it out at the top of her

voice and the word *Switzerland* echoed round the mountain. "We've made it!"

As the echo died, Heydrich's Stork appeared above them.

Otto shot out of the cockpit. "Quick, over here," he yelled.

There was an outcrop of rocks to the left of the glider and the three of them crouched behind it. Leni raised her pistol but Otto grabbed her wrist. "Don't waste the ammunition."

The plane dropped lower and the three of them waited for Heydrich to open fire. They curled up tight but nothing happened.

"Why aren't they shooting?" asked Angelika.

Otto poked his head out and the Stork swooped over their position. He ducked down again instinctively. Moments later, first one, then two, then three gray canisters, the size of tins of beans, thudded into the snow around them. Red smoke started to billow out. "He's marking our position," said Otto.

"What for?" asked Angelika.

"I don't know," said Leni.

The Stork flew straight down the mountain towards the valley. Then above them came the deep growl of a heavier aircraft. The cloud was clearing and, as they looked up, a transport plane burst over the summit.

"There's the reason, Angelika," said Otto.

The three of them watched as tiny white figures started to spill out of the rear door of the plane, strands of cord attached to them. Within a minute there were thirty or so mushroom-shaped parachute canopies floating down towards them. Paratroopers.

"What do we do now?" asked Angelika.

There was only one thing to do.

"Run!" shouted Otto.

43

Heydrich kept the plane in a steep descent. His right thigh was starting to ache now from working the heavy rudder pedals. He glanced down at the bullet wound. It was superficial, a slicing cut through the top of the muscle, but it had soaked his breeches with blood and the cold mountain air made it burn. That young girl was either a crack shot or had the luck of the devil. The side of the mountain suddenly loomed large in front of him and he pulled the stick back, increased the throttle. The plane climbed sharply. *Concentrate!* he told himself.

He looked ahead, then banked the plane, hunting for a suitable landing place. Below the tree line, the hillside leveled out onto the valley floor. A mountain river ran through the valley, copses of trees growing along its banks. He decided there was just enough space and level ground to put down. The extended landing gear that gave the plane its distinctive name,

Stork, absorbed the hard and bumpy landing, and the plane rolled to a halt.

Heydrich unstrapped and jumped out. "Give me the radio and get me a field dressing."

General Müller nodded and handed down the radio's microphone to him. Heydrich had taken the precaution of bringing Müller, his most trusted subordinate, the head of the Gestapo itself. If anyone could help Heydrich finish the job it was he. He was a heavyset man, with jet-black hair, dark eyes, and thin lips set hard.

While Müller attended to Heydrich's order and also unloaded their weapons, the third passenger in the plane gingerly climbed out. It was Straniak, now looking even more nauseated and fearful. He leaned against the plane's fuselage and took long, slow breaths.

Within minutes Heydrich was confirming that Alpine paratroopers had deployed on the mountain. He considered contacting the Führer at the Berghof but decided against it. Better to wait until he had successfully completed the mission than bring false hope.

Müller handed him a dressing and bandage, and Heydrich quickly and expertly applied it to the wound above his knee. It had stopped bleeding and the throbbing pain acted as a stimulant to him.

"Hand me the glasses," he said to Müller, who passed him a pair of high-powered binoculars. Directly in front of him was a pasture and a mountain track that led up towards a ravine. He could make out the track winding through the rocks and up to the tree line. Above that the mountain rose up.

If he climbed fast it would take no more than a couple of hours to reach the snowfield, by which time the paratroopers would have chased their quarry into his waiting arms. He struck out for the track.

Müller and Straniak fell in behind him. Müller had the submachine guns in his arms. Several grenades poked out the front of his tunic. He passed one of the submachine guns to Heydrich, who racked the slide.

"Perhaps you do not need me anymore?" said Straniak weakly.

"Nonsense, Herr Straniak, these children are like quicksilver. Until I have my boot on their throats I will not be confident of success."

Herr Straniak appeared to deflate some more.

"Remember, Herr Straniak, there is no higher honor than to serve the Führer. Now, let us finish this business."

44

BAD NEWS

Since the sun had come up over the Bodensee, MacPherson had taken to scanning the shoreline every fifteen minutes or so with a pair of powerful naval binoculars. They were still moored up on the swimming pontoon, and Durand had arranged a couple of fishing rods off the stern of the launch. The children had not appeared, as he had hoped they would, and he was becoming increasingly anxious. Several German police launches had been patrolling at first light, but they had headed back to shore some time ago and it was then that MacPherson had first got a sinking feeling.

As he put the glasses down and took out his pipe, he heard the sound of a motor launch coming towards them. Turning, he immediately made out the speedboat from the boathouse.

"It's your pilot!" exclaimed Durand. She quickly tipped her

coffee away over the side and hurried towards the stern rope tying them up to the pontoon.

Bracken came racing up, throwing the speedboat hard into reverse to avoid a collision.

"Urgent information from London, sir, radio intercept from Berlin to the Swiss authorities." He was breathless.

"Well, go on, spit it out, man!" shouted MacPherson.

"Foreign Minister von Ribbentrop has informed the Swiss that German paratroopers have crossed the border in the Engadin. They are conducting search-and-rescue operations and any attempt to resist or interfere will result in the gravest consequences for the Federation."

"The Engadin?" Durand frowned. "That's miles from here."

MacPherson knew the message had to be about the children. But why had they crossed the border so far south of the rendezvous point?

"You have a car at the villa?" he said to Durand.

"Several," she replied. The launch was already floating free of the pontoon as she hit the starter button.

"Then let's get a bloody move on," barked MacPherson.

Durand punched the launch into gear and opened the throttle wide. The launch rose up and blasted across the lake, Bracken giving chase.

As soon as the boat touched the jetty, MacPherson leaped off and strode up the lawn towards the villa. Durand was right behind him, leaving Bracken to moor both boats.

MacPherson's lungs were on fire by the time they reached the garage block. A series of elegant cars was lined up inside.

"We'll take the Rolls," Durand said. "It's fast and tough."

"Guns?" MacPherson's own Webley was strapped across his chest.

The woman opened the trunk of the claret Rolls-Royce Phantom III. Beside a wicker picnic basket and a tartan-patterned thermos flask lay two Thompson submachine guns with a dozen fifty-round drum magazines, and a sawn-off pump-action shotgun.

"Good girl," said MacPherson softly, and climbed into the car. Durand jumped behind the wheel and backed the car out of the garage at speed, the wheels shrieking on the concrete. Then she spun the wheel and the massive limousine swung round in a squealing one-eighty-degree turn and leaped across the driveway, spraying gravel from its tires.

MacPherson had understood Ribbentrop's message for what it was. Search and rescue was one way of putting it. Seek and kill was another.

"How fast can we get to the Engadin?" he said to Durand.

"Maybe an hour, if there's no traffic."

An hour.

He prayed it would be enough.

45

BOOM

Leni lost count of how many times they fell flat on their faces. Each time they had to drag themselves out of the deep snow and keep struggling down the mountain. It was so hard. There was an icy crust but it had weak spots, and suddenly you broke through and sank three feet down into the powder beneath. They all had to keep pulling each other out.

Right now, Otto was helping Angelika as best he could. Leni made her way a little ahead of them. Yet again she plunged up to her waist in the snow.

"Help me," she cried, her teeth chattering.

"In a minute!" Otto shouted back, getting Angelika free again. They were woefully underdressed for this altitude. Unless they got themselves down the mountain soon they wouldn't last long.

The first of the paratroopers had landed about five hundred yards above them by the shattered glider and were expertly and swiftly pulling in their chutes. The others were dropping onto the mountainside every few seconds. Some began to strap on snowshoes while others were using skis. They would be down with them in minutes.

"Up ahead, look!" Otto shouted to Leni. He was plowing forward now, leaving Angelika behind, racing to reach a long gray cylinder that was lying in the snow. It was an equipment canister that had been dropped by the plane for the troops, and its parachute was still attached and billowing in the breeze.

Leni heaved herself up and stumbled towards him, helping Angelika.

"Don't give up," she said.

"I'm trying," said Angelika weakly. She looked awfully tired and cold.

By the time Leni had reached him, Otto had cut the parachute free and got the canister open. Above them, the troops were spreading out across the snowfield in a semicircle. He started pulling everything out as fast as he could: a light machine gun, ammunition and grenade boxes, medical supplies, rations. At last he found what he was looking for — a short entrenching spade. He folded the blade out and locked it into position. Then he handed Leni the machine gun and a box of ammunition.

"Keep them busy!"

Leni dropped to the ground, folding out the bipod legs on the gun, just as she'd been taught at Wanborough Manor. She flipped open the top of the ammunition box, grasped the top of the belt, and fed it into the gun. Then she showed Angelika how to keep the heavy chain of bullets level with the receiving slot to stop it jamming. The little girl looked hesitant, but did as Leni said.

Leni flipped up the back sight and turned the wheel to five hundred yards. With her eyesight the paratroopers appeared as blurry blobs in the white snow. She took a breath, slowly let it out, and squeezed the trigger. The bullets spewed out, with almost no recoil, the machine gun sucking them out of the box, the brass belt sliding over Angelika's hands like it was alive.

Behind her, Otto raised the spade high above his head and brought it down as hard as he could on one of the canister's hinges. The spade sliced through the thin steel. He raised the tool again and cut through the second. The cigar-shaped canister was now severed in half.

"I'm out of ammo!" Leni cried. She gazed through the smoke drifting back from the gun. A number of paratroopers were now lying in the snow. Others were racing down the mountain on their snowshoes and skis.

"Jump in!" shouted Otto, and she turned to see him pointing to the top half of the canister resting on the snow.

Leni understood instantly. "Brilliant!" she said. She jumped up and grabbed Angelika's hand, then helped her into the canister.

Otto was rummaging through the equipment again.

"Let's go," yelled Leni. "They're getting close."

But Otto was holding up some type of assault rifle and a funny-looking grenade, which he dropped into the cup-shaped holder attached to the end of the barrel. A grenade launcher.

"Leave it!" Leni was panicking now. The paratroopers were almost on top of them. Bullets whizzed past their ears.

"Wait, I've got an idea," said Otto. "Get some more of these grenades." Leni knew there wasn't time to argue. She dived towards the canister and grabbed the ammunition box.

He kneeled in the snow and dug the butt of the launcher into it, then pulled the trigger. With a sharp crack the grenade was away. It exploded loudly amongst the paratroopers, a deep boom resonating around the mountains. More soldiers now lay still in the snow. "Reload!" shouted Otto.

Leni dropped another grenade into the holder.

Bang! It was away. "Keep them coming!"

An incoming bullet clanged off the side of the canister. Otto fired again. Then a third, fourth, and fifth time. It sounded like a thunderstorm.

"What are you doing? You're aiming too high!" Leni pointed to the smoke above the line of soldiers.

"No, I'm not." Otto threw the launcher away into the snow as a deeper boom echoed around them. A much deeper boom.

"Oh my God, you haven't . . ." Leni was staring up the mountain with terror.

"Quickly, into the canister," urged Otto.

Leni scrambled aboard with Angelika between her legs.

"I'm s-s-s-o cold," was all Angelika could say, her teeth chattering.

There was another tremendous noise, like a giant cracking sound. Otto was at the back of the canister, pushing it with all his strength. It slid forward a little, then dug in.

"What have you done, Otto?" Leni yelled at him. He was going to kill them!

"Stop shouting!" he yelled as he ran around to the front and lifted it up out of the snow and back onto the hard surface. He went back and started pushing again.

Another deep boom seemed to shake the whole mountain.

"Avalanche!" Leni screamed.

Otto gave a final, superhuman push and then the canister was running free and he was scrambling aboard, his legs around Leni's waist. Above them the top of the snowfield had slid away from the mountain and was rolling down, an enormous wave of white that seemed to grow and grow.

The canister hurtled down the slope, shot over a ridge, and was airborne before it slammed back onto the snow and raced away. Behind them the paratroopers were desperately trying to out-ski the massive wall of snow at it increased in size and speed. It was like a living thing about to consume them whole.

"It's going to get us!" screamed Leni.

"It was our only chance!" Otto shouted in her ear.

He grabbed her around the waist and pulled her tightly in. Leni did the same with Angelika. The roar of the avalanche was deafening now. The front edge of it, a cloud of snow, filled the air all around them.

"We'll make it!" he yelled.

"Only if we reach the tree line in time!" she yelled back.

Leni took one last look around and saw the remaining troops sucked into the maw of the advancing white wave. It swallowed them, then thundered on, hungry for more. They were like a tiny boat at the bottom of an enormous crashing breaker. But then they reached the tree line, the canister hurtling through the closely packed pines. Behind came the roar and thunder of trees being snapped and smashed. The wave was almost upon them when the canister clipped the side of a boulder and flipped over, hurling them onto the ground. Leni rolled onto her back and looked up. All she could see was white, and then it enveloped her, covering her completely.

Finally there was silence.

She lay in the darkness for a second, the air knocked out of her; then she realized her arms could move slightly across her chest. She freed first her right, then her left. Her heart was pounding and she couldn't breathe, but instinctively she started scrabbling at the snow above her, scrabbling until she met daylight and fresh air, and she gasped it in greedily. In less than a minute she had freed herself and was out of the snow.

"Otto! Angelika!" She stood up on shaky legs and looked around. She called again.

A hand shot out of the snow to the right.

She plowed her way down to it and started gouging out handfuls of snow. She worked feverishly, relentlessly, going down three feet or so, until Otto suddenly shot up towards her, gasping for breath, spitting out snow. Leni grabbed hold of him and pulled him free.

"Where's Angelika?" she asked.

Together they called out Angelika's name, then waited, listening for any sound. Finally, after the longest of pauses, they heard a faint whistle coming from the snowdrift just below them. They ran, stumbling and falling, towards it. The whistling became even fainter. They looked around desperately, trying to locate it. Then it stopped.

"No!" screamed Leni.

Otto waded into the drift to his right. "Here! I think it came from here!"

Together they started digging, shoveling the snow back between their legs like dogs unearthing a buried bone. Nothing.

"There!" said Leni, pointing to another spot. They didn't have long. She was beside herself, oblivious to the aches and pains racking her body. She kept digging, furiously, frantically, with Otto beside her.

"I've got her," he yelled. "I've got her foot."

Sure enough, there was Angelika's booted foot. They both worked even harder, until they could drag her out of her snowy tomb. Angelika's face had turned a ghastly blue.

"Let me," ordered Leni and pushed Otto aside. She rolled the girl over onto her stomach, turned her face to the side, and then started to apply strong downwards pressure across Angelika's shoulder blades. It was the latest version of the classic Silvester resuscitation technique, which they had been taught at the manor.

Otto crouched helplessly beside her. "She can't die, not after all this, it's not fair." His voice was strangled with emotion.

"Come on, Angelika, stay with us," gasped Leni.

It was hard work. It was also having no effect. The girl lay there motionless. Leni kept going for another minute, but it made no difference. She stopped and sat back on her haunches, her eyes filling with tears.

"I'm sorry, Otto . . ." She leaned down and rolled the girl over so she was lying on her back again.

"No," said Otto. "No . . ." He raised his good arm and brought his fist down hard on Angelika's chest.

"What are you doing?" cried Leni.

He struck her again. It was an instinctive attempt to shock her back to life.

And it worked.

Angelika gave a violent, wracking cough and vomited out a spray of snow and water. Then she sat up, coughing and spitting and gasping for breath. Leni threw her arms around the girl and looked at Otto, the tears in her eyes spilling over now.

After a moment, the three of them lay back in the snow, letting their beating hearts slow.

"Do you think the soldiers are all dead?" said Leni at length. All of a sudden she felt very, very tired.

"Let's hope so," said Otto dully.

Leni nodded. Maybe fifty men had been killed behind them, but all she felt was relief.

"But what about the bad man, the one who hurt Otto?" Angelika asked quietly.

Leni glanced at her. She could see that Angelika was frightened of Heydrich, too.

"I don't know," she said.

But she did know. He was somewhere on the mountain, and he was coming for them.

46

DEATH ON THE MOUNTAIN

"No one could have survived that." Müller was walking just ahead of Heydrich and Straniak. They had passed through the ravine and continued up the track. From there they had watched the avalanche swallow first the troops and then, seemingly, the children.

"They seem to have survived a great deal," Heydrich said.

He was not leaving this mountain without them, dead or alive.

He trained his binoculars on the glacier above, checking one last time for any sign of life from the Alpine troops. There was none. Only a few minutes earlier he had watched through the binoculars as the boy and girl had fired the grenades up the mountain. They had acted decisively and ruthlessly, wiping out an entire company of elite SS Mountain Infantry not long returned from Greece, battle hardened. Capturing three children should have been nothing to them. For the first time Heydrich considered the possibility of keeping the two teenagers alive when he had caught them. Their talents as double agents might be highly useful to the Reich and once he had established their true identities, Heydrich was sure the right pressure could be brought to bear to obtain their willing and faithful cooperation.

He set off again, maintaining his fast pace, the flesh wound on his thigh no longer troubling him. His Schmeisser was slung loosely around his neck, swinging like one of Straniak's pendulums. Below him on the valley floor, the Fieseler Stork was just visible, its white wings standing out against the green of the summer pasture. Straniak struggled to keep up, mopping his brow with a large spotted handkerchief. He was sweating profusely despite the colder air, and breathing heavily.

After some time, the three men crossed over a second ravine spanned by a rope bridge, which swayed under their weight. Below was a thundering torrent of glacier meltwater. Once over, they continued to follow the track to the right. Just before they reached the trees they came upon two men.

They were squat farmer types in traditional lederhosen shorts with bib fronts, carrying bolt-action hunting rifles under their arms. One of them had a dead mountain goat wrapped around his neck. It was dripping blood from a wound through the center of its forehead.

Heydrich didn't slacken his pace but his black-gloved hand tightened on the Schmeisser's grip. "We are searching for three children, lost on the mountain," he said. "Have you seen them?"

The two men shook their heads.

"There's been an avalanche," one of them said.

"I am aware of that." Heydrich could see they would be of no help.

The taller of the two was now frowning. His colleague slowly raised his rifle.

"You are SS, I think. Do you know where you are?" the farmer asked.

"I believe I do, thank you," said Heydrich. "Let us pass. We are in a great deal of a hurry."

The farmer raised his own rifle. "Don't come any closer."

"As you wish." Heydrich stood in front of them.

"This is Swiss territory. My brother and I will escort you to the police chief in Klosters."

Heydrich interrupted the man. "As I have explained, this is a rescue mission for three children who are on this mountain, possibly injured."

The men glanced at each other, uncertain.

"Explain your story to the police chief," the farmer said doggedly.

"I explain myself to only one person . . ."

Heydrich emptied the magazine's thirty-two bullets into the men's bodies in a little under four seconds. The two men spun and twisted like marionettes, before crumpling to the ground. Heydrich changed the magazine.

"And that person is Adolf Hitler."

47

HIDE-AND-SEEK

The staccato chatter of the submachine gun echoed up the mountain, sending Otto and the girls diving for cover. They'd reached the edge of the trees and were about to take a path that appeared to lead down to the valley floor. Huddled behind a large boulder, they sat and waited and listened. Eventually Otto snaked forward on his stomach to take a look. He was back in a minute or so.

"It's Heydrich with the two others. About five hundred yards down the path, heading this way." His face was as white as the snow above them.

"So? We fight our way down." Leni was gripping her pistol tightly in one hand.

"Yes," said Angelika. "Leni still has a grenade." She was flushed in the face. Otto knew she must be scared, but she was showing immense courage. He shook his head. Better to get the girls down to safety while he led Heydrich on a wild-goose chase around the mountain.

"You're a very brave girl, Angelika, but no."

"So what are we going to do?" she asked.

"We've got to be clever now, use our heads."

Leni nodded. "Otto's right."

"So, here's what we do," he said firmly. "We split up."

"No!" Both girls spoke as one.

"Wait, just hear me out." Otto could see he would have to be at his most persuasive. He spoke quietly, seriously. "Splitting up is the only way. Let me lead them up higher and away from the track. You wait until they have gone and then go down as fast as you can to the nearest village. Run the whole way if it's possible. It shouldn't take you more than thirty minutes." He leaned forward and pointed to the valley below. "Don't stop, don't look back, just go. There's the village, see?"

"They'll kill you," Leni said, her voice flat.

"Only if they catch me. And they're not going to do that, I promise you."

"What about last time?"

"Last time I was stuck in a cow barn. This time I've got the whole mountain to hide on. I'll see you down there for lunch. I'm going to have an enormous bratwurst and an orange soda." His voice was calm. He looked at her patiently.

"I'll do it," said Leni. "It's my turn."

Otto shook his head vigorously. "It's not about turns, Leni, you know that. It's about her. Giving her the best chance. I thought you'd made that clear a while ago." He could see that at last his words had hit home. "We're wasting time now. You know there's no other way."

Finally Leni nodded and took Angelika's hand. "He's right."

Angelika looked as if she might cry.

"Take this," Leni said. She reached inside her pocket and pulled out the remaining grenade.

"I was hoping it might be chocolate," said Otto.

"No such luck." She smiled tightly back at him. That moment when Otto had scolded her for a Hershey's wrapper seemed such a long time ago.

"You keep the gun and grenade. Just in case." He leaned forward and gave Angelika a tight hug. "Angelika, there's something I have to tell Leni, in private."

"You mean like a secret?"

"Yes, sort of."

Angelika nodded and moved away.

Otto lowered his voice to a whisper. "Have you thought where you'll take her?" He didn't say the words "if I don't make it down," but he could see Leni knew that was what he meant.

"Then we're agreed. We won't hand her over to MacPherson." Leni searched Otto's face.

"Yes, we're agreed." Otto said it firmly.

"I've been thinking, I've got some distant relations in Switzerland, in Berne. It's not too far from here. Cousins on my mother's side. I'm sure they would help us."

Otto nodded. "That sounds a good idea. Yes, that really does." He smiled at the idea of Angelika living with a Jewish family. No one would ever think of looking for her there. Perhaps he'd even live to visit. "Be careful," he added quickly, and then he was on his feet and moving away.

"Wait!" said Leni, but he was already out of sight.

Angelika hurried back over. "He didn't say good-bye," she said.

"That's because he's meeting us later for lunch, remember?"

Angelika nodded. Then she smiled. "I know what secret he told you."

"Oh, really? And what's that?"

"He told you he's in love with you, didn't he?"

Leni looked at Angelika, so sure she knew the truth.

"Something like that."

"Do you love him?"

Leni dropped the grenade back into her pocket.

"Now that's *my* secret, isn't it?" she said.

48

WHITE KNUCKLES

MacPherson hurried as fast as he could down the main street of Davos without drawing attention to himself. In an ideal world he would have been sprinting, barging everyone out of the way, racing flat out for the waiting Rolls-Royce. But it had been worth the stop. He'd got more accurate information from his contact in Berne. The Germans had landed troops on the south side of Piz Buin, a well-known mountain peak right on the border, not far from the town. He wrenched the door to the rear of the limousine open and dived in.

"Piz Buin? How long?" he yelled. Durand had already started the engine.

"Leave it with me, sir," she said simply, and the car rocketed forward, barreling down the street. Less than thirty minutes later the car had climbed high up into the hills,

MacPherson feeling more nauseous than he did on the roughest of seas.

They reached a fork in the road. The Rolls-Royce hit the humpback bridge just before it and flew majestically through the air for at least sixty feet. It smashed down on the rutted track, chrome hubcaps exploding off the wheels.

"Over there!" MacPherson barked, pointing at the Stork parked in the meadow about half a mile away. He had recognized it immediately as a German plane.

Seconds later the car had demolished a five-bar gate and was careening across the meadow, slipping and sliding on the morning dew. MacPherson clung on to the straps stitched into the ceiling lining as the car bounced over the grass, the engine roaring.

Durand slammed on the brakes and the big car slewed to a halt, hurling MacPherson into the rosewood dashboard for the final time.

"Well done, Durand," he managed to say as a cloud of fine dust enveloped the Rolls. A thin trail of steam was hissing from the radiator. MacPherson threw open his door and staggered out, making for the car's trunk.

He grabbed one of the Thompson submachine guns before scooping up a couple of magazines. The dust around the car had started to settle.

"Looks like my source was correct." MacPherson slapped a

magazine into the gun and racked the slide. The plane itself was empty.

"So it would seem." Durand had lit a cigarette and was smoking it fast. MacPherson handed her the other Thompson and she flicked the cigarette away, the deadweight of the machine gun requiring both hands.

"I've shot plenty of birds in my time, but I've never downed a Stork. Care to join me?" He glanced at the young woman. "Safety catch on the side there, flick it down to *A*."

Durand raised her eyebrows. She had already done it.

MacPherson nodded ruefully. "Ladies first," he said.

Durand pulled the trigger. A six-inch tongue of fire spat from the end of the barrel, empty brass bullet casings fountaining out of the side of the gun. MacPherson opened up with his own gun, hitting the canopy, the engine covering, and then — bingo! — the fuel tank. A satisfyingly large explosion enveloped the plane and it split in two, its wings folding up and inwards. Within a couple of minutes the whole thing had been consumed by flames. Only the crumpled steel tubing of the frame was left. A column of black oily smoke rose up in the morning air.

"Golly," said Durand. "Looks like it's the long way home for someone."

MacPherson glanced up at the mountain. It was time to get this girl.

49

TRICKED

Heydrich stared down through his binoculars to the valley below. His plane was now a smoldering wreck and two armed people were making their way up the mountain. Clearly the children's welcome party had arrived. That could make things a little more difficult if he didn't find them soon.

"Who are they?" asked Straniak anxiously.

"I would have thought, given your ability, Herr Straniak, that *you* would have told *me* that, not the other way round."

Heydrich was tired of the man. Since his initial pinpointing of the children in that hamlet he had singly failed to find them again with his stupid pendulum. Straniak had protested that he could do nothing if they were buried under twenty feet of snow but Heydrich was not convinced. The man was a fraud who had been lucky once, he thought. And yet Heydrich had caught the man staring at him strangely when he thought Heydrich wasn't looking. Almost as though he knew something about him . . . about what the future might hold. Remembering Straniak's strange reaction when they had first shaken hands, a chill went through him, like a shadow over his grave.

A small rockfall showered down on them. Heydrich dodged the stones bouncing past his head and looked back up the mountain. For an instant he caught a flash of a Hitler-Jugend shirt. It had to be the boy. He, at least, was alive. It was incredible.

"Up there, to the right!" he shouted to Müller, who opened fire, bullets ricocheting off the rocks.

"Come on!" Heydrich was galvanized into action. "They can't outrun us . . ."

He flew up the track. Behind him, Straniak stopped. Heydrich continued to climb. He didn't need the mystic anymore. But his wounded leg was aching badly now. And behind him, Müller was huffing and puffing from the thinner air. He was more used to the police and Gestapo offices of Berlin than the Alps. Rocks continued to bounce and fall towards them. The children were obviously hoping one might hit them. It was clearly the only weapon they had left, but they were right — a blow from even a small stone dropped from a height could be deadly.

He climbed for another five minutes, then noticed that the rocks had stopped falling towards them. He stopped and listened. He could hear nothing. Wait . . . There was something, very faint. A man's voice. Straniak's. He climbed onto a large boulder and looked down the mountain with his binoculars. Sure enough, there was Straniak frantically waving his spotted handkerchief and gesticulating wildly with his other arm. He was jabbing downwards.

Heydrich swore as he realized he'd been double-crossed. Then he saw the boy's head below them, just for an instant.

"Down!" he yelled at Müller just as he reached him, panting. "We go down!"

"What?" said Müller.

Heydrich started scrambling over the loose rocks, anxious not to lose his balance and fall. A sprained ankle would finish the chase once and for all.

Within ten minutes he had got back down to Straniak, sweat pouring down his face, flecks of spit at the corners of his mouth.

"Are you certain?"

"The pendulum cannot lie," Straniak said pompously.

Heydrich shook his head, tired of this man's pseudo-mysticism. "Well, if it does, I shall leave you on this mountain." He glanced up at Müller still stumbling over the rocks and boulders. "Keep up, Müller! We can still catch them."

50

ROPE BRIDGE

"Why are you stopping? Are you hurt?" Leni called back.

"Otto," Angelika said. "What about Otto?"

Leni felt the question like a stab to her heart. They'd both heard the machine-gun fire up the mountain. They'd found the dead farmers on the track. Leni had even had the presence of mind to grab one of their rifles. And Leni knew if Heydrich caught them they would be dead, too.

"Angelika . . ."

"We have to wait for him," Angelika insisted.

They had reached a rope bridge. It was a typical Alpine arrangement of four strong plaited ropes, two at the bottom supporting the wooden foot planks and two at the top as a handrail. Vertical ropes were attached between top and bottom to act as spindles. It looked solid but didn't feel it, swaying and bouncing as they made their way across. Angelika stopped as they reached the other side.

"We can't, Angelika. Not this time. We have to get you to safety first. Then I'll go back, I promise."

"It'll be too late by then."

"I'm sorry, but it's what Otto would want us to do," Leni said.

"You don't know that. You're just saying it to make yourself feel better."

The longer we're together, the more that girl can read me like a book, Leni thought.

"All right," she snapped. "What do you suggest we do?"

"What about that?" She pointed to the grenade clipped to Leni's belt. "We have to try, Leni. We have to."

Leni knew, in her heart, that she couldn't leave the mountain without Otto. Not after all they had been through together in the last forty-eight hours. Forty-eight hours. It felt like an eternity.

"All right. Quickly now." She led Angelika off the track. Once out of sight, Leni dropped the farmer's rifle, then pulled off one of her shoes and removed her sock. It was made of thick wool and she bit the top of it, breaking the yarn. Carefully she started to unravel it. "Make a ball," she said to Angelika, who picked up the end of the strand and started to wrap it around itself.

More shots rang out. They would have to hurry. Leni looked up the mountain and prayed that Otto was still alive.

51

CLOSING IN

Higher up the track, Otto was trying to stay ahead of his pursuers. He'd fallen over three or four times, each tumble skinning a knee or elbow. The hand Heydrich had stabbed was on fire and swollen. His head hurt, his mouth was dust dry, and he thought the little finger on his good hand might be broken. It was bent at a funny angle. Funny, too, because Otto couldn't for the life of him remember how he had done it. At least it wasn't his trigger finger.

Coming across the dead farmers had been a nasty shock but, like Leni, he'd scooped up the remaining hunting rifle. It was slung over his back now as he ran, and it thumped against his shoulder blades, adding another facet to the pain he was already suffering. As he rounded the last bend he saw the rope bridge ahead.

Otto willed himself forward, trying to put on an extra

spurt of speed to make it across before Heydrich and the others caught him. Machine-gun fire rattled out behind him, bullets fizzing past his head. The next round would probably hit him. But he was determined to make it to the bridge.

A searing pain punched into his left calf, throwing him off his feet. He hit the ground with his shoulder and rolled. There was a fair-sized boulder to his left and he crawled behind it. He unslung the rifle, then hazarded a look down at the injury. A bullet had channeled through his calf muscle, and blood was pouring out. He ignored the wound for a moment, letting the blood run into his boot, and instead pressed the rifle's butt into his left shoulder and stared down the barrel. A flash of black uniform appeared, and he fired. Returning fire sent him ducking back down. His whole body was hurting.

He worked the bolt on the rifle, ejecting the spent cartridge and feeding another into the breach. He'd have to abandon any hope of crossing the bridge now and try to hold them where he was for as long as he could. He wondered how many shots there were in the magazine. Not many, that was for sure. He popped up and fired again. A burst of machine-gun fire came back. He would be the first to run out of ammunition. He should probably save the last bullet for himself. He ejected the magazine to check. There was only one bullet. This was it. The blood was squelching in his boot, thick and viscous. If he tried to run with this leg he wouldn't get five feet before he was mown down.

"Put down your weapon!" Heydrich's voice cut through the mountain air.

Otto shook his head. Never. The only question was this: Was it better to be shot in the back or to do the job himself? He turned the rifle around and looked at the dull black, little hole. He could smell the cordite as he rested his forehead against the end of the barrel. He leaned forward and put his left thumb on the trigger, his bandaged right hand holding the muzzle against his head. It was a bit of a stretch. About a pound of pressure on the trigger and oblivion. He heard the crunch of boots on the path. They were close.

And then, before he realized what he was doing, he was on his feet, the rifle tossed aside, running and hopping down the path to the rope bridge. Behind came gunshots but no sledge-hammer punch into his back, just the hornet's buzz of bullets as they passed his head. He pumped his arms as hard as he could. He was going to make it. Then he was shoved violently forward and he sprawled onto the hard ground, skinning his left eyebrow. A second later, a boot was on the nape of his neck, pinning him down.

"You have gone as far as you will ever go, Munich Boy," said Heydrich.

Otto wiped at the blood running into his left eye and stared ahead. The rope bridge was only fifty feet away. He felt like crying. Then realized he was.

52

ENDGAME

Leni and Angelika were well hidden but still had a clear view of what had happened. Leni had the hunting rifle against her shoulder, the foresight dancing over Heydrich's black uniform. He had leaned down and dragged Otto up to his feet. By his hair. Leni wanted to scream out, even more so when she saw Otto's bloody face and leg.

"Shoot! Shoot!" Angelika urged Leni. "What are you waiting for?"

Leni took a breath, the way she'd been taught, to steady the heavy rifle. She tried to keep the sight fixed on Heydrich's torso but her vision was too blurry. It was impossible to get a clear shot. The range was well over five hundred feet and now Otto was stumbling along in front of Heydrich. She knew if she fired she'd just as likely blow Otto's head off.

Heydrich was walking him slowly towards the bridge. What was he going to do?

"I can't shoot, Angelika, my eyes aren't good enough."

"Let me do it," said Angelika.

Leni looked at her. "Do you know what you're saying?"

The girl looked back gravely, then nodded.

"Angelika . . ."

"Let me do it. I can see clearly. He's going to kill Otto."

"Are you sure?" Leni was wavering still.

"I don't care if it's a bad thing. Saving Otto is all that matters to me."

Leni nodded. Everything seemed unreal now. Only survival mattered. "All right, but I'll help you."

Leni handed the rifle to Angelika, who sagged a little at its heft.

"Here, rest the barrel on my shoulder," Leni said, kneeling down in front of her. With Leni bearing the brunt of the weight, Angelika then pressed the hard wooden stock into her own shoulder and wrapped her tiny finger around the trigger. She looked down the barrel. Leni could hear her suck in her breath. A moment passed, then the rifle jumped up from Leni's shoulder.

The bullet hit the silver Totenkopf badge on Heydrich's peaked cap and tore the hat clean off his head.

He pulled Otto into the side of the rock face, his arm around the boy's neck, the muzzle of his pistol jammed against his temple. "So you're still here!" he yelled. "Excellent."

Leni pushed the rifle to one side. She looked at Angelika. "You nearly got him, well done," she said, but she couldn't hide her disappointment. It had been their best chance of saving Otto. Angelika looked crestfallen.

"What are you doing here?" Otto called out, his voice cracking. Heydrich clipped his ear with the pistol barrel and he yelped.

"Your friend raises a good point. Why are you here? I hope it is not misplaced loyalty."

Leni and Angelika didn't move a muscle as Heydrich, with Otto now pulled tight in front of him, stepped out from his cover and approached the bridge. He shoved Otto onto the first tread. The bridge swayed slightly.

"That's far enough!" Leni called out.

Heydrich's head swiveled in their direction. "As you wish."

He drew the hammer back on his pistol. "We're waiting." His voice was almost singsong. "And we won't wait forever."

It was time for Plan B. Angelika nodded her head. Leni knew there would be no dissuading her.

"All right! You can have the girl on one condition," she shouted.

"No!" Otto shook his head. Another clip to his head prevented him from saying more.

"The girl for the boy. A simple exchange, is that it?" Heydrich shouted back.

"That's right," answered Leni.

"Why are you doing this?" Heydrich shouted back.

Leni and Angelika looked at each other. Leni didn't know what to say, but she had to say something before Heydrich worked out it was a double cross.

"She's doing it because she's in love with Otto," Angelika shouted back. Her voice was high and childish, but it carried to the rope bridge.

Otto looked confused. Heydrich scoffed.

"I agree." His voice boomed back across the ravine. "Let us be quick about it."

"Angelika will walk to the middle of the bridge," Leni shouted. She glanced at the girl. "You're sure?"

Angelika nodded. "It's going to be fine." She stood up and made her way through the bushes out onto the path.

"When she is in the middle of the bridge, let the boy go. Once he has walked past her, the girl will come to you."

Leni's voice was getting hoarse.

They were at the endgame now.

Otto waited tensely, with Heydrich's forearm clamped across his neck. He was so tired and in so much pain, he didn't even notice the muzzle of the pistol jammed against his temple. He just wanted Heydrich to let him go, accept the barter, even if he didn't understand what was going on. Perhaps Heydrich didn't, either. Perhaps that was why he was hesitating, wondering if it was all an elaborate trick. Otto didn't believe Angelika's reason and he knew that Leni would never sacrifice the girl; she just wouldn't.

"Very well!" shouted Heydrich, having made up his mind, his voice ringing in Otto's ears. "Come forward, child!"

Otto felt the vicelike grip slacken a little as Angelika emerged from a thick clump of bushes to the right, and walked slowly but purposefully towards them. She looked very calm and very serious, almost serene. Otto heard Heydrich give a small gasp, then the sound of footsteps behind them.

"Stay back!" Heydrich shouted to Müller and Straniak. Otto realized he didn't want anyone to do anything that might spook the girl.

Angelika reached the middle of the bridge and stopped. The whole thing was swinging gently from side to side. She held on to the left support rope with one hand.

Heydrich leaned forward and put his mouth next to Otto's bloody ear. "Now that this is over, Munich Boy, I'm going to find out who you really are, who your family is." His voice was soft. "And when I have, I will not only kill them, I will expunge any record of their existence. And after I have done that, I am coming for you. I will see to it that you and your family are erased from this earth now and forever." He shoved Otto forward with the heel of his hand.

Otto didn't look back. The threat had made the tears well up in his eyes and he didn't want to give that man the satisfaction of seeing him cry. His leg was burning but he limped on, finally reaching Angelika. "What's going on?" he whispered, wiping at his eyes.

Angelika smiled brightly. "You'll see. Just get to the other side as fast as you can."

Otto glanced down then, and saw that Angelika's middle finger was looped tightly with a piece of yarn that dropped to the wooden slat at her feet. There, unseen to Heydrich, more yarn had been wound around the wood. Otto frowned. What had Leni and Angelika planned?

"Go, Otto, go," Angelika said.

Otto pressed forward, thinking hard.

The instant he had passed her, Heydrich stepped onto the rope bridge.

"Come along, child!" he ordered.

But Angelika remained where she was, looking back to check Otto had reached the other end.

"Come at once!" Heydrich raised his voice. He strode forward, the bridge swaying and bouncing under his weight.

Otto turned to watch. Angelika pulled the yarn wrapped around her finger, and ran back towards him, away from Heydrich.

Then Otto realized what she had done. Remembered Leni's last grenade.

Five.

"Stop!" Heydrich yelled. He couldn't run, the bridge was too unstable. He dropped to one knee, tried to take aim with his pistol.

Four.

Angelika was catching up with Otto. Heydrich fired, but the swaying bridge meant the bullet went harmlessly wide.

Three.

Heydrich had to grab at the rope to stop himself from falling over.

Two.

Heydrich got up again, staggered forward.

One.

Heydrich was almost at the middle of the bridge, Angelika a couple of steps from the end. Otto was clear.

Leni's grenade exploded, severing the ropes as cleanly as a hot knife through butter, neatly bisecting the bridge. Each half slammed back towards the opposing rock face.

On one side Angelika was holding on to the wooden treads about fifteen feet down. And on the other was Heydrich, swinging from the very bottom tread. The impact had knocked his pistol from his grasp and then he'd lost his grip on the handrope. But his right leg was lodged firmly between two treads and so he found himself hanging upside down, staring back at Angelika. Otto heard the tinny clatter of his gun as it cannoned off the rocks below.

He scrambled down the broken bridge to rescue Angelika.

"Shoot! Shoot the child!" Heydrich was desperately trying to swing himself upright so he could climb back up the shattered bridge.

Müller edged along the side of the rock wall, trying to see the child, but she was below his line of fire. A single shot rang out and Müller staggered back, clutching at his left arm. A lucky shot. Leni had used her last rifle bullet well. But Müller didn't know that.

"I'm hit," the Gestapo chief shouted out. He rolled onto one side and emptied his last magazine in the direction of the bridge.

"Hurry up, Otto!" cried Leni. She crawled out of the bushes and ran for the bridge.

Otto stretched out his hand to Angelika just as the frayed and burned rope suddenly snapped. He managed to throw himself to the side, his good hand catching the edge of a ledge. He stared down, expecting the worst, but somehow Angelika had grabbed a tree stump jutting out of the rock face.

Opposite, Heydrich had pulled himself upright and was inching his way back up the rope.

Otto edged his way down until he was leaning on the stump himself. He stretched out his hand again.

"Take it!" he urged her. She was holding on to the end of the stump with both hands, swinging gently above the ravine. Slowly she let go with her right hand and found Otto's left hand. They gripped each other's wrists.

"I'll pull you up."

There was terrible crack and the tree stump came away. Otto managed to wedge his bandaged right hand into a cleft in the rock face. He screamed with pain, but held on to Angelika, who dangled at the end of his left arm.

She stared back up at him. "I can't hold on," she whispered.

Otto felt her grip on his wrist slacken. "Yes, you can!" he said, but he knew that his bandaged hand was also going to give way. Her grip was weakening all the time, and his good hand was sweaty around her wrist. It was only a matter of time.

"You can't hold on either, can you?" she said.

"Yes, yes, I've got you," he replied, but she was beginning to slip from his grasp.

"I'm pulling you down." Angelika looked up at him, her eyes wide.

"Please, Angelika, please hold on . . . we can make it," he begged. But her hand was sliding through his, no matter how hard he tried to hold on to it.

"I can't," she said quietly. "It's all right, really . . ."

Then she was gone. Falling.

Otto shut his eyes and his good hand, now free, automatically found a handhold in the rock. He clung on to the rock face. He had so nearly joined her.

Otto opened his eyes and looked across to Heydrich, who was staring down at the ravine. Otto forced himself to look, too, and saw the broken little body at the bottom. Together they watched the meltwater catch her and roll her into the mountain cascade, before the fast-flowing torrent carried her over the rocks and away. Then he felt a hand on his wrist, pulling him up.

It was Leni. "Come on!" she yelled, and Otto struggled to climb.

"Müller!" Heydrich yelled as Otto pulled himself up over the lip of the ravine and dragged himself to his feet.

Müller emerged from his cover. He stumbled towards Heydrich, his pistol in one hand, his right arm drenched in blood from the rifle wound.

"Shoot them!" shouted Heydrich.

Müller pointed the pistol and fired, but the gun was empty. He struggled to change the magazine with his injured arm.

Otto stood and stared at Heydrich. If he managed to survive, he would do everything in his power to see that evil man dead. Then he saw Heydrich grab the gun and the magazine from Müller, heard Leni's urgent shout to run, and he turned and ran like he had across the sand at Dunkirk, not even feeling the pain from his wounded leg, until he caught up with Leni; and together they ran on and on, down the mountain, the last of Heydrich's gunshots dying in the morning air.

53

AUF WIEDERSEHEN

When Otto opened his eyes he felt a momentary surge of panic. The sun was shining brightly in his eyes and for a brief but terrible moment he wondered if he was dead. He sat up quickly, throwing off an afghan, and found himself in the back of a large limousine. He was alone, it was blindingly hot, and his shirt was soaked with sweat. Only it wasn't his Hitler-Jugend shirt, but a man's linen shirt without a collar. He pushed the door lever and clambered out.

Three figures were standing in a copse by the bank of a river. He started towards them, a sharp pain shooting up his right calf. He glanced down at the fresh bandage. A spot of blood had made it to the surface from the gunshot wound. His hand was throbbing, but it, too, had been re-dressed. As he walked, the events of the last hours came back to him, beginning to make sense. He remembered running and running, scrambling down the mountain track, and meeting MacPherson and a beautiful woman with a machine gun who said her name was Durand, then an injection in his arm and the pain floating away.

He reached the copse. A slight breeze came from the river. MacPherson and Leni were watching Durand lay a series of large, flat river stones over some freshly dug earth.

"And may God have mercy on her soul," said MacPherson, ending the makeshift service.

Leni's eyes were red from crying. Otto desperately wanted to take her hand. But he didn't.

MacPherson stepped across to Otto and patted him gently on the back. "You've got some color back in your cheeks, old chap," he said quietly.

"How are you feeling?" asked Durand.

Otto nodded. "I'm all right, really," was all he could manage before his throat became hot and tight.

MacPherson nodded. "Well done. Well done, both of you."

But Otto could see the disappointment in the admiral's eyes. He watched MacPherson and Durand walk back to the car, then looked at the anonymous grave. He couldn't believe Angelika was really lying under there, dead. Just like that.

"Did he tell you who she was?"

Leni shook her head. "He thinks we don't know."

They stood there in silence, while the grasshoppers scratched out their call.

"He must think we're idiots," said Otto. He started to walk towards MacPherson.

"Otto? What are you doing?" Leni hurried to catch up as he reached the admiral. "Don't . . . Otto."

"Time we left, I think," said MacPherson briskly.

"We know who she is — I mean, who she was," said Otto, correcting himself.

"Well, you may think you do, Otto," MacPherson said soothingly.

"No, we do, don't we, Leni?"

Leni was now beside him. She nodded.

"I see. Well, that was very enterprising of you both, but —"

"What were you going to do with her?" Leni interrupted.

"I'm sorry, I can't tell you anything else. I have my orders, too."

"You'd have ruined her life, destroyed it."

"Young lady, you are a very brave girl and you have been through a lot in the last forty-eight hours. But that does not mean you know what is right. There is a war going on, a world war, and if we lose this war — and we are doing so right now — then evil will prevail and many millions of innocent people will die. So if you ask me if the sacrifice of the life of that child, a child who could have conceivably stopped or shortened this terrible conflict, is a price worth paying, I am afraid I will tell you it is."

"The end justifies the means," said Otto.

"Yes, it does," said MacPherson.

"Well, let me tell you something." Otto was fighting to control the hot ache at the back of his throat, to keep his voice level. "She saved my life, not once but twice, and she sacrificed her own to do it. She wasn't just the daughter of someone, a tool to be used by you or the Nazis. She was a good person, a brave person." He stopped. "You wouldn't understand." He returned to the grave, with Leni following him.

"May I remind you both," called MacPherson, "that you are subject to the Official Secrets Act and that . . ." He trailed off.

"You sound like an ass," Durand said. She was leaning against the Rolls, smoking.

"I beg your pardon?"

"A pompous ass."

MacPherson stared at her, then slowly nodded. "I do, don't I?" He took out his pipe and lit it. "They're right, of course. Every innocent life is sacred. And the minute you forget that, you're on the slippery slope to hell."

At the copse, Otto kneeled down and picked up one of the stones, smashing it on another so it split into shards. He took one shard and scratched something on the largest of the flat stones covering the grave. When he'd finished, he let Leni see what he had written.

It was a simple inscription: ANGELIKA — 1931–41 — AN ANGEL.

Leni carefully set the stone at the head of the grave and they both stood up.

"You know, I really think she was," said Leni, and there was a catch in her voice.

But it was time to go.

54

A MOMENT OF TRUTH

The sun was still high at this altitude, almost ten thousand feet, but it was bitterly cold for the three men trudging up the mountain in their summer-weight clothes. Heydrich, Müller, and Straniak had been climbing for seven hours since the disaster at the rope bridge, and they had finally reached the ridge that marked the border between Switzerland and the Third Reich. It was a little after four in the afternoon.

"Five minutes," said Heydrich, calling a halt.

The two other men sank down into the snow to rest their aching limbs. Heydrich raised his binoculars and trained them down on the valley below. It was covered in shade and there was no sign of further movement. Certainly there were no units from the Swiss Army. Soon after midday, when they had stopped for a rest, he had observed through the binoculars the Rolls-Royce driving away across the meadow.

Since then there had been no further activity. Clearly, whoever had met the two survivors had not been inclined, or perhaps not been able, to mount any pursuit. Not with the bridge knocked out. The secret would be left on this mountain.

Müller joined him now. "Can we make it down by nightfall, sir?" he asked. He looked exhausted and his shoulder was caked with dried blood.

"Of course," replied Heydrich. "Keep up your courage. The mountain regiment will already be halfway up the north face by now. They will carry you down, if necessary." His words brought a look of relief to the man.

Straniak struggled to his feet. "Herr Heydrich, might I have a word in private?"

"As you wish, Herr Straniak. Müller, you may start the descent."

Müller needed no urging in the matter and quickly dropped down over the ridge, back into the German Reich. Straniak waited until he was out of earshot.

"I am not a young man anymore and I fear that I may not make it down the mountain," he said.

"Nonsense, Herr Straniak, it is a straightforward descent and tomorrow is the summer solstice. We will have light until ten o'clock tonight."

Straniak waved away the words of encouragement. "Nevertheless, if I should suffer an accident, there is something I wish to speak to you about now."

"Then speak."

"When the Führer asked me to assist you in this matter, he informed me of the child's identity in the strictest confidence. I assume you were also informed."

Heydrich nodded. "Of course."

"Well, last night at the inn, I performed a simple psychic exercise to confirm that identity." A gust of wind sent a swirl of snow gusting around the two men. "It is a straightforward but foolproof test. All that is needed is an odic picture of the girl and one of the father."

"I'm not familiar with that term."

"*Odic* means a personal object, in this case a photograph that has been charged with the energy and spirit of the individual. Normally once the pendulum is set over the child it will start to spin, coming to a halt when it is placed over a picture of the father."

"I see," said Heydrich. But he could feel something else coming. "What is your point?"

"My point is simple. When I placed the pendulum over the Führer's picture, it did not stop. It continued to spin."

Heydrich frowned, apprehension building in the pit of his stomach.

"Therefore we can say with absolute certainty that the Führer is not the father of that child." Straniak was staring at Heydrich with the zeal and conviction of his peculiar profession.

"Not the father?" Heydrich let it sink in. Had this whole thing been a wild-goose chase?

"There is, however, one exception to this."

"Go on," said Heydrich intently, oblivious to the cold mountain wind whipping at his hair.

But Straniak was saying nothing more. "The matter is now in your hands if you wish to pursue it." He stepped past him hastily, suddenly anxious that he had said too much, and began his descent.

Heydrich watched him go. Another secret best left to the mountain, perhaps? Clearly whoever Straniak was proposing was the girl's mother was either too dangerous or possibly too scandalous for him to dare to express it out loud to Heydrich. He suddenly felt a new sense of curiosity about this strange man and remembered there was still one thing that had been nagging at the back of his mind since he had met him.

"Herr Straniak," Heydrich called after him.

Straniak stopped and turned.

"When you shook my hand . . ."

"What of it?" said Straniak.

"You looked at me in a certain way, as though . . ." Heydrich almost couldn't believe he was saying this. "As though . . . you saw something."

Straniak stared back for a long moment. "I saw you in Prague, in a car, in the early morning. That is all." He turned and started his descent once more.

Prague? Prague? Heydrich shook his head. Then he felt a chill cross his heart. Perhaps, like the other matter, there was something more to his vision that Straniak would not speak of.

It was well after midnight before Heydrich was summoned to an audience with the Führer. He had sped back as fast as he could to the Berghof, but other more pressing matters had apparently prevented the Führer from seeing him immediately.

During the hours since his arrival, Heydrich had taken a hot bath, shaved, and replaced his torn and tattered uniform with a fresh one. He had eaten an excellent dinner, though he had little appetite. He remained in a state of anxiety, conscious of his failure. Now he paced outside the Berghof map room, waiting. Despite the late hour there was intense activity all around him, with secretaries coming and going and dozens of *Wehrmacht* and SS officers entering or leaving the room constantly. He nodded to those that he knew but did not engage in conversation. He had no intention of arousing anyone's curiosity through polite chitchat.

At last, just before two o'clock, he was admitted into the room. He marched straight across to the Führer. Hitler was standing, gazing over a vast map lit by pools of light.

Heydrich came to attention, saluted, and said, "I am sorry, mein Führer, but I have failed you. I do not expect you to show any clemency or mercy in this matter, and I accept any actions you wish to take for my failure." He had spent the last hour rehearsing the form of words he would use.

Hitler stared at him for a long moment. He looked tired, still dressed in his habitual white shirt and thin black tie, but seemed strangely elevated.

"Let me show you something," he said, beckoning Heydrich forward.

Heydrich came and stood next to his Führer, and looked down at the map. It showed the whole of the western continent: Europe, the Soviet Union all the way to Siberia, Mongolia, and China. The current border between the Soviet Union and the Third Reich was marked by a thick red line. Behind that line, from the Baltic coast to the Caucasus, had been arranged scores of small wooden blocks, of various shapes and colors. Each one represented a different element of the mighty Wehrmacht and SS fighting machine.

The two men gazed at the map in silence. Heydrich waited.

"The order I have just given will change the course of human history forever."

"Yes, Führer." Heydrich stared at the expanse of land stretching all the way to China.

"Five million men will create a new Fatherland for us that will last a thousand years." Hitler scanned the map. "How did Hess think by betraying his country with the secret of one little child he could possibly alter this fact?"

Heydrich remained silent.

"Today was her birthday." Hitler took off his reading glasses. "Tell me, was her death quick?"

"Yes, Führer."

He looked back at the map, then glanced back distractedly at Heydrich. "Thank you, Reinhard, for your service in this matter."

"But, Führer —" Heydrich began.

Hitler held up his hand. "The child was not supposed to exist. And your real work will commence now." He glanced up at the wall clock. It was 2:15 A.M. "Operation Barbarossa has begun."

55

HEADING HOME

Otto and Leni made their way down a limestone path beneath tall cypress trees to the jetty. They had driven back from the mountains to the villa by the lake in the morning, rested in the afternoon, and Durand had re-dressed their wounds and made them a delicious tea. MacPherson had hoped to get in the air as soon as it was dark, but dense fog had settled on the surface of the lake when the sun went down, and only now, in the small hours of the morning, had it lifted enough to allow them to take off. Otto had to use a walking stick to help him with his injured leg. He limped along, and Leni took his arm a couple of times when he stumbled.

Soon they could see the outline of the plane moored outside the boathouse. A towline was attached to a launch. They stopped and waited for Admiral MacPherson and Durand to catch up with them. The little coal of tobacco in the bowl of MacPherson's pipe glowed in the darkness.

"All set?" asked MacPherson gruffly.

Leni and Otto nodded.

"My goodness, you two deserve a medal." Durand thrust out her hand and shook first Leni's hand and then Otto's, before leaning forward to kiss Otto on the cheek. "And so good-looking." Otto felt his cheeks hot against the cool night air.

"Quickly now," ordered MacPherson. He helped the children climb up the ladder into the rear cockpit. They stepped down into it and dropped through a hatch in the floor to the cabin. Otto glanced back, and in the darkness it seemed to him that MacPherson and the woman were embracing. He looked away and hurriedly followed Leni down the ladder. It was dark in the cramped cabin, a little light seeping through the small windows.

After a minute or two MacPherson stuck his head through the hatch. "What do you think of this? More comfortable than the way you came over?" He was trying to be cheery, but Otto and Leni didn't smile.

There were three narrow canvas cots bolted to the floor and in front of them a large storage locker containing thick flying jackets and oxygen breathing equipment. Both Otto and Leni stared at the third cot and thought about the girl it was meant for.

"Get yourselves squared away," MacPherson said before disappearing from sight.

Leni and Otto lay down on the cots and fastened the safety belts across their hips. A moment or two later the launch's engine rose in pitch and then the seaplane was being towed out into the lake.

After about five minutes, Otto and Leni felt the tow-line give and the plane glided to a halt. Then the engine fired and the propeller turned. The cabin was filled with a vast throbbing sound as the revolutions built, vibrating the whole airframe, and finally the plane was moving, gathering speed, bouncing over the swell like a speedboat, shaking the cots.

And then they were airborne. There was no more juddering. Only smooth air, and the sound of equipment shifting and sliding as the plane climbed steeply away from the lake. It banked hard to the right and for an instant Otto saw the surface of the Bodensee in the moonlight, like a quivering mass of mercury.

Somewhere high above them, to the north, were six Spitfires fitted with long-range fuel tanks, waiting to shepherd them back to England. Angels of a different kind. Guardian angels. And when — if — they got there, who knew what the future held?

Otto and Leni lay still in the darkness of the cabin. In

Otto's left hand was his father's watch. Slowly he reached out with his freshly bandaged hand and found Leni's. Gently they interlaced their fingers.

"It's Rebecca," she said quietly.

Otto smiled in the darkness. "And mine is Conrad."

HISTORICAL NOTE

It is important to separate fact from fiction. While inspired by real events and historical characters, this story is a work of fiction and does not claim to be historically accurate or portray factual events or relationships.

There is no evidence to support the idea that Adolf Hitler ever fathered a child, and Angelika is a made-up character. So, too, are the characters of Otto and Leni, although during the Second World War there were thousands of displaced children from Germany, Austria, Czechoslovakia, and Poland, separated from their families and living in England.

Admiral MacPherson is also a fictional character, although the London Controlling Section was a real organization, set up to devise and coordinate military deception and covert plans during the Second World War.

WINSTON CHURCHILL led Great Britain from 1940 until 1945. His "bulldog" spirit seemed to summarize the mood of the British people even during the bad times, such as the events at DUNKIRK. For many people, his stubborn refusal to admit defeat during the Second World War has given him a reputation few other politicians have ever achieved. He died in 1965.

RUDOLF HESS was Adolf Hitler's deputy in the Nazi Party in the early 1940s. On the eve of war with the Soviet Union, he flew solo to Scotland in an attempt to negotiate peace with the United Kingdom, but was arrested and became a prisoner of war. Afterwards he was sentenced to life imprisonment. He died in 1987.

Despite the betrayal of Hess, Adolf Hitler commenced OPERATION BARBAROSSA, the invasion of the Soviet Union, with over four and half million troops. It was the largest military operation in human history, but its subsequent failure marked the turning point in the Third Reich's fortunes.

MARTIN BORMANN succeeded Hess as Hitler's gatekeeper and confidant. He remained with him to the very end inside the Führerbunker in Berlin and was one of the last to escape following Hitler's suicide on April 30, 1945. It is generally believed that he fled to Argentina.

REINHARD HEYDRICH was Lieutenant General of the SS and chief of the Reich Main Security Office. He was attacked in Prague on May 27, 1942, by a British-trained team of Czech and Slovak soldiers sent to kill him. He died from his injuries a week later. Historians regard him as the darkest figure within the Nazi elite; even Hitler christened him "The Man with the Iron Heart."

LUDWIG STRANIAK was a German mystic and a pendulum dowser. He was also an architect and astrologer and was used for his skills by the German military, not necessarily willingly.

HEINRICH MÜLLER continued to the end of the war as head of the Gestapo. Like Bormann he disappeared after Hitler's suicide. He has never been found.

ACKNOWLEDGMENTS

I could not have written this novel without the love, help, and encouragement of a great many people.

Firstly, my parents, who never batted an eyelid when I gave up my respectable job as a young barrister and jumped on a plane to Hollywood to become a screenwriter. I'm sure deep down they thought it was a foolhardy decision, but they have never shown me anything but unwavering support. Both of them served in the Second World War, my father in the Indian Army and my mother as a Wren. In 1941, when this story is set, my father was twenty-three and my mother was nineteen.

I must also thank my brother, Alec, and sister, Kate, for all the dressing up as soldiers and shooting at each other that we did as children. I think it was then that my interest in the Second World War took hold.

Love and thanks also to my wife, Debra, whom I adore and

...no is always prepared to tell me the truth about my writing, even if it hurts; and to my children, Constance, Dulcie, Edgar, and Frank, who inspired this book and to whom it is dedicated.

And of course, so many others who have helped along the way, not least, Anita, Ivan, Virginia, Nelda, and Guilio. I must also mention Foggy and Mistie, particularly Foggy, whose regular disappearances for hours on end into the woods of Hampstead Heath allow me the time to stand and think about story structure.

Turning to the book itself, I must thank: Judy, who encouraged me all the way and read the earliest draft with the sharpest of eyes; Michael Foster, esteemed agent and old friend, who read the manuscript on the spot and championed it from the get-go; Rowan, my other esteemed agent, who calmly and professionally found a home for it; my editors, Imogen and Rachel, who expertly cut and polished the rough diamond they were given; and everyone else at the Chicken House who have embraced the book and been wonderful; and lastly, Barry, the big cheese, who made it happen.